Seizing Amber

Jonathan Harris

SOURCEBOOKS LANDMARK™
AN IMPRINT OF SOURCEBOOKS, INC.®
NAPERVILLE, ILLINOIS

Published by Sourcebooks, Inc.
P.O. Box 4410, Naperville, Illinois 60567-4410
(630) 961-3900
FAX: (630) 961-2168
www.sourcebooks.com

Library of Congress Cataloging-in-Publication Data

Harris, Jonathan, 1962–
        Seizing amber / Jonathan Harris
                p. cm.
        ISBN 1-57071-712-5
        1. World War, 1939–1945—Confiscations and contributions—Fiction. 2. Intelligence officers—Fiction. 3. Art treasures in war—Fiction. 4. Amber art objects—Fiction. 5. Medici, House of—Fiction. I. Title.

PS3608.A783 C48 2001
813'.6—dc21
                                                            2001031326

Printed and bound in the United States of America
        LB 10 9 8 7 6 5 4 3 2 1

To my beautiful wife, Trace

ACKNOWLEDGMENTS

E.M. Forster once said that "the final test of a novel will be our affection for it, as it is the test of our friends." I have had the great good fortune of wonderful friends.

I would like to thank my wife, Trace, for all her love and support, and for her neverending contributions to this book.

Among those who believed, Andrew Steinberg believed first and most. He has supported and helped me in more ways than I can recount. Andrew is a modern day witch, his advice always true.

It was through Andrew that I was introduced to my agent, Alice Martell. Alice's unflagging enthusiasm and professional guidance have been a godsend. It is modest to say that Alice gives all literary agents a good name.

My thanks to every one at Sourcebooks who has worked so hard and especially to my editor, Hillel Black. Galileo said that writing is the mortal enemy of good health. Not when you have an editor like Hillel.

Laurence Rosenthal has been a great friend, supporter, and critical reader of many, many drafts. Thank you, Laurence. Dr. Robert Klein has been my medical advisor, both a spinner of ideas and an indispensable resource. Tricia Giese, Marianna Gracey, Wynn Miller, Connie Tavel and Plato Wang are friends who came through in the clutch.

I would like to thank my mother, Sherry, and her mother, Rose, for giving me the love of books. My father, Joseph, for always being there for me. And my dog, Mike, for steadfastly sleeping by my side while I work.

PART ONE

"Let him who seeks continue seeking until he finds. When he finds he will become troubled."
—*The Gnostic Gospel of Thomas*

1

Ivo Jenkins shifted his weight, 288 pounds according to the hotel room scale, his new diet doing no good at all. His goal was 260, so that he would look good in a new tux for his baby girl's wedding. But dropping the pounds would have to wait: even if he had promised his wife and even if he was looking more and more like a black Sydney Greenstreet. His business being so often about the waiting—God favoring the patient and all that. Even if God maybe hadn't meant to apply that particular rule to him. He picked up the phone and called room service, contemplating something rare.

It was nearly eleven on a warm summer night in the nation's capital. He slid over to the heavy suitcase that he'd let the bellhop carry up to the room and removed a metallic box the size of a stereo receiver. Dangling from its back were a jumble of cords and cables, too many for Ivo's taste. He preferred the old ways. But a man had to keep up with his profession: after all, slow buffalo got shot.

He placed the box on a cheap veneer dresser and plugged the thinnest of the wires into a power outlet, bending the prongs slightly so as to fit them into the much-abused socket. Then he ran a coaxial cable from the box to the room's television set. A small green light blinked on in the center of the box's power button, which Ivo depressed slowly with his thumb.

From the darkness of the television screen emerged a pixelated image of a bored late night newscaster. The newscaster reading scripted words from a teleprompter about an upcoming presidential election in Russia, with pictures of the candidates drifting across the screen. Seemed the Russian electorate had a choice between an old time commie with a new style western haircut, and a new style western-educated reformer with an old time bad Russian suit. Neither one of them looked to Ivo like they went much for the ladies. But you never knew, and Ivo figured that somewhere in Russia there might have been a kindred soul, a member of the professional brotherhood, who might have been interested.

Ivo personally liked to work closer to home, and he switched to the blank screen of channel 3, lowered the lights and settled back into a plaid armchair to wait, staring at the emptiness.

He sat there without moving for thirty minutes until, at exactly midnight—God how he loved punctual people—he heard a quartet of footsteps reach a pause not twenty feet from him, in front of the door to the neighboring room.

The lock opened with the click of an electronic keycard and, driven by an automated demon of its own, the television screen simultaneously flicked on in front of Ivo. In 21-inch color, a distinguished-looking white man in his early fifties stepped onto the screen and into a room identical to Ivo's own, right down to the plaid armchair. The man was lean and muscular, with silver gray hair, a square movie star jaw and a smile. A Charlton Heston type, wearing a two-thousand-dollar, hand-tailored, blue pinstripe suit. Soon enough Charlton was joined by another type altogether, a thin girl of maybe fifteen. She had long straight hair, light skin, and an oval face that belonged to a Modigliani portrait. Had Modigliani painted black girls.

Charlton took his clothes off first, carefully and methodically: his pants draped with a perfect crease over a hanger, the jacket added and the set hung in the closet, his shirt and tie meriting a hanger of their own, well-shined shoes placed together under the foot of the bed, socks neatly folded and laid on a chair where they were thereafter joined by his white jockey shorts. All done in a manner that was meticulous—the manner of a man who had regular habits, who believed in an ordered world and his place in it.

As the girl slid off her own skirt, she stole a single glance at Charlton standing there naked. She turned and offered a self-conscious glance in a mirror, then just looked away.

They did more than enough. Did it twice, maybe a hat trick. After a while, Ivo closed his eyes and stopped watching. The girl was still a child, her body not fully developed, her breasts and

hips more sharp than full. Charlton gave it to her best he could and when he was finally done, he dried his dick off with a tissue, stepped back into his fine clothing, handed the girl a couple of hundreds and went out the way he'd come in. Smiling.

In return, Ivo Jenkins allowed himself the thinnest of possible smiles. Like its blood relatives, politics and sex, blackmail is a dark art of the possible. And Charlton was about to learn just how very possible blackmail could be.

• • •

An unlabeled videocassette arrived via messenger the next afternoon at the still distinguished man's well-ordered office. A typed Post-It note suggesting, helpfully, that perhaps it would be best to view the tape in private.

And so it was only that evening, watching in his living room as the first frame of the tape rolled, his wife an unlocked door away in the next room, that he realized the facts of his situation, and fear and anger took hold of James Washington Lancaster.

2

They met in a small park in a neglected part of the capital.

Ivo's choice of location was more practical than symbolic—although James Lancaster would certainly look out of place in this particular neighborhood, the appearance of the FBI would be truly remarkable, and therein lay all the protection Ivo figured he needed.

Nevertheless, in keeping with his practice, Ivo arrived early to proof the site, taking a long stroll through the park before settling down on a green bench with peeling paint. A group of young black children were playing noisily on a jungle gym less than fifteen feet away from where he sat. Just another underemployed man, mellowing in the afternoon sun, eating sunflower seeds out of a paper lunch bag.

Holding onto his punctuality, Lancaster appeared perfectly on time, walking stiffly from the edge of the park to the foot of the bench. He looked Ivo up and down.

"Please sit, sir," Ivo suggested politely.

James Lancaster stood still.

"Who do you work for?" Lancaster asked, demanding to know, a tone of disgust in his voice, a failure of imagination preventing him from understanding that the man who sat before him chewing seeds had orchestrated this scenario without guidance from betters.

"I work alone, a free agent so to speak."

Ivo now turned his gaze towards the children playing nearby, reminding James Lancaster of the not altogether private nature of the setting he had chosen. The noisy children would soon enough get under Lancaster's skin. That was unfortunate for him. It was so important to keep cool in this business. Any business, really. But this sort in particular, where letting emotions run free always worked against you.

"Sit or stand, sir," Ivo added, "Whatever you like. But may I suggest that we'll attract less attention if you sit."

James Lancaster stiffly placed himself as far from Ivo as he could manage on the small bench. As if Ivo Jenkins was the one doing something he shouldn't have been proud of. As if a simple piece of blackmail was worse than giving seven stiff inches to a teenage girl while your wife of thirty years stayed up and waited for you to come home. Adultery, prostitution, and statutory rape being forgotten crimes in this country, Ivo supposed.

"I won't pay blackmail."

"Excuse me, sir?"

"I said, I won't pay your goddamned blackmail." The word blackmail uttered with a rather ugly, unfortunate hiss. A tone Ivo never appreciated.

Ivo cracked a seed between his teeth and spat the shell to the ground. "Please. You and me, sir, we are past time for moral indignation. How old do you think that girl was? Fifteen? You have a daughter that age." Ivo picked a couple more seeds out of the lunch bag. "Good for my diet," he said, sliding the bag towards Lancaster. "Go ahead, have some."

Lancaster kept his hands stiffly at his side.

"Suit yourself," Ivo shrugged.

"I've already spoken with Director Spellman—"

"—of the FBI. Yes, went to college with him, didn't you? Princeton. Lovely school." Ivo craned his head around the park, seeing only the nearby children and a quintet of old men playing cards and drinking beer. "Don't see old Laurence Spellman or any of his men here, do you?"

Lancaster chose not to answer, although Ivo waited.

From a battered leather folio which he'd laid near his feet, Ivo removed two sheets of white paper, 8½ x 11. He handed the top sheet to James Lancaster.

It was a neatly typed list: a five bedroom house in Virginia; a vacation home in Nantucket; two Jaguars, one a convertible, both silver; a money market account at Riggs National Bank of Washington; a stock account with Smith Barney; life insurance policies, three, with a combined cash surrender value in excess of $450,000; a lesser painting by an overrated modernist, purchased on a trip to Paris…a man's possessions, acquired over a lifetime of work. Owned jointly with his wife, some five million or so.

Ivo took a moment, then handed James Lancaster the second sheet of paper, which appeared on its surface to be similar to the first: a stock account with Morgan Stanley Private banking, a 40 percent interest in a New York real estate limited partnership, yet another life insurance policy…

"I believe," Ivo said, pointing to the second sheet, "those are the extras your wife does not know about. Some $500,000, roughly. Am I correct, sir?"

But James Lancaster still wasn't answering. He stared down at the pieces of paper, his fear and anger and disgust now commingled with the indignity of the violation. This cheap blackmailer had exhumed his life. Had watched and taped him fucking. And now, wanted his money.

"I take it by your silence that the list is accurate," Ivo said, his cheeks rolling as he spoke. "You can be assured that in all my dealings I believe in the five Ps: Proper Preparation Prevents Poor Performance. I am prepared. I have been planning this for some time, you must realize. Regular habits are a killer. Every Thursday night: the same hotel, same room, same time. A large mistake, sir. Made for nice footage though…plenty of time to plan the lighting."

"I've dealt with ruthless men before," the words mumbled by Lancaster, as much to himself as to Ivo.

"Maybe, sir, at some polished oval table up on the forty-second floor of a fancy office tower. All nice and polite. But I don't play by the Marquis of Queensberry rules—'a man hanging on the ropes in a helpless state, with his toes off the ground shall be considered down.' That would be rule number five. It doesn't apply here, sir. Take my word for it."

"Please," Lancaster said slowly, sarcastically, trying to gather himself together, fighting the image now dancing in his mind—a beaten man, his back arched against the third rope, naked, exposed, his arms unable to cover, waiting for the next blow to land—to the head, to the heart…had to fight that image. He forced it from his thoughts and spoke in a smooth baritone, a stage voice befitting a Public Man of Integrity and Influence, even a scared one. "No legitimate news organization will ever run that tape. And even if one might, all your leverage would evaporate the instant the tape was shown. It would be rather like shooting your only hostage. I won't pay blackmail, and if you release the tape then it loses all its value." Lancaster gained strength, ready to come off the ropes and throw punches. "Perhaps a token payment can be arranged to compensate you for your expenses."

Ivo smiled, enjoying the performance. He lived off men with sterling public reputations and fine pedigrees. James Washington Lancaster, no different. The right schools, the right firms, the right friends. And now Ivo Jenkins from 144th Street in Harlem had him by the lemons, squeezing tight. That was hard to take for a man like Lancaster, and it was to be expected that he would get his back up at some point.

But it was Janis Joplin who'd understood the rules of the game best: "Freedom's just another word for nothin' left to lose." Associate Justice James Lancaster of the Supreme Court, now he had a lot to lose.

Ivo spat another shell to the ground. "I don't believe you've been listening to me, sir. Did I mention taking the tape to the news? I don't think so. So far, only two people in the world have seen that tape: me and you. And, even though some might rate your performance impressive—and they will rate your performance—do you think the president and first lady will still have you over for dinner once they get their copy of the tape? Think your wife won't leave you the day she gets her copy? Fifty-fifty, I'd say, that is if she was my wife. You'll have to supply your own odds. And those are just the first two copies. One copy a day to someone near and dear to you or your career. Each day a new viewing. I figure it will take about a week for the rumors to start. Before long, people will be paying good money for a bootleg—senators and congressmen and all the lobbyists. You know how the lobbyists love their trash. Believe me, the newspapers are way down on my list. And I haven't even mentioned the Internet." Ivo paused to let

9

reality work on the justice for a moment, reality being his friend here.

"So here's the deal, sir. I'm about to propose a number you can live with, and you're going to pay it. That's what's gonna happen. $500,000. That's the number. For your wife's sake you can keep the rest. Keep the job. Still be married. Kids won't know. Don't play clean, well, I don't believe we need to go over that again."

James Lancaster wiped some sweat away from his eyes with his palm, but that was sweaty too, and the sweat just kind of smeared around. A skinny girl was climbing on the nearby steel contraption and shouting nonsense at her friends, the sound waves shooting right through his nerves. Through the nerves of the man on the ropes. Telling him to stay there and try to cover up. It was all he could do. This fat man had won. The fat man knew it. Lancaster knew it. The girl knew it. They all fucking knew it.

"Do we understand each other, sir? $500,000, then I'll leave you alone. Forever."

Forever…forever…forever…the word seemed to catch in the air. On the ropes…forever. As the word hung there, as Lancaster hung there, a new understanding descended upon the justice. One that displaced the fear and the anger and the violation. There was no way to cover up. This nightmare would go on forever.

"Yes, thank you…now I believe I do rather understand," the justice stuttered haltingly. "I pay and in six months or a year or two years, you're back demanding more." Lancaster offered a wry smile, one Ivo had seen before and even come to expect. "No deal, I'm afraid."

"I'll give you my word, sir."

"Your word," Lancaster scoffed. He'd spent his life drafting and negotiating written contracts that were enforceable in court. But there was no way to enforce a deal with a black-mailer. And the justice stood to leave, to take a loser's chance with the federal bureau.

Casually, Ivo ground a shell into the dirt with his heel.

"There is another way—more expensive than trusting my good word."

"Oh really...and what's that?"

Ivo stood and removed his wallet from the back pocket of his pants, then fished out a creased white business card which he handed to the justice. On the card was a neatly typed name.

"Mister Ashland's price is $100,000, sir. I believe you will find his services to be worth every penny."

11

3

New York.

With the thumb and forefinger of his left hand, Isaiah Hawkins gripped a thin metal pin capped by a bright red round plastic head. Tacked on the wall in front of him was a map of the world, eight feet wide by six feet tall. It was a new map and had only arrived that morning, to replace an older version that had lined the west wall of his office for the past year. It had taken three months for this new map to go from design to printing to arrival in his office and, during that period, national borders had been shuffled in several places in west Africa, another country had been born from the ashes of the Soviet Union, and a tin pan dictator of an Asian archipelago had claimed yet another island as his own. Each of these recent events were already reflected in the array of digitized multimedia images, updated every twenty-four hours and rotatable in space, should anyone wish to rotate them, which were at Isaiah's disposal via the Agency's computers. But he preferred the inefficient paper map, its very out-of-datedness a constant reminder of the ephemeral nature of nations and of men.

The movements of his eyes reflected those of his life, drifting from the eastern coast of the United States down and across the Atlantic Ocean to the western coast of Africa. Then, a voice lightly intruded.

"Admiring your world, Isaiah?"

Isaiah Hawkins took a last look at his map before turning deliberately in the direction of the voice. The speaker was his assistant, Anne, with him ever since he'd returned to the States. Standing next to her in the doorway to his office was a man of ordinary build, in his forties, with deeply intelligent eyes.

"Admiring is for the historians, Anne," Isaiah said warmly, his voice a low rumble of cigarette smoke and years. "Am I correct, Professor?"

"That, or reviling," Professor Alexander Greene corrected, stepping forward to clasp Isaiah's outstretched hand. "Of course,

12

the true historians never have counted me as a member. Battles and generals and grand political revolutions being more their thing. Art is so much tamer than all that."

They settled into leather chairs on either side of Isaiah's desk. Isaiah unwrapped a fresh pack of Kents. It was the only perk worthy of envy that had come with this job—New York City's jumble of anti-smoking ordinances having no jurisdiction over him or his people. Not that it made him happy. Thirty years of freedom and chaos in the field, reduced to needing a special federal exemption to smoke in his own office. He lit a cigarette with a tarnished silver lighter and leaned deeper into his chair, taking his time. Always taking his time.

Isaiah had played minor league baseball back when, and the professor knew that game's sense of time and place had determined Isaiah's nature. Still, he couldn't help wondering if maybe God hadn't half intended Isaiah Hawkins for football. Men who were six and a half feet tall, two hundred and fifty pounds, and with the wingspan of an albatross were meant to rush the passer. But then Isaiah's talents had been directed to other purposes.

"I met a young woman this morning," the professor began. "Pretty blonde girl, by the name of Sarah Ridell. From Texas or Oklahoma if I had to guess. Looked mid-twenties, but could be older. Either way, she had the look men want. If you've got the time and money and inclination for that sort of thing."

"What do you have time and inclination for, Professor?"

"Rumors."

"What kind of rumors?"

"The kind that you are interested in, Isaiah. That a pretty blonde woman has information about a phantom. Rare that a true work of artistic genius goes missing. Rarer still when it isn't found for half a century. But you know that already."

Isaiah stubbed out his cigarette. Professor Greene hadn't mentioned the piece by name. He didn't need to. Art was outside Isaiah Hawkins' ordinary sphere of interest. There was only one piece in the world worth discussing with Isaiah Hawkins. The one Isaiah had put Professor Alexander Greene on retainer for, in case he stumbled across interesting information. That was the famed Amber Room of Peter the Great, and a personal obsession of Isaiah Hawkins. Someone else could chase all the other phantoms.

"So you met the woman, Sarah Ridell. I'm assuming her information is for sale. And is expensive."

"Quite," the professor replied.

"And you believe her—that she has something. Enough to push ahead at least."

Professor Greene pressed his hands together and held them awkwardly to his lips, like he was praying and hadn't had much practice at it.

"Yes, I do. But you know the condition, Isaiah. Most people in my world are collectors. They care about possession. I know you do as well. But I don't. Art historians don't possess, they preserve. The Amber Room has been presumed lost for fifty years, and if it stays lost for another fifty, so be it. Desire can be an awful temptation. I've seen it lead people to risk destroying something beautiful, if the other option is someone else possessing it. But I can't be responsible for that type of recklessness."

Isaiah leaned back in his chair. Alexander Greene had made this point before, when Isaiah had approached him about collaborating in their mutual searches for the Amber Room. Perhaps they had different motives, but they shared the same goal. So why not work together? That had been Isaiah's pitch, and the professor had gone along quite easily, helped naturally by the financial incentives. So difficult living in New York on a professor's salary.

"I understand, Alexander."

"And what about your people? Will they understand?"

His people? Isaiah lit another cigarette. Always get your people. Something his mentor had imprinted on him three decades ago. Still one of the best pieces of advice he'd ever received. Get your people. Not the honest people or the decent people or the truthful or caring or any-other-impressive-adjective people. Not the people the Agency sent around either. Get your own people. People you know.

People whose flaws you already understood. Preferably people you owned. People Isaiah Hawkins could use right now.

"Don't worry, Professor. You'll be satisfied with my people." Isaiah Hawkins left unsaid the unpleasant reality. Professor Alexander Greene of Columbia University was one of his people, and had been from the moment he cashed his first check.

After the professor had left, Isaiah returned to his map. For a moment he glanced at Africa, where he'd first fought the Agency's wars and those of his friends, and where in certain bars one could still hear stories told about the White Zulu. Other stories were told in other places.

Then the Agency had called him to leave the field, to take his turn overseeing this map. And he, all the while, wishing to still be down there on the ground where sudden opportunities of the type brought by luck, Alexander Greene, and a woman named Sarah Ridell would be exploited or lost.

He slid a step to his left, the map's west, so that he was standing directly in front of Europe. A series of map pins—red, green, and yellow dots—jutted out from the typewritten names of Europe's great capital cities: Prague, Vienna, Berlin. The green dots were his. His people in place. The red dots belonged to others. The yellow dots were the toss-ups, places where more innings needed to be played before a winner would emerge.

Belgrade was a yellow dot—in the former Yugoslavia, there wasn't anyone of talent who wasn't playing multiple sides. But that pin was of small matter. Belgrade was an insignificant capital of a still less significant country. A harsh assessment perhaps, but no less true for being so. The game lay elsewhere.

In the upper left corner of the map, not far from Iceland, was a bullpen of unused pins. Isaiah selected a yellow one. He swept the pin along the map from left to right, arcing it slowly across Scandinavia and the Baltics, and across the Volga river until it hovered over the very heart of Russia. He pushed the pin into the map with precision...his man in Moscow, the most important dot of all.

4

Ivo Jenkins looked out a window of a different and better hotel, seeing the Washington Monument shining brightly against a half-crescent moon. God, I love my work, he announced to himself. Justice Lancaster had just called and his barely audible voice still rang loud in Ivo's ears. The man was ready to be played, and Ivo picked up the phone to dial a number he knew by touch. Two…one…two…

Anand Ashland was reading poetry when the call came into the study of his Manhattan townhouse. Unfortunately, verse and Anand's particular line of work made an ill-fitting pair, and he knew as soon as he heard Ivo's voice that he would not be returning to Eliot that evening. He answered the phone in his own soft manner, "Ivo, how is your world?"

"Lovely. I'm living large, loving life. I take it, however, that I'm interrupting your most laudable efforts to understand human nature through fine literature. A doomed enterprise, that is, compared to my own efforts. That is, compared to a videotape of the justice putting his wand—"

"Ivo, spare me the details, please. I'm reading Eliot."

"Now, what's that Eliot says, 'April is the cruelest month'?"

"'The Wasteland.' I'm suitably impressed, Ivo. But it's not April."

"No matter. I got my ass drafted in April. April 1965. I know what the man was talking about. That was one tough month, yes sir. But this summer is looking fine. F-I-N-E. I've got the justice by the proverbial balls, and my price for letting go is half a million. He wants assurance that I don't give him another squeeze in a year or so. There's a clean hundred in it for you, my friend."

Anand Ashland looked over at a sepia photograph of his light-skinned father and his darker-skinned grandfather that hung on the wall of his home and hesitated, considering the implications and the price.

Ivo Jenkins felt the hesitation and added, "He's a real prick, too."

"Prickdom," Anand replied, dragging out each letter like a don at an English boarding school, "is not the question." Still, the answer was clear—this line of work being the Ashland family business for over two hundred years on three continents.

Later that night, Anand stood in front of a set of shelves filled end to end and then some with hard- and soft-backed books, the spines of the books creased and battered. Ritual mattered and every commission deserved its own quote, or so his father had always maintained. Anand's hand drifted over the volumes, trying Browning, then Swift, before lighting upon Melville. He opened the book like a medieval seer who told fortunes by opening the Bible to a random page and selecting a line. The lines intended for this reading were halfway down the page:

> Delight is to him who gives no quarter in the truth, and kills, burns, and destroys all sin though he pluck it out from under the robes of Senators and Judges.

5

They met this time in a room at the Watergate Hotel, because it was public and because Ivo knew that the Watergate's magical symbolism would wear on Justice Lancaster's thoughts.

The justice arrived last, clutching a black leather briefcase and wearing the exact outfit he'd worn to his film session—same suit, same tie, same shoes—right down to the same white jockey shorts for all Ivo knew. Which was either an irony one would not have supposed the justice capable of, or a certain obtuseness which could only be admired.

James Lancaster immediately focused on the third man in the suite: early forties, olive skin, slender build, jet black eyes and hair, wearing an exquisitely tailored suit; the cut and fabric of his whole being speaking of inherited wealth. He looked Caucasian, but James Washington Lancaster couldn't be sure. Mr. Ashland, nevertheless. A man whom he had never met, who was part of this parade, and to whom he was being asked to pay $100,000 for his own good. A slice of the surreal. The justice made his fist ever tighter around the leather handle of his briefcase, so that the blood fled the knuckles of his hand.

"I assume, sir, that you have checked Mister Ashland's references by now?"

James Lancaster nodded noncommittally. As if this Anand Ashland were a cardiac surgeon, he'd been given a list of three names: David McKinney, the senior senator from Illinois; Peter Rousch, a vice-chairman of Morgan Stanley; and Kirkwood Williams, a Broadway player. The justice knew Senator McKinney, having met him at parties over the years, so he'd started there. At least that way he could attempt to laugh it off if necessary. McKinney had not laughed. Neither had Rousch, nor Williams. Each of them had vouched for Anand Ashland, without details, of course, of the circumstances under which they had come into Mister Ashland's particular orbit.

"Then you know that Anand Ashland's word is beyond reproach," Ivo stated.

"I know what I was told," the justice replied. He turned to Anand. "I would appreciate some details. Exactly what will you deliver for my hundred thousand?"

"The intent is that I deliver nothing," Anand said, clipping the words short as he reached into a leather briefcase of his own and removed two videocassettes which he held secure in his hand. One marked with a green label, the other red.

"I believe, Judge, you are already familiar with one of these tapes. As for the other..." Anand paused here and motioned in the direction of Ivo. "You are of course aware of our associate's profession. But neither the government nor his children have been so informed. They believe he earns his rather substantial income through the ownership of several inner city fast food chicken franchises—quite successful I'm told. But not, I'm afraid, as lucrative as this type of endeavor. I'm sure you can appreciate that."

The justice gripped his leather bag even tighter, his expression making it plenty clear that, no, he did not appreciate any of this. Nor understand it.

Anand raised the tape with the red label and continued. "Surely a man in your position, Justice Lancaster, can see how our friend would not wish his career made public. The police would certainly find it interesting, his family painful. This tape contains a full confession to his involvement in your predicament, as well as a series of prior projects he has undertaken. You may view it as a loaded gun. If our friend breaks his word and attempts to blackmail you again, I will release this tape to the police and to his family. By the same token, to prevent you from engaging in discussions with FBI Director Spellman or any of his brethren, I will keep a tape of your transgressions. Both tapes, locked in a vault to which I hold the only key. Assuming, of course, all payments are made by you in advance."

Lancaster ran his free hand across his mouth. His mouth dry, his hand sweaty, the taste bitter. The proposal remarkable: through the dual tapes, they would be placed on equal footing, he and this blackmailer, both of them on the ropes, naked, exposed. But only so long as he paid. If he didn't pay, if Lancaster left the room with his precious money, it was only he who would be left naked.

The justice could think of few men with nerve and smarts enough to better their position by proposing to expose themselves to jeopardy. But, with the connivance of this Anand Ashland, this blackmailer had just done exactly that.

And it was that recognition of his opponent's will, more than anything else, that convinced James Lancaster of the rightness of paying for his indulgences. The justice flared his nostrils and breathed deeply, sweat dripping down his back.

"Now, the money please," Ivo said politely.

Lancaster let loose the grip on his briefcase and handed it to Ivo, a surge of nausea hitting him as he let go.

Ivo counted the bills carefully. Ten stacks of hundreds, fifty thousand per stack. Two more stacks for Anand. Six hundred thousand total. It was all there. And it restored the blackmailer's primitive faith in man.

After the justice had gone, Ivo poured two glasses of fine whiskey from a tall bottle he'd been saving for the right occasion. One glass for himself and one for Anand. They drank a toast to the excesses of men, upon which they lived, then set the glasses down, alongside a better portion of the money the justice had paid.

Anand had already shifted his commission into his own bag, and Ivo contemplated the remainder, his money now. "That girl," Ivo started, speaking with a hesitancy that only rarely crept into his voice, "the one the justice was with…she was only fifteen. Just a girl. No family. No future. Tossed away…already."

It was a ritual of theirs and didn't require any further discussion.

Anand reached into his bag and removed $10,000. A sum Ivo would match five times over. Money which would find its way to the girl for an education. And for their karma, all of theirs, including James Lancaster's.

Finally, Anand stood to leave, "I have to get back to New York."

"Anything we can talk about—professionally, I mean?"

Anand hesitated. A summons from Isaiah Hawkins was most definitely not something one could talk about. "Not yet."

6

Anand slipped into the fluorescent lit room, the last of four to arrive. Isaiah Hawkins had asked him to come here—to a musty chamber carved out of the earth a hundred feet below Central Park, in the depths of the American Museum of Natural History—for a briefing session. The topic and the other participants were not disclosed in advance.

Already seated at an old wood library table was a woman in perhaps her early thirties, a stranger to Anand. She was quite pretty; slight, with green eyes and black hair, cut very short and dyed with a tint of dark red. A thin black top, summer cashmere, clung to her body and she looked every bit a downtown New Yorker, and no part Agency, except for her tan. Her bare arms and face had a rich permanent tone, of the type that was not acquired in a city tanning booth or long summer weekends in the Hamptons. That tan came from someplace else, and it gave her away as the type of person whom Isaiah Hawkins might have collected.

At the front of the room, standing next to a projection screen, was a man of medium height and build, in his late forties, wearing khakis and a sports jacket. He had a soft look, unexpected for someone dealing with Isaiah Hawkins. On the screen next to him, a glistening yellow gem the size of a man's fist shone brightly. Frozen inside the gem was a bee, perfectly preserved—the stinger distinctly visible, as were the veins on its wings.

Isaiah Hawkins was across the table, his long arms and legs spilling out of the same-sized chair which held Anand comfortably and all but swallowed the woman with the smile. Isaiah's hair, silver forever, had thinned since the last time Anand had seen him, perhaps a year back.

The tan woman invited Anand to sit next to her. "Kathryn Blaire," she said, casually, offering a subversive, twinkling smile. Perhaps her way of saying that she too had been summoned, although it could have meant any number of other things, or nothing at all.

"A pleasure, Ms. Blaire. My name is Anand Ashland."

"Yes, I know. Isaiah has already told me something of you. Interesting profession you have. Nice to be working with you."

Anand slid his chair back from the table and sat down. How nice of Isaiah to fill in Kathryn Blaire and all.

"Thanks for joining us, Anand." Isaiah said simply. He motioned towards the man standing at the projection screen. "Anand, this is Professor Alexander Greene. Alexander is a professor of art history at Columbia University and a curator here at the American Museum of Natural History. His specialty is amber. He is going to be working with us on this project. I've asked Alexander to prepare a presentation to get you and Kathryn up to speed." Isaiah paused. "Why don't you get started, Professor."

"Thank you, Isaiah. Glad to meet you, Ms. Blaire, and Mister Ashland." Professor Alexander Greene's voice had one of those East Coast WASP accents that defied geographical precision. "I don't know how much Isaiah has told you so far, but it all starts with amber."

Professor Greene pointed at the screen with a laser pen, focusing directly on the gem with the imprisoned bee. "This is a piece of fossilized tree resin—amber. This example is forty million years old and comes from a site near the Baltic Sea. It was formed when a bee, this bee, got stuck in resin oozing from the bark of a tree. The bee never escaped, the tree died, the resin hardened. About one out of every hundred pieces has an insect of some kind trapped in it. Biological scientists love amber because it offers a window to the past, a chance to study the features and the DNA of creatures that existed millions of years ago. In essence, amber does for insects what mummification did for King Tut. Interesting. Compelling to some. The Jurassic Park of it all. However, I'm not here for dead insects and neither are you. We're after something much more valuable."

Another click of the remote and the projected bee was replaced by a necklace. A glistening double strand of beads

wrapped around the long neck of a beautiful African woman.

"Jewelry and beauty. It's where the game has been since the Stone Age. Upstairs on the second floor of this Museum, in the Cantrill Gallery, you can see amber pieces carved during the Neolithic era. The Phoenicians traded amber jewelry. As did the Romans. A small piece of amber jewelry was worth more than a female slave during the reign of Nero—not that I recommend the reign of Nero as an enlightened example. And from jewelry, we move to art."

Professor Alexander Greene clicked again. The necklace was replaced by a black and white picture of a high ceilinged room with brilliant paneling. Greene stepped back from the screen to get a better view of the picture, as if admiring it himself.

"The stuff of fables," he said, his voice lowered to a whisper. "And the reason we are here. This is the Amber Room. Imagine, if you will, Kathryn and Anand, walls lined floor to ceiling in a colored mosaic. More than one hundred thousand pieces of amber—yellow, red, blue, green, and clear—polished, carved, some with etched images, all formed into an intricate, stunning vision."

Kathryn Blaire raised her hand, appeared to feel a bit sheepish for doing so, but got the professor's attention in any event. Her voice a raspy cross between Kathleen Turner and Billie Holiday. "I thought amber was, well, amber in color. Golden."

"Most amber jewelry is," Alexander Greene replied. "The other colors are quite rare. But beautiful. I wish I could show you, but this black and white photo is all we have of the Amber Room."

"Why is that?" Kathryn asked.

"World War II to be precise," Greene said with a half smile. "But I have to begin two hundred years earlier. The Amber Room was designed in the early 1700s for Frederick I of Prussia, by a German master craftsman named Wolfram and a French jeweler named Tusso, using pieces of amber that the Prussian kings had collected over decades. When finished and installed at Frederick's palace of Mon Bijou, the Amber Room had twelve panels, each sixteen feet high, along with desks, chairs, and tables, all of amber.

"But the Room did not stay there long. When Frederick I died, he was succeeded by his son, Frederick William, an eccentric of the first order with a particular obsession for giants, some twelve hundred of which he gathered into two battalions known as the Giants of Potsdam. Although Frederick William was quite willing to pay for his giants, and tried breeding them as well, it seems that the best way of collecting giants at that time was to trade for them. Therefore, Frederick William swapped the Amber Room to his friend Peter the Great—the Peter the Great—for fifty giants collected by Peter throughout the Russian empire. Quite a good trade for Tsar Peter. After all, one could argue that the lives of even giant warriors are temporal things: flesh to be bought, sold, and killed in battle. But the Amber Room is timeless.

"Turns out, Peter was a better trader than decorator. The Tsar's palace had thirty-foot ceilings, and the panels were only sixteen feet high. So Peter left the panels to sit in their shipping crates for some thirty years, while the giants died off. Eventually, Peter's daughter Elizabeth retained an Italian architect named Rastreli, who incorporated the panels into larger ones that included mirrors and Italian mosaics and hung the redesigned panels at the Tsar's palace in Tsarkoye-Selo near St. Petersburg. There they remained for the next two centuries. The photograph we have been looking at was taken in 1930 at Tsarkoye-Selo."

"Then what happened?" Kathryn asked, giving the professor a cue he hardly needed, but nonetheless appreciated.

"The Nazis happened, Ms. Blaire," Alexander Greene replied simply. "As the German army conquered territory, the Nazi leadership engaged in a systematic program of looting Europe's great works of art. The spoils of war and all that. Nothing new. All told, the Nazis captured tens of thousands of objects of art, many of them for Hitler's personal collection. The Nazi advance on Leningrad caught the Russians by surprise, before the Amber Room could be protected. Some of the desks and chairs and other miscellaneous objects, such as some small mirrors, were packed away and hidden, but the amber panels were left in place. When the Nazis captured the palace at Tsarkoye-Selo, they promptly shipped the panels to East Prussia, to an old Bohemian castle in Königsberg where they were displayed as a war trophy."

A sense of regret now crept into the professor's voice. "Königsberg castle, which had survived eight hundred years of Teutonic warfare, was destroyed in one day by an RAF bombing mission in August 1944. Eight months later, Russian troops captured the city after a battle in which forty thousand German soldiers were killed. Most of Königsberg was completely destroyed. As for the Amber Room—it simply disappeared."

"What?" Anand asked, as in his experience, valuable objects never simply disappear. People made them disappear—and reappear in other places.

Professor Greene took a sip of water and joined the others at the table, relieved now that the lecture portion was over. "Most believe it was destroyed in the bombing, Mister Ashland. Others, more cynical, believe that Russian troops recovered the Room and spirited it back to Russia. But I have never believed that. The Amber Room belonged to the Russians. The giants for the Room. A deal. The Russians could have taken it back to Tsarkoye-Selo openly and freely. Either way, the Amber Room—except for a few of the minor objects saved from the Nazis and which surface from time to time—has never been seen since the end of the war."

Isaiah Hawkins had taken out a pack of cigarettes from his pocket and now he tapped the bottom of the pack against the knuckle of his thumb. He took one for himself and offered the pack to Kathryn Blaire. Not offering any to the others, presumably because he knew they did not smoke, the way he knew everything about them. Kathryn Blaire took a cigarette anxiously, almost greedily. Smoke from their twin fires swirling into air like thin gray spires. One thing quite evident to all, although the professor had not said the words. The Amber Room, missing since the end of World War II, was somehow in play. And of interest to Isaiah Hawkins and the Agency.

Professor Greene turned his head to look back at the picture of the Room. There was a look on his face that Anand Ashland recognized. Searching for a lost treasure, after all, was a lifetime of false leads and con artists. This was not the first time Alexander Greene had allowed himself to believe the Amber Room might be within his grasp.

Isaiah slowly tapped the ash off his cigarette into an ashtray. He looked carefully at Anand and Kathryn, as if deciding just now whether to continue, whether to inform them of the reason he had called them both to this meeting. Knowing they were both wondering why the Agency was interested in a lost work of art. Even a legendary one.

Isaiah rested the cigarette against the lip of the ashtray and spoke to Kathryn and Anand as a pair. "Professor Greene believes new information regarding the Amber Room is available. He came to me in part because he knows I am interested in seeing the Room recovered. More to the point, I have resources unavailable to him. Such as you. But you are no doubt wondering why I care."

Isaiah focused his gaze on Kathryn Blaire, who was leaning forward like she was waiting expectantly for an answer to that question. That was Kathryn Blaire. She liked to know why. Sitting next to her, Anand Ashland was impassive. If there was a deal to guarantee, he would do it. *Why* wasn't an issue for Anand Ashland.

"Fact is," Isaiah said precisely, "I have no business caring about the Amber Room, and neither does the Agency. But the Gospel of Luke, 6:27, advises us to love our enemies and give unto our enemies that which they want. For the past four decades the Russians have been my enemy, and I've finally taken Luke to heart.

"As you all know, the Russians are in the last weeks of a presidential election. A former Red Army general, Sergei Mikhailov, is running as a communist against the current vice president, Nikolai Lysenko, who has positioned himself as the democratic heir to Gorbachev and Yeltsin. General Mikhailov is a tough, nasty son of a bitch. Dropped four thousand bombs an hour on the city of Grozny during the war in Chechnya. Would have been twice that number if he had the supplies. General Mikhailov has himself taken to heart the Russian faith in power—that the mandate to rule does not come from doing right, but from being strong. To that point, he's running as a communist, as the successor to Lenin and Stalin. He's not doing so because he believes, but because the communist myth is still resonant. It evokes a Russia and a party that won a world war, had an empire, and was feared and respected. That would contrast with the facts of today: no empire, a deteriorating military, and a third-world economy filled with corruption.

"The general's opponent, Nikolai Lysenko, the current vice president, is a do-gooding reformer. His great ambition is to get Russia on the right path economically, so that with luck, Russian standards of living will equal that of Denmark by the next generation. It doesn't sound sexy, but it's the right ambition.

"General Mikhailov is ahead right now in the polls by eight points. I don't suppose that's a great surprise, given the general's promises to restore Mother Russia to glory. But our object here is simple. We don't want the general to win. We don't need a military buildup in Russia, we don't need the general running around thinking he is the Tsar, we don't need him causing trouble in the Balkans, and we don't need him in control of Russia's nuclear weapons. I'm too old for that. And I don't need to tell you that just because the general may be elected democratically he is a good guy. Hitler was elected democratically, so were most of the assholes running Africa as dictators. On the other hand, if the vice president wins, we can expect Russia to keep cutting military spending and concentrate on domestic policy. That's a win, and that's where the Amber Room comes in.

"The Russians see the Amber Room as an icon—a symbol of national sovereignty that was stolen from them during the war. The Russians are like children that way, symbols of their past greatness matter deeply to them. But let's not forget they lost twenty-five million people winning World War II. They did fight a great war.

"We are going to find the Amber Room and present it to the current Russian government the week of the election as a symbol of friendship. A staggering quantity of Russian television time—controlled by the current government—will be devoted to well-staged images of Vice President Lysenko in the Amber Room taking the credit for its return. It will show he cares about national pride, he will bump in the polls and, I believe, he will win. Why? because at the end of the day, I'm betting the Russian people really do want Denmark's standard of living for their children more than they want a military buildup, they just want a little national stature along the way. Any questions?"

But Isaiah knew there wouldn't be any questions. Love your enemies. It was good, but it wasn't quite right—a man in his chosen occupation was defined by his enemies. In Isaiah's case, that enemy had been the Soviet Union and the communist party. Maybe he had sounded just now like an unrepentant cold warrior who regretted the collapse of communism, but that wasn't it. God had given him the Cold War, he had enjoyed it, and damned if he was going to lose it now through a democratic election. There was more to it than that of course, but Isaiah Hawkins felt no need to go into that in this room.

Across the table, Anand smiled to himself. It seemed like a nice story to him. Happy, happy. A gift of the Amber Room to the Russians—influence an election, help world peace. Very nice. A win, Isaiah called it. But Isaiah Hawkins didn't hand out a lot of gifts, even Trojan horses. And happy, happy wasn't becoming on him.

Kathryn Blaire stood, as if she was anxious to get going. Her rasp interrupted Anand's thoughts, "What comes next, Isaiah?"

"We wait. Professor Greene's source is a young woman named Sarah Ridell. She is to contact him to arrange the next meeting. Our job is to be prepared. Any other questions?"

There were plenty of questions, but no one bothered asking them, because Isaiah Hawkins kept the whole truth only for himself anyway. That's the way this game was to be played.

7

Sarah Ridell didn't keep anyone waiting. Her message arrived the next day, written longhand, in a rounded script, on a pretty card with a picture of yellow and purple tulips.

Dear Professor,

May I suggest the sculpture garden at the Museum of Modern Art tomorrow at noon?

I will come alone. You may bring with you anyone you wish. But please do not make the error of believing that the object of your desire may be recovered through false means.

Sarah

Isaiah Hawkins reassembled his team that evening and they each read the note to themselves, without comment. Then Isaiah turned to Kathryn Blaire, rather than Anand or the professor, because he trusted her instincts where this woman Sarah was concerned. Troubled women being Kathryn's particular metier. That and money.

Kathryn drew her finger across the tulips. She'd always felt that tulips were meant to be her flower, ever since she'd received a single, white tulip from her first lover. She was seventeen. It was quaint. The tulip, not the lover. He was the first in a seemingly inexhaustible and oftentimes random sequence of handsome, charming, or wealthy disappointments—most of them her fault—that composed her love life. And what did the tulips mean here? Nothing as far as Kathryn Blaire could tell. Just that a woman had selected the card, but they already knew that. Rather, the clues she saw ran elsewhere.

"Assuming it's her handwriting, I see three things. She's young; look how rounded and flowing her script is. She's an amateur; a professional wouldn't have handwritten that note.

And, she underestimates the stakes; the last line—it's too mannered. I mean, how the fuck else would the Amber Room be recovered except by false means?"

"You got all that from the note?" Professor Greene asked, clearly impressed.

Kathryn smiled. "Not exactly, Professor. I did some homework on Ms. Ridell between yesterday and today. She is twenty-eight years old. Lives in an apartment on East 73rd Street. Moved here from Oklahoma a couple of years back. Graduate of University of Oklahoma and OU law school. Doesn't have a job that I could find yet. Apartment is rented, owned by a cutout New Cayman corporation. My guess is she's screwing the real owner and doesn't pay much cash rent. I'll know better later in the week. We'll be watching the apartment starting tonight. She's no one's fool. But this isn't her usual gig. She's got issues here. But who doesn't?"

8

At 11:00 the next day, an hour early, Professor Greene and Kathryn Blaire arrived at MOMA, bought their tickets, and walked back to the outdoor sculpture garden. It was just the two of them, Anand having been given the day off by Isaiah, held in reserve as it were.

While the professor waited nervously on a small bench checking his watch, Kathryn enjoyed the summer sunshine best she could. All things being equal, and they hardly ever were, she would've preferred to be back on the beach, her beach. Isaiah had thought differently. She could see his point, especially the way he'd made it, and here she was. His girl, back on the job.

With an hour to kill, she opted for art appreciation over constant vigilance, starting with a nice little statue, and then moving on to Picasso. She decided, after some hesitation, that she rather liked the Spaniard's anorexic metal Goat—because she supposed you had to like Picasso if you were to be considered modern. And she liked Henry Moore's Large Torso because of the way its oversized curves looked warm even in bronze. But when she stood in front of Rodin's Monument to Balzac, her mind wandered straight to memories of her old partner at the Agency, Gray Taylor. Rodin was Gray's God, Gray having taken more than one trip to Paris, a city and people he otherwise detested, just to visit the Rodin Gardens. He said you could see the whole life of the man sculpted in each of Rodin's works: you could see the good and the bad, and the truth which lay somewhere in between. Which may have said something about Rodin, or maybe about Gray.

Gray had always seen the ambiguity. Seen through the surface of men and circumstances the way a painter sees through a complex color straight to the underlying pigments. Except unlike painting, their job tended not to get any clearer when the individual streams were isolated, just more muddled.

And that, Kathryn suspected, was why Isaiah had paired

them up. Because where Gray saw things as they might have truly been and gave pause, all she had ever admitted to believing in were opportunities to exploit. She supposed that to admit to anything more—to having doubts, hopes, or faith— even to herself, would have been showing weakness. And Kathryn Blaire didn't show weakness; she had decided that a long time ago.

Kathryn was still thinking of all that when, at five minutes past noon, Sarah Ridell stepped through the double glass doors that lead from the Museum gallery to the outdoor garden. She was a young woman with long sandy blonde hair, soft features, light green eyes, delicate lips and an ever so slightly crooked nose that only made her look more beautiful. She was wearing a fashionable black pants suit and seemed like the type of smart young woman who would be at home in a Park Avenue law firm or investment bank, had she gone to the right schools.

Alexander Greene stood to greet her, and took her hand politely.

"Professor Greene, so glad you could come," Sarah said, her voice trailing a hint of a plains accent. She turned towards Kathryn and, as she turned, Kathryn noticed a small scar on her left cheek. "And you are?" Sarah asked.

"Kathryn Blaire. I'm working with Alexander, Professor Greene that is. I'm the money."

Sarah looked Kathryn up and down, trying to decide just where that money came from. Or, more to the point, whether the money was real. "How do I know you can deliver, Ms. Blaire?"

Kathryn smiled back, a different smile than the one she'd given Anand. "Same way we know whether you can, I suppose. Little bit of instinct. Little bit of background research. How much money are we talking about anyway?"

"I don't believe we're at that point yet, Ms. Blaire. The people I represent—"

"The people you represent?" Kathryn interrupted. "I thought—"

Sarah looked at her sharply. "Neither you nor Professor Greene can possibly believe I would be so innocent as to put myself out here if I personally had the information. I have been hired to represent someone else…as their attorney."

"Their attorney?" Kathryn questioned intuitively, impulsively. And she regretted the question the instant it escaped her lips.

"Excuse me?" Sarah bristled.

"Never mind," Kathryn said quickly. After all, it was obvious. People always hired twenty-eight-year-old girls from Oklahoma to handle situations like this. No way Sarah Ridell had been hired so that if the authorities came down or something went wrong, she'd be the one to take the hit while her clients pulled back and disappeared into the ether. That wasn't the way the world worked anymore. New world order, and all that. She, Kathryn Blaire, had just been out of the loop too long. Too much time on the beach. Sarah Ridell was an attorney, not a fall girl.

Professor Greene looked at Kathryn crossly, the way Isaiah had suggested in the likely event it seemed right. "Now, Sarah, what exactly is it that your clients wish to propose?"

Sarah Ridell sidled closer to the professor, as if Kathryn were no longer there. "We are asking for an initial payment of one million dollars. After which, you will be provided information leading directly to the Amber Room."

"A name and an address, am I correct?" Professor Greene asked.

"A name, Professor. And a city. That ought to be enough, I would think. Payment due three days from today."

"Three days…" Greene stuttered, actually surprised they'd been given so much time.

Sarah smiled her best southern smile. "With five million more due immediately upon recovery of the Room. Of course, I'll need some assurance the five million will be paid once you have the Room. We can work out those details later, after the first million has been paid."

"What's your take?" Kathryn asked.

"My fee is my business."

Kathryn replied coolly, "I'm sure it is."

Sarah handed the professor a folded slip of paper. "That's the number of a private bank account in Switzerland. As I said, the first million needs to be deposited within seventy-two hours, or I am authorized to make a deal with others who might be interested." Gently, she placed her hand on the professor's arm. "I can only imagine what the Amber Room must mean to you. I'd like to do this deal with you, I really would. Don't let other people take it away from you."

Then Sarah released Professor Greene and began to detach herself from the group, looking around rapidly as she did, to see whether anyone was waiting to intercept her. There wasn't, because that was not the way Isaiah had chosen. Rather, his instructions had been quite clear, to let this play out for now the way Sarah Ridell chose. But Kathryn Blaire didn't like what she felt, and she caught up to Sarah as she was walking away, taking hold of Sarah's arm.

"You don't want to hear this," Kathryn told her, "because the money seems like too much to resist and, believe me, I know that feeling. But you're the fall girl here. You're out of your league, girl."

"Thanks for the advice, Ms. Blaire. But I'm not a girl anymore, and I ain't never been out of my league."

"That's what everyone thinks the first time, Sarah," Kathryn Blaire replied softly, relaxing her grip and letting Sarah walk away. Sarah Ridell was right, she wasn't a girl anymore. But that didn't mean she wasn't about to get hurt.

•　　　•　　　•

"Do you believe her?"

Isaiah finished putting flame to tobacco while the question hung in the room. He was halfway through his second pack of Kents for the day; two packs a day for some forty-five years and long ago he'd realized that the smarter thing to do would've been to stop smoking and put the money saved into

Kent stock. But then he'd never believed all of life was about being smart or about making money.

"Well, do you believe her?" Professor Greene repeated.

Isaiah watched a wave of smoke climb from the end of his cigarette before answering. "It's not that simple, never is. I suspect some of what she said is true and some false. Some of it she believes herself, and some she doesn't. And just because she believes something, doesn't make her right. The real question here, Professor, is whether to pay the money. And I think we come to the same answer whether we believe her or not."

"Why?" asked Greene.

"Because we have to pay to keep playing," Isaiah said simply. "A bunch of irises was sold some years back for sixty-one million dollars. Someone's going to pay Sarah Ridell that one million if we don't. We can't take that risk. And if her information turns out bad, I don't mind our odds of getting that one million back."

Isaiah paused and looked over the other members of the team, assembled once again in the war room in the basement of the Museum of Natural History. He knew Anand would be questioning whether his services were needed to arrange a guarantee. But it was too early for that. Better to wait until Sarah Ridell went for the five million, then introduce Anand.

Isaiah turned to Kathryn instead. "Take care of the payment. But not until day three. And make sure to place a trace on the money. I want to know everyone who handles it. Understood?"

"Yeah...sure," she said, in a hesitant manner that Anand and Professor Greene took for momentary distraction.

"What about Sarah?" Anand asked.

"We watch her for the next three days. See what we learn before sending the money. Maybe she'll make a mistake."

Kathryn picked up the thread and pushed it. "I think we should approach her, Isaiah. Try to turn her. She's not safe with the clients she has, or with their information. Turning her would be better for us, better for her."

Isaiah exhaled a stream of white smoke. "Better for her isn't

our concern. And, as for us, I like playing the game straight up for now."

"I've just got a bad feeling that once the money is paid, Sarah Ridell becomes very expendable," Kathryn replied.

"We're watching her apartment, aren't we?" the professor asked.

Kathryn looked over at him crossways. Yeah, they were watching Sarah's apartment. Kathryn, and a couple of free-lancers, including some dubious associate of Anand's—taking turns peeping, seeing what turned up. But watching and doing something were two very different things. "She's not a pro, Isaiah. Watching isn't enough here. Not if something goes wrong."

"Possibly," Isaiah said. "But she has put herself into this. And no one's appointed us her guardian angels. We keep watch on her apartment, pay the one million at the appointed time. That's it."

"I still don't like it," Kathryn pressed, her face openly draining of all its easygoing sparkle.

Isaiah, rather calmly, let her anger drift past him. Most of the Agency's people had too much concern for their own careers to openly challenge him. That's why he'd stopped using them for everything but the routine turns and writing reports. Writing reports, they were good at that. Not Kathryn Blaire. She didn't give a damn about her career. Just not the way she'd been hardwired according to the Agency shrinks:

"She's an extreme type T, Isaiah. An outlier on the Z-Triple S—the Zuckerman Sensation Seeking Scale, as modified by Bernouilli for the Agency. She's not in the normal range. Not even close. It's most likely biological and hereditary—a deficiency of the monoamine oxidase enzyme, causing a significant diminution in her ability to feel psychological arousal. She'll take risks that aren't worth it."

"Isn't that why we're here. To take risks, Doctor?"

"Maybe. But she'll do it just for the rush. For the thrill, physical or mental."

The doctor—a woman named Cummings who'd vetted all of the Agency's field hires for the past decade—looked down at the computerized printout of Kathryn's test results, seeing a five inch spike where there should have been a flat plateau. She pulled at her earlobe. A mannerism that could've perhaps used its own studying.

"Just so you know, Isaiah. I'm going to recommend against it. Hiring her, that is. In my assessment report."

Isaiah shrugged. "The test...it's self-reporting, multiple-choice, right? One hundred or so questions, you select the answer that most nearly describes how you feel?"

"That's right."

"And the questions are pretty obvious as to which way they go on the scale. Do you prefer many sexual partners or a constant relationship? Or, do you think skydiving would be an excellent way to spend an afternoon?"

"What's your point, Isaiah?"

"So she could've lied."

"Sure. Plenty do. But I don't believe she did. I spent three days with her, running her through the TAT, Jungian word association, Stanford-Binet IQ...I can usually tell when they lie."

"I know you can, Doctor. That's why I like you. But she couldn't be bothered to lie. She's off the charts the wrong way, she knows it, and she doesn't care if we know it. That's the vig here. Most people are more afraid than anything of making a mistake. Not this girl. The only thing she's afraid of is not getting a chance to make a play."

"She's not as hard as you think she is, Isaiah."

"I didn't say she's hard, Doctor. I'm not looking for hard—hard I've got plenty of, sitting in offices on every floor. I said she's got nerve, and those are the difficult ones to find."

And she had gambled and made mistakes. Enough that, objectively, it didn't matter any longer whether she cared about her career. She didn't have a career left worth giving a damn about. That was all right. Not many of Isaiah's best

people had careers. But they had lives and they made plays, and this Sarah Ridell had touched a nerve in Kathryn Blaire.

Isaiah lit another smoke. "None of us like it, Kathryn. It's not about the liking."

She shrugged her shoulders, "Well, that settles it. If you don't care whether you like it, then let's pay the money and fuck the girl, I guess."

9

Alone in her high-rise apartment, Sarah Ridell felt strangely safe. Even more so when she slipped across her living room to stand in front of the long window which ran the full width of the room and rose to the ceiling from waist height. Elliot had insisted on having thin metal venetian blinds installed, the type that could be finely adjusted to let in streams of light and shadow or no light at all. Now she pulled the blinds all the way up to let in the evening and pressed her face against the glass. It was surprisingly warm.

She looked down upon Lexington Avenue, fighting vertigo to focus on the small figures thirty-nine floors below. The sun had pretty much dimmed, and she strained to make out a woman in a reddish jacket walking a barely visible dog. Next to the woman, a bald man was reading a paper while leaning against a street lamp, the light of the lamp reflecting off of his round head. Nearby, a yellow cab stood idling by the curb waiting for a fare to climb in. None of those scenes looked at all out of place in this neighborhood.

Of course, the type of people she was trying to spot couldn't be expected to look out of place. Besides, she realized she was probably looking in the wrong direction anyway. A much better view into her apartment would be afforded from another angle altogether.

She lifted her head up and looked through the glass and straight across a bridge of air to a tall white brick building that rose up across the street. Every day for the last two years she'd woken up to the sight of that building and she hated it. The brick was so ugly and dirty and heavy. But that's where she guessed they would be, in an apartment, most likely on the thirty-ninth or fortieth floor. They would be staring right at her, watching her, waiting for her to make a false move.

They being Kathryn Blaire and her people.

A million dollar up-front payment just wasn't going to be made lightly, and Kathryn Blaire and her people would be

watching right up until the very moment the wire transfer was due. They'd be watching her every motion, hoping that she would make a mistake and lead them to her client, or give away the information they were supposed to pay for, or perhaps give herself away as a fraud.

And so long as Kathryn and her people were out there, Sarah Ridell felt safe. Because so long as they did not know the truth, they would protect her.

•　　　•　　　•

Ivo Jenkins leaned back into the soft leather chair, its cushions still remembering the shape of its last occupant—a woman about one-third his weight. The air in the small apartment still gray with the remains of her cigarettes. Anand hadn't told him much about her, other than her name, Kathryn Blaire. Anand hadn't told him much about anything. Just offered him money for a job.

Ivo positioned the chair so that he faced directly toward the window, straight out across Lexington Avenue toward a steel and glass high-rise. It was almost close enough to do the job with natural eyesight. In fact, his predecessor in this chair, the skinny woman named Kathryn, had skipped the binocs. But that was casual of her, more laid back than Ivo liked to play it, and he unpacked a set of army issue favorites from a case the size of a thick Baptist Bible.

He aimed the lenses across the street at the apartment directly opposite him, adjusted the focus until he could just about see the fuzz on an apricot, then dropped his line of sight one story down and one apartment over to the left. 725 Lexington Avenue, apartment 39G.

The high-powered lenses took him straight into the living room: white walls, a glass and chrome coffee table, black halogen lamps, unfortunate modern art posters on the walls, a rounded Italian black leather couch. The whole thing not his style, but then, he hadn't been hired to give decorating points.

A white girl with shoulder length sandy blonde hair was

stretched out on the couch, wearing a silk bathrobe, and Ivo drew her face into the glasses.

She was pretty, real pretty, in an Ellen Barkin kind of way, with a crooked nose and small scar on the side of her cheek. And she matched the picture Anand had given him that afternoon of a young woman standing in a museum sculpture garden. Anand hadn't told him the girl's name and Ivo hadn't asked. Just watch the apartment from eight at night to eight in the morning and take pictures of any visitors, Anand had said. Three grand a night. Don't know how many nights. No problems with the law. His word on it. Someone else would be handling the day shift.

Ivo stared some more at his assignment. Yeah, she was pretty. But she was also worth 3K a night, just to be watched. And that said more than enough.

•   •   •

Sarah Ridell drew her bathrobe a little closer around her waist, and slipped Mozart's *Jupiter* into her CD player. It was a triumphant piece of music, perhaps a bit out of place, but for the first time in an awful long time, Sarah Ridell felt in control of her destiny.

Just off to her side, on the glass and chrome coffee table (not her first choice of furnishings, but then, she hadn't paid for it) rested a picture of the girl she'd once been. Eighteen, blue jeans and boots, leaning against the front fender of Jimmy Saunders' new pick-up. That was back in Johnson City, Oklahoma. A picture of the girl who couldn't miss. Smart as a whip, everyone in town said. And would you look at those tits, the men would add, when they thought she wasn't listening. Jealous of Jimmy, all of them.

Jimmy Saunders was the slickest ballplayer ever to come out of Rayburn High, a shortstop who could catch anything and had an arm like a lesser god. The Dodgers drafted him in the second round. They figured he'd learn to hit the curve. Last she'd heard, Jimmy was back home, selling cars at Bill Fowler's

Ford dealership.

Her eyes drew tight and she wondered if Jimmy ever still thought about her. She hoped he did, because those times had been right. More right than anytime since. Until now. She laid the picture face down on the table.

Elliot would be coming over soon and she had to get prepped for the evening. She had to be perfect tonight. But not because he'd paid for it, although that was good enough reason most nights.

Elliot came over every Tuesday and Thursday night to claim what he was paying for. Or more accurately, who he was paying for. Maybe that wasn't a real pretty way of putting it, but she had never lied to herself, not once. She had understood the truth: Elliot owned this apartment and everything in it, he paid for her clothes, paid for her phone calls to her friends, for her workouts, her haircuts, her birth control pills, and everything else in her life. Elliot could whisper that she was his lover all he wanted. But she was his fuck. Plain and simple. And when he got tired of her, he would take it all away. He'd move on to a new girl, younger and with better tits, and she'd be left like Jimmy Saunders, going back to Johnson City with nothing.

That was the way the script had been written. The way that particular script always went. Except Elliot had screwed up and given her an opening, figuring she'd be too dumb to walk on through.

Elliot bragging to her about his new client, Bianca. A wealthy and very private woman who had retained Elliot and his firm to put in a secret offer on an antique mirror that would be coming up for sale from a private seller.

A mirror? she'd said.

Yes. A mirror. Which the client believed came from the Amber Room, Elliot said.

The Amber Room?

So Elliot told her all about the Amber Room, talking down to her for having never heard of it. Asking her if they had museums in Johnson City. Patronizing her with information he'd just learned himself. Then wanting to screw.

The very next morning she'd walked down to the New York Public Library and done some learning of her own. Her plan pretty much formulating itself right there under the high arched ceiling of the main reading room.

Step One—getting the word out that she had information on the Amber Room. That was easy, requiring only a little time spent drinking martinis and speaking a bit too loosely in a couple of clubs frequented by the art crowd.

Step Two—reeling in Professor Greene. Even easier. He had heard the rumors and sought her out.

Step Three—setting up Elliot.

Tonight was all about Step Three. Oh yes, she would be perfect for Elliot tonight. Do her hair. Put on a slip of a dress. Laugh at his jokes. Give him a first class fuck and a blow job, too. Cook him dinner if he wanted that. And all the while Kathryn Blaire and her people would be watching—with the blinds wide open and the lights on. They'd be watching Elliot and taking pictures and believing that she was working for him. That she was his fall girl.

Then when the million was paid, she'd turn over to Professor Greene and Kathryn Blaire the name of Elliot's client and the information about the mirror and disappear. If that brought the professor and Kathryn Blaire to the Amber Room, it was fine with her. And, if it didn't, that was fine too. Either way, it would be Elliot's problem.

It would be up to Elliot to explain to his client or to Kathryn Blaire or both what was going on. Except, no matter what he said, the answer would be obvious to everyone. Elliot Rosewater was a powerful man, Sarah Ridell was his toy and he'd used her to sell information on the Amber Room. To sell out his client, as well.

Too bad Elliot hadn't done any of that. Too bad for Elliot, that is. But then, Elliot wasn't the type to take pity on the less fortunate.

•   •   •

Ivo adjusted his focus. The pretty girl had changed into a midnight blue slip. Nothing over it. Nothing under it. Some women were just made to wear lingerie. She'd tidied up the apartment, too. Answered the door with a radiant smile. Got no gift of flowers, nor anything else in return for her troubles, not even much of a smile, though she was damn sure worth it. Ivo let the girl drift out of his field of vision and focused on her visitor.

He didn't recognize the man by his face—a soft chin, thin nose, and hawkish eyes—but by his look, which Ivo had seen so many times before: on men who got their happily-married-with-two-children-uptight-suburban cocks waxed a couple of nights a week by the same girl, at the same apartment, and at the same time. The only variable being that sometimes the girl would get dinner at a fancy restaurant first.

Not tonight. Tonight the pretty blonde girl started on top, with her back arched toward the sky, and her breasts working their way half-in and half-out of the blue silk as she moved to the rhythm. A fine sight, indeed. Fine enough that Ivo felt it. But that was no way to work, it was unprofessional, and he shrugged off that feeling, like he always did except when it was his wife. Then he put the glasses down. Picture time.

He'd brought his Canon 1N and high speed Kodak film—Ektachrome P1600 color and T-MAX P3200 black and white—and he opened the back of the camera while thinking about his choice of film. Everyone else he knew in the business used color these days, but he still preferred black and white. Black and white was the first color of blackmail. The color of film noir. And with her crooked nose, this girl had looks that definitely said noir. Ivo loaded the T-Max P3200, pointed the camera, and zoomed in.

Click. A nice shot of the naked, happy couple. Click. A close up of the man's face. Click. The man's hands on her breasts. Click. Her tongue licking his chest. Click. The sound of money. Click. Her tongue elsewhere. Click. Click. The blonde girl doing all the work, all the sweating, while the man lay on his back with his eyes closed and his arms folded behind his head.

Ivo took a picture and sighed. For what this had to be costing, the man should have been working it more.

As for the girl, Ivo could only imagine what she was getting out of this. She had to be getting something, because it couldn't be about the sex for her. Of course, it never was when a pretty twenty-something girl was hooked up with a rich, married, probably powerful, middle-age man. But this, this really wasn't about the sex. Not for her. Click. Click. Click.

The girl was on top again, like she was loving it, leaning back and laughing. Click. Then the man jerked up, and, just like that, they were finished.

While the girl laid herself down on the sheets, the man coolly picked himself off the bed and dried his dick off with a tissue. Just like they all did. Not much of a dick either.

Twenty minutes later, all showered and neatly dressed in his gray suit, the man walked out of the apartment and back into his life. With the same smile possessed by pretty much all who starred in Ivo's photo shoots.

Show over. Another night, another three thousand dollars well earned. A smile came to Ivo's countenance and he recited the Blackmailer's Prayer: Thank you God. Thank you for rich men and young girls. Yes indeed, he was sure to deliver unto Anand exactly what Anand must have wanted. Delight being unto him who gave no quarter in the ugly truth.

The girl was still lying on the bed, her eyes closed. Ivo put his camera down and walked to the kitchen of the apartment. A take-out bag was sitting on the counter, and he unwrapped a couple of all-beef patties which he'd bought hours earlier. His latest burgers in a week-long fest of burgers. Nothing the microwave couldn't bring back to life. At peace with the world, Ivo Jenkins had no idea what was coming.

Even when it happened, he didn't fully comprehend it at first—except that he'd known a lot of bad in his life and knew its language. The noise sounded like a drinking glass shattering, although that wasn't it. It was too large, and too much glass. He spun and looked towards the girl's apartment and saw nothing. The lights blacked out. Then the scream hit him,

a shock wave ripping across the night. He followed the scream with his eyes until he saw it. Saw her. Against the mirrored face of the steel and glass building, she was a single silhouette falling to the ground. She was soaring, but not in the way she'd dreamed. And Ivo watched helplessly as she fell, as she fell all the way down.

The blonde girl exploded when she hit the ground. There was nothing neat about it, the way it was in the movies when a body falls from the thirty-ninth floor of a building. In the movies, the dead body just kind of lies there in a small pool of blood: a made-up stunt double ready to get up and walk away. But the blonde girl with the pretty face and crooked nose lay in pieces: arms, legs, and the rest. And there wasn't a thing Ivo Jenkins could have done to save her.

10

It was two-thirty that morning. Kathryn Blaire sat alone in an old Adirondack chair on the deck of her apartment, looking off at an old flatiron building lit by streetlamps. Someone nearby was playing Billie Holiday on the stereo, and the music and words drifted through the warm night.

Kathryn knew she would not go to sleep that night, and she could not stop thinking about the dead girl. She wished to be someplace where mistakes didn't have consequences, and some years before, she might have found that place in a handful of pills or a smoke that had to be hand rolled, or a man who would be soon forgotten. But she didn't have the energy for that tonight.

It had been quite a homecoming for Kathryn Blaire already. Two years since she'd left New York, taking a kind of self-directed, self-destructive, self-funded leave from the Agency, and brought back by Isaiah Hawkins to this.

Been away, she'd told an inquiring neighbor.

"Where?"

Been away.

Her apartment was still in good shape. So was the girl who had been house-sitting. The girl was a baby-faced freshman at NYU when she'd responded to Kathryn's ad. Now she was a junior, prettier, still sweet, and with a nice-looking boyfriend. She didn't seem to mind much at all that Kathryn had returned. Life was flexible that way when you were twenty, smart, and pretty, and knew everything was going to turn out all right.

Kathryn hoped it all came true for the girl...and found her mind veering back to Sarah Ridell. She couldn't help it. Couldn't help imagining what it would be like falling thirty-nine stories. Would it be the fear that she felt most? Or would it be the physical sensations: broken glass, wind, a sense of speed, weightlessness? Or would it be just surprise—that this is how it was going to end? She wondered what Sarah Ridell

thought of as she fell. A lover? God? Family? An old pet? Did she think of the Amber Room? Kathryn doubted it.

Sarah Ridell must have closed her eyes and prayed for an angel to save her. But the world didn't believe in angels anymore, and so there weren't any available to answer her prayers. Maybe, if Isaiah had chosen differently, Kathryn might have been that angel. But it hadn't gone that way, she hadn't fought Isaiah hard enough. And the girl was dead.

The game would go on. It always did. There were photographs to be developed. A man to be identified and located. They would find him soon enough, and learn what he was doing with Sarah Ridell. But they'd keep their eyes on the ball. Isaiah Hawkins was not one to get distracted from his goals, and justice for the girl wouldn't be high on the agenda. Isaiah wanted the Amber Room. It was all that mattered. And if some bastard had coincidentally screwed Sarah Ridell and then killed her, well that was a concern for someone else.

That was Isaiah Hawkins, that was the Agency, and she...well, she loved it, and was repelled by it, and maybe she needed it. Nearly two years running away, wanting to be free from the hardness, and all the while maybe lying to herself. More than the freedom, was it the roller coaster she needed— the risk, the energy, the wins and the losses and the pressure, the bets on chance and on people—the opportunity to play in Isaiah Hawkins' game?

She closed her eyes and whispered, *I'm sorry, Sarah.* Reaching out for Sarah Ridell in the in between. Praying for understanding. Billie singing, "Hush now, don't explain..."

11

The dead girl's scream ran right through Ivo all night. Watching that girl fall was about the worst thing he'd witnessed, maybe ever. At least all of God's losers in that piece-of-shit jungle war had known what was going down— the only question being who was gonna be spared and who wasn't. But that pretty girl had no idea she was going to die that night, and no time to say her prayers.

The girl had a name now: Sarah Ridell. She had other things too: parents, friends, ambitions, hopes, loves, hates, disappointments, a whole story. Ivo figured he'd stolen part of that story, told in a row of 8x10s he was now hanging to dry in a crooked line in his dark room.

Stories. That's why he had gotten started working behind the camera. To capture people's stories. Then he'd come back from the war and learned he'd become the daily double—unemployed and unemployable. A man had to eat and he knew two things: recon and photography. The rest was easy. Especially the money.

Sometimes Ivo Jenkins still liked to pretend that someday he would be a photographer of the city, a latter-day Weegee, taking pictures of crime scenes and prettied-up politicians. He would shoot shoeshine hustlers in old sneakers, mixed couples sneaking kisses, drug addicts coming down from their highs, white cops straight out of high school and walking the beat uptown. He would shoot the lives people led, not the lies they told.

You see, photographs froze the truth. And that's why Ivo loved them so. Too many people loved words, and words weren't so often about the truth. Words were about denying, explaining, rationalizing, and lying. Mostly lying. Truth was that Justice James Washington Lancaster liked to buy fifteen-year-old black girls. Truth was that a man without grace liked to stop off on his way home and get screwed by a pretty girl with a crooked nose. Truth was that the girl with the crooked nose was dead. And, truth was, Ivo Jenkins was the girl's last best witness, courtesy of Anand Ashland. Damn him.

Ivo carefully lifted another 8x10 out of a chemical bath. He hung it on the line to dry with the others and, in the damped orange darkroom light, looked down the row of black and whites. At the far end was a color picture he had taken a year before, of a powerful police official having an interlude with his twenty-two-year-old, finely shaped, Australian housekeeper. He'd been saving that picture for a rainy day, in case he needed it, and had left it hanging on the line just because. Because in his business you had to love law enforcement officers, household help with a sexy accent, tan breasts, and no morals when it came to fucking. But not this day…

His eyes drifted slowly, hesitantly, down the row of photos. He saw faces, torsos, legs, lips. He saw Sarah Ridell bending down to give her last visitor a kiss, and the man placing his hand on her breast. He saw images the man's wife ought never see. He saw the man and the girl finishing. The girl leaning back and laughing. Leaning back and laughing…sweet…sweet Jesus. Ivo stared at the photo and heard her scream again. Sweet Jesus.

What should I do, honey? he asked Sarah Ridell, in his gravelly voice, unclipping the final picture from the line and cradling it in his hands. What should I do, Sarah Ridell?

It was supposed to be a different story hanging on that line. Or at least so he'd believed. One night in a pretty girl's life. A lover caught on film, with consequences to be determined as a business matter. It wasn't supposed to be a morality tale ending in murder. Or maybe, now that he thought about it, a tale beginning in murder. He wasn't even sure where he had entered the story.

About all he was sure of was that Anand Ashland had done Ivo Jenkins wrong by putting him in the middle of it.

What to do, Sarah Ridell? Mail copies to the police anonymously? They wouldn't be good evidence in court that way. Go to the cops in person? That was the dream of every blackmailer, sashaying into a New York City police station one fine day with black and whites of a wealthy man putting it to a dead girl. He almost laughed, almost cried. His eyes staring at the picture of the girl: the one of her leaning back and laughing.

•   •   •

Ivo tapped a thick manila envelope against Anand Ashland's desk, a lovely old banker's desk set in a corner of Anand's study. The manila envelope made a heavy thunk with each tap. "He fucked her. You know that. Before killing her."

"Yes, you told me over the phone," Anand replied. "Does that make it worse? The pictures, Ivo, may I have them."

"That deal, three grand per night, it ended last night. Pictures have a new price now." Ivo let the envelope fall from his hand to the coffee table. Thunk. "See how much the people you're working for value these. You know the price."

"And if they won't meet it?"

"Haven't decided. Haven't had to yet."

Anand picked up the heavy envelope and held it to the light, unable to see anything. He supposed that Sarah Ridell didn't look like a woman who deserved to die, but how many did?

•   •   •

Just after sunup, Rebecca Ashland went downstairs to Anand's study. Her husband was lying on the couch with his eyes closed, his treasured book of poems—by Coleridge, Wordsworth, Keats, and all the others—still in his hands. A manila envelope, clasped shut, on the floor near him.

It was a necessary gift of his, the sleep into which he could will himself. The other worlds to which he could escape. And, believing that he could hear her, she told him that she loved him. She always did. Always had.

Rebecca Ashland leaned down and kissed her husband of so many years on the cheek. She didn't know about Isaiah Hawkins or the Amber Room. She didn't know how Anand's father had met Isaiah in the intelligence service after the war. Just as she didn't know of Ivo Jenkins or Kathryn Blaire or of a southern girl named Sarah Ridell who'd flown close to the sun. She didn't know any of it. Only that he loved her.

PART TWO

Perhaps an angel in hell flies in her
own little cloud of paradise.
—*Meister Eckhardt*

12

In 1589, Galileo Galilei calculated that the acceleration of any falling body is thirty-two feet per second. He proved this by dropping two lead balls of unequal size and weight off of the leaning tower of Pisa (which was already leaning, even back then). The two balls hit the ground at the same time, destroying forever the notion that bodies of unequal size or weight fall at different speeds. Using Galileo's insight as a starting point, Homicide Detective Ben Russo of New York's twenty-fourth precinct calculated that, depending on wind conditions, it took Sarah Ridell six seconds more or less to fall from the window of her thirty-ninth floor apartment to the ground. Which was not a pretty thought at all.

The Ridell death had landed on Russo's desk with his morning coffee, completing a special week. Even for a homicide cop. Three deaths: an eighteen-year-old kid impaled through the chest on an iron fence post, a thirty-five-year-old Korean woman shot to death with a bow and arrow in midtown Manhattan, and now this. Like knives and guns were suddenly out of fashion or something. He shouldn't have even caught this last case, except some high flyer (they wouldn't tell him who) had called headquarters and specifically asked for Ben Russo. His lucky fucking day.

He began typing a preliminary report on Sarah Ridell, hunting and pecking on the same old manual typewriter he had used for the past twenty-five years.

Probable Cause of Death: defenestration. That was one he didn't get to use very often. It came from the Latin *fenestra* meaning window, which he remembered from his days with the nuns. But that didn't make it a healthy commentary on his fellow man, that tossing someone out a window had its own separate entry in the dictionary. Of course, there was a chance that Sarah Ridell had committed suicide. Which, depending on how you looked at it, was either better or worse. But Ben Russo didn't think she had jumped. With all the pharmaceuticals available these days, hardly anyone killed themselves anymore by jumping out of a window. It was just so messy, envisioning yourself in a pool of bloody pieces on the ground. And there were always guns, if you wished a mess.

Witnesses: None. The first cops on the scene had interviewed Sarah Ridell's neighbors during the night. No one saw anything unusual. Of course, all the neighbors had taken the time to describe Sarah Ridell as a nice, quiet girl. That ran according to form. If a pretty young white girl got killed, four to one said the neighbors called her a nice, quiet girl on the first pass. It was only later that the inevitable details came out: heroin, or a bad choice in boyfriends, or high-priced hooking. Fact of the matter was that pretty young girls minding their own business tended not to get dropped thirty-nine stories. Not that it never happened that way, but the odds were against it. Later, he'd make his own visit to the girl's building to see if the neighbors might be more forthcoming with his kind of information.

But first, Ben Russo really wanted to know the answer to just one question, the one which had jumped into his mind as he went through the dead girl's personal address book: what was a young woman from Johnson City, Oklahoma (population 181 according to the latest almanac), doing with John Nicholas Osborne's address and phone number?

The 103 lawyers of Osborne, Crane & Rosewater occupied four floors of New York City's most expensive office space, everything about the offices designed to make a statement. Dark wood paneling everywhere, richly colored wool carpeting, oak tables with matching oak and burgundy leather chairs, a reception desk airlifted straight out of an old French hotel, and an arrogant receptionist with a stiff upper class British accent. Too bad Ben Russo knew that the statement was a lie.

Osborne, Crane & Rosewater was New York's most profitable law firm, but not part of the club. The firm had been started from nothing in the early 1970s by a threesome of ethnic guys on the make: John Nicholas (Jack) Osborne, a catholic school boy from Queens and Fordham who'd passed the bar the same year Ben Russo graduated from the police academy; Isaac Crane, an orthodox Jew straight out of Brooklyn; and Elliot Rosewater, another Jewish homeboy with a dual degree from NYU in law and business and the smartest of the three. They'd made Osborne, Crane & Rosewater by representing clients whom the old-line firms looked down on, anyone with a numbered account, corrupt leaders of foreign governments being particular specialties. They had a reputation for working all hours, for getting good results, and for writing up their bills with the heaviest pencils in town. All of which Ben Russo thought was fine. In fact, he liked to see the local boys make it big. But no amount of oak or burgundy leather was ever going make Osborne, Crane & Rosewater a part of the WASP establishment. And Ben Russo didn't have a lot of patience for pretenders.

Still, Jack Osborne tried to play the perfect host.

"Detective Russo, please take a seat," he said, pointing to an uncomfortable-looking antique couch in his office. Louis XIV or someone like that.

Russo sat slowly, eyeing Osborne. The man was beyond pale. In fact, it was questionable whether anyone that pasty could still be alive. "Sorry to bother you, Mister Osborne—"

"Please, Detective, you can call me Jack."

"Yeah, well. Jack, let me get right to it. Your name came up in connection with an investigation."

"My name?"

"Afraid so. A nice, quiet girl by the name of Sarah Ridell died last night. Fell from a thirty-ninth–story window. Or maybe she jumped. I'm not sure which yet."

"My God...how horrible," muttered Osborne, with a perfect touch of $500 per hour shock and compassion in his voice. "How old was she?"

"Twenty-eight."

"My God..." Osborne muttered again. "That's the same age as my oldest daughter. I can only imagine how her family must feel."

"Not good, Jack. They feel not good. Do you mind if I ask you a few questions?"

"No. Go right ahead, Detective. Anything I can do to help. You said my name came up. I'm not sure I understand."

"How well did you know her, Jack?"

"Excuse me?"

"I asked how well you knew her?"

Jack Osborne cupped his hands over his mouth and blew into them, like he was deep in thought. Then he ran his newly warmed hands over his pale bald head. A vein in his forehead throbbed in blue and red. "What did you say her name was?"

"Sarah Ridell. R-i-d-e-l-l. From Oklahoma—Johnson City. She moved to New York after graduating from the University of Oklahoma law school."

"Sarah Ridell...Sarah Ridell..." Osborne looked lost. "University of Oklahoma you said?"

"She graduated three years ago."

Osborne closed his eyes, squeezed the bridge of his nose with his thumb and forefinger, and seemed to search his mind. His throbbing vein slowed a fraction, and he opened his eyes brightly, as if a forgotten synapse had just been activated. "Blonde girl...sandy blonde. Very pretty?"

"Hard to tell right now, Jack."

A hint of sympathetic blood flowed through Osborne's translucent vampire cheeks. "Yes, of course. I'm sorry. I'll have to check my files, Detective. But, I do seem to remember her. I believe your Sarah Ridell met one of our partners at a restaurant or a party or some such thing. Made an impression on him, and was brought in for an interview. You understand, we wouldn't ordinarily hire anyone from the University of Oklahoma, or even interview someone from there."

"Yeah, sure I understand," Russo nodded. I understand you perfectly.

"Anyway," Osborne said, with a shrug. "It must not have worked out—the interview, that is; not everyone is cut out for Osborne, Crane & Rosewater. Let me check with our recruiting coordinator, Ms. Baker, she'll know for sure."

Osborne reached for the phone, but before he could dial the second digit, Russo cut him off.

"I didn't ask if she'd interviewed with the firm, Jack. I asked you how well you knew her."

"Come, Detective. I've just told you."

"I meant, how well you knew her personally."

"Please, Detective," Osborne replied. "I'm trying to help you. What leads you to believe I know…that I knew this girl personally?"

"Her address book. Your name was in it."

Jack Osborne narrowed the space separating him from the detective with a glare designed for intimidating. But its effect was lost on the cop who just stared back dumbly. Osborne addressed him in a voice shimmering with studied disgust and impatience. "Lots of people have the firm's name in their Rolodex, Detective. I assume Ms. Ridell had our name because she interviewed here. Now, if you would just let me check with—"

"I didn't say Rolodex. And I didn't say the firm's name. I said your name was in her personal address book with a star next to it. Jack Osborne, and a big star. So let me ask you again, exactly how well did you know her? And what did you have to do to earn a big star, Jack?"

The veins in Osborne's head rose like a flooded river and his words were spat from his lips, "I can throw you out of here right now. Right fucking now."

"Maybe you should," Ben Russo said, speaking so calmly it was unnerving. It was a fine line between rattling a suspect into making a mistake and getting tossed out of an interview with nothing. Russo was straddling that line and Osborne was used to dealing with deteriorating situations as a lawyer. But somehow dealing with other people's ugly problems never quite prepared anyone for ugliness of their very own.

"Maybe you should throw me out, Jack. But I won't go away. When I saw your name in Sarah Ridell's address book, I figured it was something that needed to be checked out. I had no real reason to believe you had anything to do with her death. Personally, I still don't. But I know you knew her. Want my best guess? Maybe you met her while she was temping and looking for a law job. You talked up how important you were, brought her in for an interview, screwed her a half-dozen times, and then said, 'Sorry, honey, the job just didn't work out.' So here's a piece of advice, Jack. If I'm guessing more or less right, let me know and I can get on with my life. Otherwise, I'm going to keep digging. And when I keep digging, other people, like maybe your wife, are going to find out what I'm digging into. That's the way it is, Jack."

The blue-red vein throbbed. Never talk to the cops alone was a mantra Jack Osborne never tired of repeating to his clients. But it all came down to judging one's adversary. Judging his ability to handle this cop.

"Speaking hypothetically, Detective, I might have met a young woman while she was waiting tables at an Italian place not far from here. Nice restaurant, not much of a job for a woman with a law degree. I might have asked her out, letting it slip that I was a name partner at this law firm. She might have accepted, thinking it would help her get an interview. You can assume the rest, detective. Hypothetically, that is."

"You sleep with her?"

"We might have spent the evening together."

"How often?"

"Might have done it five, six times. Wouldn't have been much of an affair, really."

"What else?"

"There is nothing else, Detective. I slept with her a couple of times—hypothetically, like I said. I might have arranged an interview for her, and I never would've seen her again. She would not have been offered a position at Osborne, Crane. Even if we did hire attorneys from the University of Oklahoma, her grades at law school were not up to our standards. We only hire those who graduate in the top five percent of their class. This woman would have been top five, but barely. I would have asked my secretary to make arrangements to help her find a job. You understand, Detective, this firm has a clear rule against partners sleeping with associates. It wouldn't have been prudent to offer her a position. Hypothetically, of course."

Lovely, thought Russo. Didn't even matter that Sarah Ridell might have made the grade. Too bad she didn't know those were the rules. Russo wanted to ask Osborne if having his secretary make a few calls made him feel any better about himself, but held off. He also wanted to ask where Osborne graduated in his class, but skipped that one as well because he knew the answer. "Did she ever mention anything to you about being scared, or having a problem?"

"Really, it was some time ago, Detective. To be honest, I don't think we really would have talked all that much."

Russo moved on. "When's the last time you saw her?"

"I never saw her again. Assuming I ever did. Any other questions, Detective?"

"Yeah. Why'd you lie to me before?"

"Surely, Detective. Some girl with whom I might have had an insignificant dalliance, past tense, dies. Falls out of a window, for God's sake. My only interest, and the interest of the firm, is in keeping our name out of the papers. What else did you expect?"

"Not much, Jack." Russo picked himself off of the Louis whatever couch and started to leave. "I'll be in touch if I have anything else. Thank you."

"One moment, Detective."

"Yes?"

"After you called this morning—to say you wished to see me—I called the commissioner of police and asked about you. The commissioner is a long acquaintance of mine. But, I'm sure you knew that. He assured me that you were a man who knew how to keep private matters private."

"Really? Irish Mike said that?"

"Yes, Commissioner O'Malley said that."

Russo smiled. "Did he also say he'd fire me if I crossed you?"

"Nothing so crude as that, Detective," Osborne said with his

61

best false chuckle. "Thanks for coming down. My secretary will show you the way out now."

Ben Russo left the offices of Osborne, Crane & Rosewater knowing he'd be back. A quarter century on the job told him that. If it had happened the way Jack Osborne said—a simple matter of morality—Osborne would've tried to handle the matter differently. He would've treated Ben like one of the boys from the old neighborhood, and explained that it could've happened to anyone. Which it could have. But that wasn't the play Jack Osborne had made.

13

Anand's expensive shoes tapped lightly against the soft concrete floor as he made his way down a musty subterranean hallway of the Natural History Museum.

According to Professor Greene, the museum's labyrinth of underground corridors had been built in the 1870s and worked on continuously ever since, with rooms and hallways opened, reconfigured, walled up, and forgotten. No accurate plans existed anymore, if they ever did. And, every so often, someone would break down a wall and find a long forgotten chamber filled with a mountain of mammoth bones, or fossils, or human brains preserved in solution—the study of Natural History and the evolution of species being a sometimes messy business.

Anand turned a corner, another long narrow corridor opened in front of him, and at the end of the corridor stood Kathryn Blaire. As he approached, Anand was surprised to realize just how small and lithe she was, five foot four on a tall day and maybe a potato chip over a hundred and ten pounds. Not exactly Agency issue size, but not delicate either. Isaiah Hawkins didn't have much use for delicate.

Anand's whisper was instinctive but unnecessary, as he and Kathryn were quite alone. His question still a surprise. "Did you get photographs, Ms. Blaire? Last night, of Sarah Ridell's visitor?"

"No. He came after I left. But your associate, Ivo, was there with his camera."

"Unfortunate."

Kathryn looked at Anand with a puzzled expression. "Why? Did he fuck up?"

"Not at all, not his style."

Anand handed Kathryn the thick sealed manila envelope from Ivo. But as she began to undo the metal clasp at the top of the envelope, he said, "There is an issue."

"What's the matter?" she bristled.

"The price."

Kathryn nodded her head slowly, thinking that now she understood why Anand had asked to meet her alone. Her hand held still on the envelope clasp. "Isaiah controls the purse, not me, Mister Ashland. You'll have to ask him for the money. If that's where you're going."

"Ivo believes we put him in an awkward position, Ms. Blaire, that we made him a witness to a murder. That is not his usual business, and he believes our deal with him has been violated. A position to which I am not unsympathetic."

"How righteous of him, and you," Kathryn said with a cynical smile. "Exactly what did you say Ivo's usual business was?"

Anand glanced at the envelope he'd carefully placed in her hand, thereby giving her control, or at least the illusion thereof. Making his job easier. "The choice is yours, Ms. Blaire. But I should advise you that Ivo is considering sending a duplicate set of those pictures to the police, which might have the effect of throwing sand in our gears."

Kathryn smiled again, her best cynical smile getting a workout now. "So what's his price? Ten thousand dollars and he forgets about the murder? Or are his sensitivities more expensive than that. Perhaps twenty thousand? Tell me, what's his price? And yours?"

"I think you misunderstand me. I never suggested that Ivo wants more money. He doesn't. Ivo wants to be certain that Sarah Ridell and her killer each get their due."

"No money?"

"Just the three thousand agreed to. And no free pass from you for the man in the pictures if he killed Sarah Ridell."

She hesitated. No money? If you couldn't buy off a blackmailer with money, who could you buy? The world had gone sideways once again.

"How come you came to me with this, instead of Isaiah?"

"The official reason…" Anand cleared his throat. "The official reason would be that Isaiah placed you in charge of the surveillance operation, and therefore I believed I had an obligation to come to you. Unofficially, let's say that I'd heard

you were the type of individual who would know how to handle this situation, Ms. Blaire."

"Really. What did you hear?"

Anand thought about what he'd been told by his sources: that Kathryn Blaire was Isaiah's best and most resourceful girl. That is, until one fine winter day a few years back when she skipped the country and the Agency with almost three million dollars that she had skimmed out of an extralegal Agency operation. Word was that her old partner had tracked her down to a small town outside Mexico City, then let her go, in return for a share of the takings. Kathryn Blaire hadn't been seen since, that is until just recently, when she'd returned for reasons only Isaiah knew. Disgraced and defrocked, but back. Flexibly moral perhaps; but far, far from incompetent. Just the person to satisfy Ivo's conditions.

"I heard you understood how fluid situations can be. How accommodations must sometimes be made." Anand glanced again at the envelope in her hand. "Do we have a deal, Ms. Blaire?"

Her finger tapped on the envelope clasp. The moral circumstances were plenty good enough for her. Way better than usual. But there were still the facts to consider. She took several steps away from Anand, and she hesitated again. "May I check the goods first?"

"Go ahead. Thank you for asking."

With a flick of her nail, she opened the clasp and slid the photos out. Right on top was a glossy of Sarah Ridell giving the man a class-A blow job while his face stared unknowingly straight at the camera. "Yes, we have a deal," she said. "And call me Kathryn."

14

On the East Side of the park, Ben Russo's anticipated transformation of Sarah Ridell was already well underway, courtesy of Ida Stone, a forty-plus, blonde-from-the-bottle divorcée who lived in the apartment next to Sarah Ridell's.

A man—Ida didn't know his name—about fifty years old, with a soft body but hard eyes had been coming around for at least a year. He visited Sarah Ridell once or twice a week. On Tuesdays and Thursdays. But she wasn't sure if he'd been there the night Sarah died. It wasn't, she explained carefully, like she was keeping tabs on Sarah Ridell. She'd just noticed this man because…well, how couldn't she? It was disgusting, a man like that—in his fifties and no doubt married. A pretty young girl like Sarah should have been dating men her own age. Right, detective? Not that Sarah deserved what happened to her. God forbid the very thought. Still…Ida dropped her voice and confided a secret: the walls were thin and she heard them sometimes, you know, heard them in bed. It was shameless. Wasn't it, detective?

Ben Russo nodded his head and heard Ida Stone out to the end. There was nothing like a murder to bring out the best in people. He had learned that lesson long before and it wasn't ever going to change. But Ida Stone's bitter envy of a pretty girl who still laughed in bed was more sad than anything else. And he forgave her because he needed her information, and because he figured it wasn't easy spending your time alone but for jealous memories. No, he knew that wouldn't be easy at all. Thank God he had his Maria to keep him company. A smile came to his face just at the thought of her name, Maria Antonia Russo. He had twenty-five years on a job he loved and twenty-four years married to the best woman in all the five boroughs. He couldn't wait to get home to her. He would tell her all about his day over a bowl of risotto and a glass of red wine. But he would leave out the part about Ida Stone.

"Would you say this man, Ms. Ridell's visitor, was unusually pale looking?" he asked, when the words had stopped rushing from Ida Stone's mouth.

"No, Detective. Soft looking, hard eyes, like I said. But not particularly pale. Must be a different man than the one you had in mind. I would've noticed if she'd had two of them."

Ben thanked her and called for a police sketch artist to come up and see what could be done. Then he took the elevator back down to the ground floor.

A pot-bellied doorman with slicked-back, get-the-gray-out formula hair was behind the front desk, and Ben approached him, doing his best now to walk like a cop. The pot-bellied man shuffling his feet while Ben read the man's nametag, Walter T. Well, Walter T. looked nervous.

Ben flashed his badge. "Detective Russo, I'd like to ask you a few questions."

"Sure...go ahead."

"You on duty last night?"

"No. That was Tony's shift," Walter said, too fast. "I usually work the day shift. Tony will be back tonight if you want to see him."

"That's alright. Why don't you tell me about Sarah Ridell."

"I didn't know her real well. She hadn't lived here long. Year and a half maybe. She always seemed like a nice, quiet girl."

"What else, Walter?"

"Good tipper."

"Boyfriends?"

"Not that I remember."

"You're sure?"

"Yeah, like I said. Not that I remember. Like I said, I work the day shift."

"Right...right," Ben repeated, nodding his head slowly while Walter T. shuffled his feet some more. "Day shift. Could be. On the other hand, I'm thinking maybe the boyfriend was a good tipper, too."

"Don't know what you're talking about, detective."

"Really?" Russo lowered his voice to just above a whisper, so that Walter T. had to lean in to hear the words. "Not smart,

Walter. Not smart at all. You see, I'm a betting man. And I'm betting that you know the boyfriend. I'm also betting you handle certain transactions here at this building. Rich guy in 40A wants a funky lady or a boy for the evening. You take care of it. Same thing for the powder. You and half the other door-men in this city. A matter between you and my brethren at vice. They choose to look the other way, that's between you and them. I work homicide. It's been a lousy week and I do want to know about Sarah Ridell. So you got a choice. You can start talking about the boyfriend, or you can come down with me to the station and explain how you afford your lifestyle on a doorman's salary. What's it going be, Walter?"

Walter T. cleared his throat, but nothing came out.

"The one who came by twice a week, Walter. Want to tell me about him? Whoever he is, he didn't tip enough for you to take a bust for him. Am I right?"

Walter T. shuffled more slowly. He wasn't stupid. A twenty dollar tip every Tuesday and Thursday wasn't worth fucking up his angle. Besides, the girl was dead, there weren't going to be any more Tuesday honey runs, and there sure weren't going be any more tips. "There was a guy—"

"Not a guy, Walter. I want the name."

"Don't know." Walter T. put his hands up in the air, like he was innocent. "I'm not bullshitting you. A white guy in his fifties. Came by limo and usually stayed for a couple of hours. You know, long enough for a good bang or two. Sometimes they went out to dinner first. Like I said, I don't know the guy's name, but he's money. I could tell that."

"How about other men?"

"Other guys sometimes went up. But no one regular."

"She a pro?" Russo asked.

"I...ah...I don't know."

"Give me your best guess, Walter. Because I'm figuring you would know if any professionals are working in this building. Please don't disappoint me now."

Walter shook his head, "No."

"No what? No Sarah Ridell wasn't a pro? Or no, you

don't know?"

"No. She wasn't a pro for Christ's sake. Stop busting my balls."

"Yeah, sure. What about drugs?"

"She wasn't the type."

"You're sure?"

"I'd know." Walter T. pulled a big white handkerchief out of his pocket and wiped his fleshy face. "That's all I know. Are we done now, Detective? We got a deal, right?"

Russo stepped back and eased off. "Yeah, we got a deal. One more question. You said the boyfriend came by limo, what's the name of the limo company?"

Walter T. took a slip of paper out of his wallet and handed it to Russo. "This is their number. You know, sometimes I call them for cars."

And get a cut on every call.

Ben Russo left that last thought unsaid, took the card, and went straight to the phone: 1-800-BIGCARS. Ida Stone's soft man would have a name and an address soon enough. A wife and kids, too, probably.

15

Early that evening, with some substantial legwork of her own behind her, Kathryn Blaire passed the 8x10s around the wooden library table.

At the head of the table, Isaiah Hawkins examined each picture in turn, slowly and carefully, professionally, having seen many of their like in his day. He admired the quality of the work. The pictures of Sarah Ridell and her male visitor were clear, precise, and showed multiple angles. Other pictures perfectly framed to capture both the participants' faces as well as the compromising action. Mister Ivo Jenkins knew his business.

Professor Greene was not capable of viewing the show with the same detachment. It wasn't his business and Sarah Ridell, after all, was dead. That changed things, made the photos even more pornographic somehow.

Anand didn't bother looking at the pictures again. He'd seen enough of them.

Professor Greene raised his head and looked at Isaiah, "Who is he, the son of a bitch in these pictures?"

Isaiah pushed his chair back and stretched his legs out. "What have you learned, Kathryn?"

"Man's name is Elliot Rosewater. Name partner at a fancy Park Avenue law firm, Osborne, Crane & Rosewater. Married, two children. Seems to have been a regular event, him and Sarah Ridell. The usual financial arrangements."

"You mean, she was a hooker?" Professor Greene asked. He looked down at a picture of Sarah Ridell's naked torso and let out a small whistle.

"No, I don't, Professor," Kathryn spat out, annoyed, the only woman in the room. So tired of being the only woman in the room. "I mean, there were financial arrangements. She was his mistress. It isn't that simple."

Isaiah impatiently tapped a finger on the table.

"What else, Kathryn?"

"I don't know what else. I haven't found anything yet tying

Rosewater to the Amber Room, if that's what you mean."

"But you're on it, right?" the professor asked, although it wasn't his place to ask that question.

"Yeah, I'm on it. Should know more by the morning. Got a plan and everything, if that's all right with you, Professor Greene."

She stood to leave and get on with whatever she had in mind, but Isaiah slowed her with a glance. "The professor has prepared a memorandum on the most tenable of the theories regarding the disappearance of the Amber Room. I want you to read it."

"Good," she said, taking a copy of the memo from the table and rolling it into a baton in her hand. Nice of the professor to do something value-added.

"And one other thing, Kathryn," Isaiah said. "With Sarah Ridell dead, we won't need to wire transfer the million dollars."

"I figured as much," she said deadpan, and kept walking out the door.

16

To: Isaiah Hawkins
From: Alexander Greene
Re: Investigations into the Amber Room

The last confirmed sighting of the Amber Room took place at Königsberg Castle in the spring of 1944, prior to a series of devastating bombing raids conducted by the RAF against Königsberg in the summer of that year. When the city was subsequently captured by Russian forces, neither the Amber Room, nor conclusive evidence of its destruction was found.

Among serious art historians there have been a plethora of theories, ranging from the plausible to the absurd, offered to explain the disappearance of the Room. This memorandum addresses the five most likely scenarios. I caution that these are just speculative theories.

* 1. The Nazis moved the Amber Room to a safe location outside Königsberg in the late summer of 1944, just prior to the bombing raids. Such a measure would have been consistent with the extraordinary efforts undertaken by the German high command to remove valuable works of art from war zones to protected locations within the Reich. Indeed, as a result of these efforts, out of the several hundred thousand pieces of art looted by the Germans, less than a dozen truly priceless pieces were ultimately lost or destroyed in the war, the Amber Room included.

The principal German repository for the stolen art was in the Austrian mountains at Alt Aussee, a site which had been a salt mine before the war. Hitler's personal collection of some two thousand pieces, along with many other valuable works, were hidden at Alt Aussee—in chambers deep inside the mountain, where they were believed safe from Allied bombs.

Unfortunately, as the Reich collapsed, the local Gauleiter attempted to blow up the mine and all its contents from the inside in an effort to follow Hitler's orders that the retreating

Nazi forces should "scorch the earth." The Gauleiter's attempt failed, but only after Alt Aussee's curators (tipped to the attempt) had fearfully scattered the most important works to the mine's most remote chambers.

The art repository at Alt Aussee was discovered by the American 3rd Army as it swept through Austria, and the mine's chambers were searched exhaustively by Allied personnel. The Amber Room was not found. However, many still believe that works of great value, including the Amber Room, could remain hidden in that labyrinth, possibly in chambers sealed off and hidden by explosions.

2. The Amber Room was transported by train to a location in Eastern Germany. It is known that the East German secret police made significant efforts after the war to find the Amber Room within East Germany—with no success. While this theory has serious proponents, including Professor Karl Wertman of the Smithsonian Institution, a fine scholar whose views are entitled to serious respect, I personally find it unlikely. Given the powers of persuasion available to the Stasi, their failure to locate the Room would indicate to me that the Room is not to be found in East Germany.

3. The Amber Room was sunk with the *Wilhelm Gustloff*. The final German ship to leave the port of Königsberg was the *Wilhelm Gustloff*. It departed in January 1945 with five thousand refugees aboard, and was sunk almost immediately by Soviet torpedoes. Although undersea investigations are notoriously spotty affairs, divers have investigated the wreck and have failed to find the Amber Room. Despite this attempt, rumors persist that the Room was aboard that ship.

4. The Room was hidden within Königsberg by a German officer named Erick Koch. After the war, a number of Königsberg residents came forward (separately) to inform Russian authorities about the activities of a Nazi officer named Erick Koch. They stated that Koch had been given charge of the Room with orders to protect it in the event of an Allied offensive. This has been authenticated by German military records.

The residents further stated that Koch was a frequent visitor to a brewery located along the shores of a nearby lake (improbably named Swan Lake), and reportedly had learned of an underground icehouse there which had not been used since 1912. It was alleged that Koch arranged to have the Amber Room panels secreted to the icehouse in late July 1944, in advance of the Russian invasion.

On the basis of these statements, Koch was arrested by the Russians and interrogated at length. It is unclear exactly what he told them, although there are persistent rumors that Koch, in a disoriented mental state, claimed that the Amber Room had been hidden under an old Roman Catholic church. As of 1944, there had been no Roman Catholic churches in Königsberg for hundreds of years due to the Protestant Reformation. But the Swan Lake brewery was built next to the ruins of a thirteenth century castle which would likely have contained a church. The Russians reportedly searched the area around the brewery and the castle ruins thoroughly and failed to find the Room.

As for Koch, his fate is unknown. Survivors of the Soviet gulags have reported the presence, as late as the mid-1970s, of a German officer who spoke of a fabulous room belonging to Peter the Great. This man has never been positively identified as Koch.

5. The Room was in fact recovered by the Russians. In the course of my joint investigations with Isaiah Hawkins, a final theory has emerged. In the early-1980s, a Russian defector by the name of Mikhail Shokovitch informed the Agency that the Amber Room had been recovered by the Russians from Königsberg. Shokovitch asserts that the Room was secretly transported back to Moscow to be installed in Stalin's personal residence. However, rather than being so used, the Room remained in storage until being sold by Stalin to a private collector in the early 1950s along with some other items, also of apparently great value.

We have been unable to confirm any of the details offered by Shokovitch. In sum, fifty years after the Amber Room's disappearance, all we have is theories and rumors based on the slimmest slivers of fact.

17

The skinny delivery boy never saw the straight right hand. Truth is, it wouldn't have mattered even if he had. The boy had no chin, and out cold is out cold.

Kathryn quickly dragged the body (the boy's arms still clutching a brown bag) into a nearby alley, where she wiped a flash of blood off her knuckles and paused to wonder if her hand would scar. Hard to tell from the minimal light offered by the closest streetlamp. But she thought it might. Damn. Whatever…occupational hazard.

She stripped the boy straight down to his boxers, and put his navy blue cotton uniform on over her own tight clothes. The uniform was about three sizes too tall for her, but she made it work with a hip-hop, baggy look, perfectly accessorized by a Yankee cap pulled low over her face. Then she checked herself in a hand-mirror and glanced at her watch, 11:45 P.M.. Last chance, dinnertime at Osborne, Crane & Rosewater. A delivery she had counted on. Driven law firm associates and the closest available Chinese restaurant having a more regular nightly relationship than most husbands and wives.

She walked out of the alley carrying the brown bag—a still warm serving of mu shu pork, pot stickers, and brown rice. Osborne, Crane & Rosewater's office was just a two block walk away, at 335 Park Avenue. The delivery boy was left to his dreams.

A few minutes later, Kathryn swung through a revolving glass door and into the lobby of a sixty story granite and glass tower, where she was greeted by the sound of low flying reggae music. Peter Tosh, she thought.

A young black woman was stationed behind the security counter, the music coming from a nearby boom box.

"Where you going, honey?"

Kathryn shuffled over, placed the bag of food up on the black marble counter, and pointed to the pale green delivery slip. All the while keeping the Yankee cap tucked low over her eyes. "For E. Visser, at Osborne, Crane & Rosewater."

"Sign here," the guard said, motioning toward an open ledger book, while picking up the house phone to notify that skinny prick Visser that his food was on the way.

"Sure." Kathryn put a scrawled black line in the book, and her mind gently tapped into the music. It was a loose thing, reggae. Hard to clasp your arms around, easy to feel the essence. The essence and the looseness slipping inside her, something to envy. It was so tight, this job. And, without knowing it consciously, but knowing it for certain nevertheless, she reached for a little of that looseness, a casual chance taken. A calling card left behind, perhaps. Every girl, after all, needed a calling card.

"Peter Tosh, right?" Kathryn asked softly.

"Yeah, *Legalize It*."

"Thought so."

When the elevator let Kathryn Blaire out at the thirty-fifth floor, Eric Visser was already waiting for her. A young associate who looked like he'd been up all night for the past several nights, he numbly led her through the firm's glass security doors, down a hallway, and into a conference room where he apparently wished to eat his dinner.

She left the food near his pile of papers, he handed her twenty-five bucks and took a receipt, then he went straight back to marking up an eighty page, single-spaced bank loan agreement while absently shoveling in cold Chinese food.

While Visser booked billable hours, Kathryn slipped out of the conference room. Back in the hall, she took three steps towards the elevator before darting left down a long corridor.

Elliot Rosewater's prime corner office was marked with a polished brass nametag on an oak door. The door was locked. Kathryn reached into a small bag strapped to her waist, taking out a pair of black leather gloves and putting them on, then pulling out a ghost key.

The key worked its magic, the tumbler turned, and she pushed the door open, the light from the hall enabling her to take an instant inventory: antiquey looking wood furniture, stacks of paper everywhere, diplomas and photographs on the walls, and a small banker's lamp on the desk. She closed the door behind her quietly, relocked it, and turned on the small desk lamp.

18

On the corner of the desk, a color photograph smiled up at Kathryn: a soft-faced man, his arm around a nice looking woman of perhaps forty-five. Funny, the soft-faced man had looked so different in Ivo Jenkin's photos.

It was just past midnight, Elliot Rosewater had long since left the office and wouldn't be back until morning, figure 6:00 A.M. at the earliest. That was plenty of time. But now for the hard part—what the hell was she looking for? That was always the hard part on these types of efforts, because you never knew until you found it. Sort of like the Supreme Court's famous decision on pornography. Because she had to start somewhere, she began with the papers stacked on Rosewater's desk.

● ● ●

Almost at the very same moment, Elliot Rosewater stepped out of a black limousine thirty-five floors below. He'd been busy all night with clients, buying dinner and kissing ass and pretending that everything was fine. Fine...not exactly.

Jack Osborne had given him a heads up about Detective Russo's visit. Jack claimed not to have given the cop much of anything, but whether Jack had or hadn't didn't really much matter. The cop would figure out sooner or later that Sarah Ridell had been passed down the firm's letterhead from Osborne to Rosewater, that he'd been banging her for over a year, and that he'd been with her the night she fell. But the cop wouldn't be able to tie him directly to Sarah's death, not so long as he made sure that nothing was left to chance.

With a determined stride, Rosewater pushed through the revolving door leading into 335 Park, where the sounds of bewildering music suddenly assaulted him. He stared at the night watchwoman but said nothing, making a mental note to inform the building's owner in the morning. That woman would have to go. Then he stepped into the elevator, pushed

35, and went back to thinking about Sarah.

Her death was a shame. She'd been a helluva fuck. Best he'd ever had. But good things weren't meant to last forever. More important than the regrets were making sure that he got his story set for Detective Russo. He rehearsed his words one more time:

"Yes, I was with Sarah that night. I'd been seeing her for a year, Detective. You already know that. But these things always have to end, and I told her so that evening. I told her that Jennifer, my wife, was getting suspicious and I couldn't take the risk of being seen with her anymore...Of course, that wasn't completely true. My wife didn't know a thing...Still doesn't. But, it seemed the best way to get out cleanly. It wasn't as if I'd ever intended to leave my wife for her, Detective...and Sarah knew that. I'd never even hinted I would marry her.

"Anyway, Sarah started crying, wouldn't stop, even threatened to kill herself. Of course, I didn't believe her. I figured she'd get over it. Especially after I told her that I would take care of her financially. One hundred thousand dollars. A lot of money, detective. That seemed to calm her down a little, we talked some more, and I finally left to go home. Next thing I knew was what I'd read in the newspaper...tragic...absolutely tragic..."

The elevator reached the thirty-fifth floor and Elliot Rosewater got off and pushed through the firm's glass security doors, still going over his story, wondering whether one hundred thousand sounded cheap. Probably not to a cop. What did Russo make? Fifty thousand a year, if he was lucky. He'd buy the hundred thousand. Just like getting him to buy the whole story wouldn't be too hard. Half a dozen people got themselves murdered in New York City every week, week after week, year after year. Sarah Ridell was a nobody from nowhere, and after a couple of weeks she would be forgotten. The case would be closed as a suicide, and everyone would move on. Nor would it be much harder keeping his name out of the papers. He'd been doing favors for publishers for years

for a moment just like this. Sarah Ridell's death was not going to ruin him, no fucking way. Not so long as he could handle the other one...

Bianca. That was the name Elliot Rosewater wished he'd never heard of. Wished he'd never been contacted by her about that damned mirror, even if it was part of the legendary Amber Room. If you didn't have the Room, why bother with some mirror? And if you did have the Room, it was some hell of a risk to take, exposing yourself just to get the mirror.

But he had been retained by Bianca. He had accepted Bianca's money. And he had bragged about it all to Sarah Ridell, as if he needed to impress Miss Johnson City, Oklahoma.

With that in mind, Elliot Rosewater turned down the corridor leading to his office. He reached into his pocket for his keys, and felt a strange iron pendant he'd received by courier from Bianca earlier that day, without explanation. He'd put the pendant into his pocket and almost forgotten about it and now he took it out along with his keys. Cast into the pendant was a picture he didn't understand, and he looked down at it as he absently inserted the key into the lock.

•　　•　　•

On the other side of that office door, Kathryn Blaire's attention had been fixed on Elliot Rosewater's calendar, one of those entered on a computer and then printed out in hard copy. It was the type of program where you could draw with a stylus and her eyes stared at a doodle entered for 5:00 A.M. the next morning, six balls sketched on some sort of triangle. Absorbed as she was, she didn't hear Rosewater's footsteps, didn't notice anything until the sound of jangling keys made her arteries pound with blood. Instantly, she cut the desk light, slid silently against the wall near the door, and held her breath. Please, she prayed, just be the cleaning service.

The keys scraped against the lock, the doorknob turned, and the oak door was pushed open into the office. Backlit by the lights from the hall, Elliot Rosewater stepped into the room. He stood there for an instant, not noticing her as he looked down at something he was holding in his hand.

Then he flipped the light switch, bathing Kathryn in a blue-green fluorescent aura. For an instant, he stared at her, paralyzed, trying to decipher who she was. Not three feet away, Kathryn Blaire stared back, uncertain herself.

Rosewater opened his mouth, haltingly, "Wh...Who are..."

Kathryn's training took over. Her fist answered Rosewater in the gut, taking the wind and his voice from him and doubling him over. She reached out with both hands, grabbed the lapels of his jacket and yanked him back up towards her. So that they were staring right at each other, as she slammed her knee into his balls. His body sagged. He staggered backwards and dropped to his knees, his free hand clutching at his groin. There was no comprehension in his face, his eyes begged her to stop, and he looked like he was going to vomit. But there were no points for mercy and she ripped a kick into his jaw, knocking him flat onto his back. Driven by adrenaline, she rocked back to kick him again...but Elliot Rosewater wasn't groaning anymore. He wasn't moving at all.

She held her swing in mid-air, then slowly dropped her leg to the ground. She stood over him, fighting the rush. The rush that would stay with her until morning. The high she loved and feared...and had to control. She had to finish the job. Do what she believed in best—exploit the opportunity.

Close the door, Kathryn.

Elliot Rosewater was sprawled lengthwise on his back, with one hand still clutching his balls and the other making a tight fist held arm's length above his head. She bent down over his torso, put her ear against his chest and placed two fingers against his neck. He was unconscious, but his breathing, jumbled as it was with her own, seemed all right. His pulse, too. Elliot Rosewater would wake up sore, but he'd get over it.

She slid up to the arm extended over his head and pried open his fist, surprised to see he was holding a pendant—a heavy flat circle of cast iron hanging from a metal link chain.

The back side of the pendant was completely smooth. On the front, an image had been cast into the metal: a picture of a young man hanging upside down from a tree by one leg. The young man's free leg bent at the knee so as to cross behind the bound leg, and the man's arms crossed behind his back.

It looked cool. And vaguely familiar. But Kathryn couldn't place it and she stuck it into the pocket of her blue delivery uniform. She looked around the rest of the office, seeing all the stacks of paper Rosewater had accumulated. Papers on the desk, on the credenza, on the floor. All of it giving her pause. She no longer had the kind of time it would take to work through the papers.

One thing she knew, in a mess of clutter like this, Elliot Rosewater would have needed a place or two to put the stuff he really cared about it. So she started looking for that place. And she found it behind Rosewater's framed NYU diploma: like magic, a shiny steel safe sunk into the wall.

Cracking safes without explosives was an art, one Kathryn wasn't particularly skilled at. But this wasn't the sort of safe any serious player in her business would have ever paid money for. It was more like a good looking toy, and within minutes she had it open.

It was empty—the way a clear mind with one sparkling idea is empty. Because dead in the center of the chamber was an invitation addressed to Elliot Rosewater from the Sintra Art Gallery.

She slipped the invite into her pocket without opening it. No time to worry about that now—she knew for a fact she'd found what she was looking for. It just worked that way. She stepped carefully around Elliot Rosewater and walked out the door.

•   •   •

Later, the rush still strong, Kathryn lay down on her bed. The delivery boy's uniform heaped in a pile on her hardwood floor. Her body naked but for a tattoo below her navel. The iron pendant and the invitation in her hands. She remembered that she'd been looking at Rosewater's calendar when she first

81

heard the jangle of his keys—at a notation with six balls on a triangle—and she supposed now that she should have taken the calendar too. But she was too tired to beat herself up over it, and she put her head down to sleep.

Her dreams overtook her almost at once, random and displaced bits of her life anxious to circle up to the surface, as if they were paying passengers on the devil's ferris wheel.

She found herself driving once again through the parched Mexican desert. Gray having found her hiding at an old Hacienda in the silver hills, and then letting her go. Not, as some claimed, in exchange for a slice of the money she'd taken. He wouldn't take any of it. No, he'd let her go because they were partners. Because he owed her. And mostly because she loved him and wanted him to come with her, but he knew that it could never work—her lifestyle and his sense of severe loyalty being simply incompatible, perhaps selfishly so.

So he'd let her walk away, drive away actually, straight down a half-paved, dusty, high-desert road in an old, green convertible Jaguar. The money stuffed in a fake Vuitton bag on the seat beside her. So empty it turned out. Not the money. She loved the money and always would. It was her dream of freedom that proved an illusion.

All that time eyeing the money, just waiting for the right opening…and she'd known with a final certainty that she'd made a mistake the very instant Gray had slipped out of the range of the rearview mirror. What good was freedom if you were adrift alone?

She tried now to focus her shifting mind on Gray's image, but it faded away again, replaced in her dreams by a new vista. Then that too disappeared into its own haze.

Her dreams continued without pause. The faces of friends, and others who were not friends, came forward then withdrew. And when she saw Elliot Rosewater's face staring back at her, Kathryn woke with a start and opened her eyes to see a thin stream of moonlight shining through a window. It was a gorgeous crescent moon. Beautiful. And she put her head down for a while longer.

19

It was not yet eight in the morning when Ben Russo parked his car straight outside 335 Park, right behind an ambulance. An overnight cross-check of fingerprints picked up from Sarah Ridell's bed frame against those the state bar kept on file for all attorneys had eliminated any doubt—Sarah Ridell's last night had been spent screwing Elliot Rosewater. And Ben planned to kickstart the new day by paying Jack Osborne's partner a surprise visit.

The ambulance driver, a burly man with a double chin, thick forearms, and a cheap hairpiece, yawned as the detective got out of his car.

"What's going on?" Russo asked.

"Don't know. Heart attack, probably. My radio busted on me soon as we got here. Seen the prissy mayor on the tube last night talking about getting cellular phones for emergency services. Who's he kidding—we can't even get a decent two-way fucking radio. Third time in two months my radio's busted. I'll tell you, this city's all fucked up good."

Russo nodded, as if a man with twenty-five years on the force needed to be convinced that the city was all fucked up good. He stepped past the driver and, tilting his head back, stared up at the granite building, imagining all the over-stressed, overweight, overachievers sitting hunched over their desks. There must be a heart attack every week. And he told himself, for not the first or last time, that he should've been a doctor like his blessed mother said. He began to question that non-decision even more when he arrived at the thirty-fifth floor.

The usually pristine reception area of Osborne, Crane & Rosewater was in disarray. Jack Osborne stood in the center of the open space, at the head of a loose circle of some twenty men and women, most of them crying. Osborne himself was giving a hug to a heavyset woman in a blue polyester dress. Then another hug, to a woman with purple eye liner running down her cheek and onto Osborne's suit. Funny, Russo hadn't figured Osborne for the public hugging type. He went up and tapped his hand on Osborne's shoulder.

The lawyer spun around and looked at Russo like he'd been expecting to see him. "Thank God you're finally here. It was horrible. Just horrible. An associate found him this morning."

"Found who?"

"Rosewater…Elliot."

Russo took a moment to register the information and find the right words. "How is he?"

Osborne didn't answer straight off, like maybe he didn't hear the question. Or maybe Russo was a complete fucking idiot.

"I asked, how is he?" Russo repeated.

"How is he?" Osborne paused. "Not well, detective. Not well at all."

●   ●   ●

It was a little later that morning when Ivo Jenkins left his home to go to the local newsstand. It was a ritual of his, walking down to Muhammad Shah's each morning to pick up the tabloids. Kindred spirits, Ivo and the publishers of the tabs, men whose livelihood depended on human behavior of the sleazy kind.

Because it was a particularly lovely summer morning and because Ivo still needed to lose that weight, he took the long route, getting some extra exercise before approaching the kiosk filled with magazines and papers.

"What's news, Muhammad?" he called out to his favorite vendor.

"Big news, big man," Muhammad Shah replied with his everpresent cheerfulness. "You got to read all 'bout it, like they say."

"Oh, yeah?"

"Oh, yes. Full front page. Little fellow like me gets himself knocked around, it doesn't make the front page. That's the way it is. Way it's always gonna be. But this was big time." Muhammad held up the paper so that Ivo could read the ninety-six-point type headline, and see the photo, taken on a better day, of Elliot Rosewater's soft smiling face.

Ivo stared silently at that soft smile. A black and white image of Sarah Ridell leaning back and laughing filled his mind. It seemed Anand's people had come calling on behalf of Sarah Ridell. With enthusiasm. And that was just fine. He stuffed the newspaper in a garbage can near the steps to his home.

•   •   •

Dressed in a plush green velvet robe, Kathryn Blaire was eating a breakfast of corn flakes, and listening to Otis Rush sing the blues, when the music died down and was replaced by the drone of a radio newscaster:

...sources within the police department have informed WAMC that well-known attorney Elliot Rosewater of Osborne, Crane & Rosewater...

She was still eating when it hit her that the news report was wrong.

...police commissioner Michael O'Malley is expected to hold a press conference later this morning...

Had to be wrong.

...according to sources close to the family, a private service is planned at two o'clock on...

It had to be wrong. Elliot Rosewater was alive.

In a near trance, while the newscast continued with its lies, Kathryn replayed the fight, Tai-chi-like against the air. A slow motion punch, stomach high. Both hands shooting out to grab his lapels, her knee driving up. Then, a finishing kick. She reached back for another and held up. Gut. Nuts. Jaw. That was it. Just enough to disable, like she had been taught. Elliot Rosewater was out cold. But very much alive. She hadn't killed him...she hadn't meant to kill him.

Her mind slowly absorbed the truth, and paused. Judge not, lest ye be judged, and she was not ready to pass judgment on herself yet. Instead, her thoughts skipped to the relative comfort offered by a rational assessment of the impact and consequences: they needed Elliot Rosewater alive. The evidence and clues she had found in his office might prove valuable, but with Sarah Ridell already dead, Rosewater's death was potentially devastating to their hopes of finding the Amber Room. No comfort there. First assignment since she'd been called back and she had just recklessly killed their best lead. Isaiah Hawkins would not be pleased. Not at all.

She closed her eyes, and the judgment flowed. She tried to stop herself, but it didn't work. How couldn't she judge? She had just killed a man, may God forgive her, and had fucked everything up while doing it.

•   •   •

At the station house, Ben Russo picked up the coroner's preliminary report from the fax machine. It read more clinically than it must have felt:

> VISIBLE INJURIES: bruising on abdomen consistent with internal bleeding; fractured mandible; bruised testicles; traces of vomit and dried blood found in mouth.
> APPROXIMATE TIME OF DEATH: 4:00 a.m.
> PROBABLE CAUSE OF DEATH: internal bleeding

Fight and life over. Elliot Rosewater, his prime suspect in the Ridell murder, beaten like a stupid drunk in the wrong bar. Lovely.

20

In his office high in an anonymous New York skyscraper, Isaiah Hawkins listened to Kathryn's story the way a conductor listens to his orchestra play a difficult symphony: evaluating each note and, quite separately, judging the texture and flow of the whole.

Isaiah radiated absolute calm, something Kathryn had seen him do so many times before. It was his gift, the ability to slow things down until he was ready, as if he could personally suspend the laws of time and relativity. Still, his cigarette obeyed the laws of physics, burning down steadily as he flicked the ashes into a styrofoam cup that he'd fashioned into a makeshift ashtray. Deciding her fate while using a two cent cup as an ashtray. The contradictions that were Isaiah Hawkins piling up like the ashes.

"Enough," Isaiah finally said, holding up one hand to physically reinforce the single word. His judgment on her actions. On killing Elliot Rosewater. One word. Enough.

A wisp of smoke escaped from the tip of Kathryn's own cigarette, merging into the semi-permanent white haze that had formed in the atmosphere of the locked office, and she nervously fingered the heavy chain dangling around her neck.

"Is that it?" Isaiah asked, watching her gesture. "The pendant you were telling me about?"

"Yeah...didn't want to lose it." She lifted the chain and pendant over her head and handed it to him.

Isaiah looked the pendant over, then gave it back to her almost casually, as if to say, so what. Not much to die for. Not like the invitation to the Sintra Gallery which was already lying on his desk. Nice work on her part, stealing the invitation from Rosewater's safe while he lay dying not more than five feet away. Nice work, if you had the nerve for it.

Kathryn put the pendant back around her neck, and thought about what to say next, knowing it didn't really matter. Isaiah would only let the conversation go where he wanted it to. "It gives us something to work with, anyway, Isaiah. The pendant and the invitation."

Isaiah nodded noncommittally. Maybe it gave them something

to work with. Maybe not. They would see where Kathryn took it. And where she took it would determine her future.

Isaiah stood up slowly, like an aging fullback getting up from a hard tackle. And for the first time, Kathryn thought he looked old.

"Let's just get what we came for, Kathryn," he said. Then he stubbed out his cigarette against the bottom of the styrofoam cup, the meeting over. Kathryn's career intact for another day.

•   •   •

"Thanks for coming," Kathryn said, her voice thinner than usual, as she opened the door to her loft, the pendant still dangling from around her neck. She began to explain, even while Anand was still standing in the doorway, "It didn't happen like you think. The thing with Elliot Rosewater, I mean. You know what I mean."

Anand closed the door behind him. "There's no need to explain, Kathryn. It doesn't matter."

She looked at him strangely. It was, after all, her life they were speaking of, not to mention Elliot Rosewater's. "It does to me."

"And perhaps to Isaiah, but perhaps not, and certainly not to me."

There was, after all, nothing left to discuss. Anand supposed she'd found what she needed in Rosewater's office, found Rosewater there as well and killed him. Or something along those lines. The photos paid for. A deal with Ivo honored. The Amber Room soon within their grasp. And, with an excess of casualness and detachment, Anand paused to look around the apartment. The loft was designed like a minimalist art gallery, with high ceilings, no doors between rooms, huge works of art hanging on white walls, bare wood floors, and a giant skylight. It was a lovely space.

"This yours?" he asked.

"Yes…I own it." Kathryn answered haltingly, distracted.

Anand took a step towards a poster-sized black and white photograph of a nude woman with a script tattoo below her navel. Words in ink making an interesting suggestion. The woman resembled Kathryn, but the lighting in the picture was dark and Anand couldn't be certain. Or didn't wish to look closely enough

to be certain.

"You don't understand," she went on. "I didn't kill him. Not on purpose."

"Please—by accident or with purpose—it does not matter to me." There was no need to explain. It wasn't that kind of business. A moment of introspection, perhaps. A beat of concern. That was all one could afford. He looked at her more closely. "Are you all right?"

She clenched her hand, noticing a little stiffness. "I'm fine, I guess."

"Anyone see you at Rosewater's office?"

"No...I mean, a couple of people saw me, but no one paid me any attention."

"Fingerprints?"

She thought of the pair of gloves still piled on the floor near her bed. "No."

"Would it be impolite then for me to ask whether you found what we were looking for?"

She shrugged and decided not to mention the invitation for the Sintra Gallery for later that evening, preferring to handle that herself. But she lifted the metal pendant from around her neck and held it out toward him. "What do you think of this?"

Anand examined it briefly, but carefully, making no comment.

"There's one other thing, I suppose," she added. "I had just started going through Rosewater's calendar when he surprised me. There was an odd notation...a drawing...six balls on a triangle. But I forgot about it in the excitement...forgot to take it with me."

"You can't go back there."

"Left it right on top of the desk," she said with a small, half smile.

Anand smiled too. Seemed Kathryn Blaire had started moving past the explaining stage herself. And pretty quickly.

21

Ben Russo ran his finger down an opera schedule he'd pulled off the Internet and dreamt of his wife. Gaetano Donizetti's *Lucia di Lammermoor* was playing at La Scala in Milan the next week, with Jane Eaglen as Lucia. He didn't know Eaglen...didn't know enough about opera, other than that he liked it. But he knew that La Scala wouldn't have anyone center stage unless she could really open up and give it a ride. And he knew his Maria would sparkle the night he finally took her to La Scala. There were a thousand reasons they had never gone, all the good and bad reasons people find not to do things they want to. And there was one reason he knew he had to take her. She would absolutely sparkle...

Reluctantly, he tucked the opera schedule in the drawer of his city issue, gunmetal gray desk. The drawer stuck, like it always did, and he slammed it hard with an open palm just to close it about halfway. The squad room had another twenty desks just like it, all of them bought in 1963. The greatest year ever for port, or so he was told, but a lousy year for desks.

It was nearly 8:00 P.M., past time to go home, the end of a long day that had started with that ambulance driver. But before leaving, he always spent some time reviewing his notes. A twenty-year habit that paid enough dividends to justify the investment.

He started with his notes from an interview, taken just before lunch with one Aristotle Long, a skinny Chinese boy with an outstanding name and a nice shiner over one eye.

Aristotle had come in and given a story to a couple of cops at the 33rd. Told them he worked for a restaurant named Hunan Harvest and that he'd been on his way to Osborne, Crane & Rosewater around midnight with a delivery when he got sucker-punched coming 'round a corner. A couple hours later, he'd woken up in an alley, stripped to his boxers, socks, and sneakers, his uniform and food delivery stolen.

It wasn't as if the department had the resources to pursue

crimes of food, and ninety-nine times out of one hundred, the boys at the 33rd would've told Aristotle to take some aspirin and be more careful the next time. But two things about his story stuck out.

One, he was positive he got creamed by a girl. Not that women couldn't be hungry and broke; but desperate women tended to find a different way to get a meal. Two, when the owner of Hunan Harvest called Osborne, Crane & Rosewater in the morning to apologize and to explain the missed delivery, it turned out that the food had shown up, and just about right on time. It had even been paid for. The cops at the 33rd had managed to put two and two together and called Ben.

Next stop for Ben after interviewing Aristotle had been back to Osborne, Crane, to interview one Eric Visser, the associate who had ordered the dinner. Visser had only the dimmest memory of the entire event. He hadn't really noticed much about the delivery person, except it was a woman.

Dark hair, light hair?

Eric Visser couldn't say.

Tall, short, heavy, thin?

He kind of thought she was thin. Certainly not fat, anyway. He did remember paying her. He'd kept the receipt and submitted it to the firm for reimbursement. That was firm policy, Visser explained. If an associate ate dinner at the office after 8:30, the firm would charge the client, tacking on a 20 percent markup, and reimburse the associate. But no, he could not recall walking her out to an elevator. He'd been too busy working on an important loan document to pay attention to that. He was sorry he didn't remember more. It was just that he usually ate at the office four or five nights a week, and he didn't much pay attention to the delivery person. It was just a delivery person, right? Ben let him go without any more questions after that. The kid had probably gone to law school to help people. After two years at Osborne, Crane, he was already three-quarters of the way to becoming a complete asshole.

The only other person at 335 Park Avenue who'd seen anything was the night watchwoman, Latisha Dixon.

"Sure, I remember her," Latisha told Russo. "White woman. Small and thin. Had a Yankee hat pulled down pretty low over her face. Didn't get much of a look at her...now that I think about it. I remember thinking it was strange, them having a white girl delivering and all. Usually it's some tall, skinny Chinese boy. But you know...that's their business. As long as someone upstairs says it's OK, I'll send them up."

"Do you remember seeing her leave?" Russo asked.

"My job is to ask people questions on the way in. What happens after that, you know, that ain't my nevermind. Women come up, maybe they stay a little longer than they should. Same thing with some pretty looking men. Either way, my eyes are closed. You know what I'm saying? The people paying my salary, they don't want Latisha Dixon paying too close attention to their business and all." She paused. "Girl knew who Peter Tosh was...if that helps."

"Peter who?"

"Tosh...you know. Peter Tosh. One of the guys founded the Wailers. With Bob Marley. Reggae God."

"No. Didn't know that," Russo said, with a sigh.

Ben put his notes back down on his desk. No one else at Osborne, Crane had seen anything. None of the cleaning people, none of the other lawyers who'd worked late that night. He would've liked to ask Jack Osborne some more questions—it being such a happy coincidence that Jack and Elliot Rosewater were both screwing Sarah Ridell. But Jack was out of the office, grieving, according to his secretary.

Ben knew, if they got real lucky, they might be able to pull a fingerprint from Rosewater's office. He had assigned a young cop named Stacy Sparks to supervise that task. But he didn't hold much hope of success. Too many people would've been in and out of that office every day touching things; there'd be prints all over. And the killer seemed to handle herself well—getting in, beating a man a death, cracking a safe, and getting out, all without being seen—too well to forget about wearing gloves. No matter. Hell, he already knew who he was looking for: a thin, white girl who fought dirty and liked Peter Tosh. Wonderful.

22

Kathryn sank into the old clawfoot tub in the corner of her white-tiled bathroom and let trickles of hot water run down her feet and calves. She still had two hours before that evening's opening at the Sintra Gallery, and her body seemed to float and her mind followed, seeking refuge.

To some, baths are an anachronistic killer of time, strangely out of step in today's world. But Kathryn Blaire understood their magic as a place out of time.

She'd only recently learned to take the measure of time: while she was on the run, as the last two years of her life might have been romantically called. Of course, it was an odd thing being on the run, as she was hardly ever actually moving. Mostly she was sitting tight, alone, waiting. There was an old mansion in Mexico City with a beautiful garden hidden behind adobe walls. She had stayed there under the jacaranda trees for days while waiting for the money she had stolen to wend its labyrinth path through the banking systems of three sovereign nations. There was the white-on-white hacienda in the hills, where she waited for Gray to find her. There were other places, much the same, the days blending seamlessly into one another, time a forgotten element.

Not that Isaiah Hawkins had cared about any of that when he had finally found her, when he had arrived one fine day at a luscious beach in a far corner of Brazil that was on no map…except his. And he never asked about the money either.

Never asked why she took it. There was, after all, no reason for him to ask why. He had always understood her motives better than she had understood them herself. The money just lying there, slippery, in an Agency account, but not legally of the Agency. Slushy money. Finders keepers money. A magic pot of gold belonging to anyone who possessed it. Money that could buy her freedom, so she believed. Driving all other thoughts from her mind, the way angels were driven from heaven.

But he hadn't even asked for the money back. Instead, Isaiah had simply suggested she come back with him. Like a God giving her a second chance…if not absolution.

She hadn't questioned why, either. Isaiah Hawkins was complex in ways that neither she nor anyone else would ever fully understand. But she understood enough. She had her money and her secrets and now Isaiah owned her.

She belonged to Isaiah Hawkins, and that was a deal she could live with because she was thrilled to be back. Back where she belonged. Alive. In the game. And, instead of setting things right, everything was going wrong.

Sarah Ridell, their lead to the Amber Room, had been killed under her watch. Sure, it was Ivo Jenkins actually doing the looking from across the street, but that watch was her responsibility. Then she'd gone and clumsily killed Elliot Rosewater right in his own office, leaving him to die all alone on the floor. Maybe Elliot Rosewater had deserved it—if he had killed Sarah Ridell like it seemed. But maybe he didn't, and she would have to deal with that somehow, someplace, best she could. But not now. Not until this was over and she knew the truth. She quietly said a small prayer asking for luck at the gallery that night.

Then she stepped out of the bath and toweled off, staring at her reflection in the mirror. She didn't think she looked like a killer—not standing there naked anyway. She was too flimsy: too skinny, too short, and too vulnerable. Naked women weren't capable of killing, she didn't think. Not even ones who had been trained to hit first and hard and fast, and never to hesitate. So she pulled on her clothes—black cotton panties, black leather pants, a tight black cotton t-shirt, tie-up black leather half-boots—and then walked back to the mirror.

Even dressed she didn't look like a killer. Still too flimsy. But it seemed that's what she was. Her eyes strayed to a long scuff at the toe of her right boot. She'd been wearing the boots at Rosewater's office. That scuff was the truth. No matter what she wanted to believe, she was a killer and a thief. A person not to be trusted. One of Isaiah's people, for so long as he needed her.

23

In the light darkness of the city night, Ivo Jenkins climbed the granite steps leading to 335 Park Avenue. Just that morning he'd thought he was done with Elliot Rosewater forever. His mistake.

He took the last of the stairs and pushed through a revolving glass door into a brightly lit lobby. The sounds of "Many Rivers to Cross" drifted through the large space—seemingly from the security desk, where a pretty young black woman stood watching him. Ivo shook his head, no wonder he had been hired for this assignment.

Latisha Dixon eyed him back with considerable concern. She was lucky to still have her job, what with the murder and all, and she knew it. In fact, she figured there was only one reason she was still around: if the dead lawyer's widow sued it would look worse for the security company if she'd been fired—it would be like admitting she had done something wrong. Which she hadn't. And she wasn't going to this time either. As Ivo moved towards her, she mentally noted everything about him: his bald head, his age, the color of his eyes, the clothes he was wearing, the leather portfolio he was carrying, the camera slung over his shoulder…No way she wasn't going to be able to describe him to the cops if she had to, not like that delivery woman who'd suckered her by wearing her cap down over her eyes.

Ivo came to a stop right in front of her.

"Who are you here to see?" she asked, an edge in her voice, not happy at all about seeing a three-hundred-pound behemoth strolling into her lobby near midnight.

"I'm not here to see anyone except you, honey."

Even before he'd finished the "e" in honey, she was reaching for her walkie talkie. "Then you better leave. I'm not interested in what you got."

"Now it's not like that," Ivo said with a broad, simple smile, placing the leather portfolio up on her desk and pointing to his camera. "I'm a photographer, see. I got a deal with a book publisher and everything. It's legit. Straight up. Here," he opened the folio to its first page, "go ahead and look."

Tentatively, at first, Latisha Dixon flipped through the pages, looking at the black and white glossies. She took them in one at a time: an aging hostess in a luxurious bar, a vibrant young waitress in a cheap and dirty diner, a toll booth collector wiping the soot off his face with a monogrammed handkerchief, a young cop walking an early morning beat. "These are good," she said softly, holding the photo of the cop up to the light, a nice looking young cop, on patrol on Lenox Avenue. It was a real good picture. Good as anything she'd ever seen in the magazines.

"I'm working on finishing the series," Ivo said, "and I'm walking past this building tonight and I saw you, all lit up by the lobby lights. Framed, you know what I mean. And I said to myself, I just got to have her picture. What do you say?"

"I don't know..."

She looked at the photos again, their allure drawing her in, battling against her fears for her job, what with the man's murder and all, and against all her natural suspicions. She knew about that Internet stuff and all. How pictures got around. She raised her eyebrows and stared at Ivo. "You're not gonna ask me to show you my titties or nothing like that, are you? Because I don't do that kind of thing."

"Got no interest in that." Ivo held up his wedding ring, then took a delicate, admiring glance at her chest. "Not that you don't look fine. OK?"

"Yeah, OK. Now you understand, I can't leave my desk. I need this job. And, I don't have any makeup on or nothing."

"That's the way I want you. Just the way you are. Oh, yes," he said, lifting the camera to his eye, looking at her through the lens and snapping a picture. Capturing her. "You look perfect. Oh, yes. Now look this way." Click, click, click. And, as he took the pictures, he saw Anand Ashland slip quietly into the building, behind Latisha Dixon, and into an elevator.

The elevator stopped on 35 and, wearing a conservative blue

pinstripe suit, blue shirt, and rep tie, Anand entered Osborne, Crane, looking like he belonged.

Three yellow strips of police tape stretched across an otherwise open door to Elliot Rosewater's office and Anand ducked between the waist high strip and the knee high one.

Rosewater's calendar was sitting right out on the desk, exactly where Kathryn said she'd left it, like a gift from heaven. The type of apparent luck that never happened. Anand rapidly turned through the computer generated pages looking for the entry she had described. Except...except there were no entries for the past week. Nor for the week before that. They were gone, ripped from the book. Anand figured by either the cops, Kathryn, or anyone with an interest in hiding their dealings with Rosewater. That left a lot of possibilities. But no reasons to panic.

Instead, he moved quickly to his backup plan, and powered on Rosewater's office computer where a mirror copy of the calendar should be stored in its memory. He moved quickly through the computer's file structure, finding the location on the hard drive where the calendar data belonged, then a whispered string of language he didn't usually use escaped from his lips. The computer calendar data file had been wiped clean as well. A nice job. Thorough, it seemed.

Still...there were other ways.

Anand knew enough about computers and the Agency to have learned a couple of things. Despite all the high-profile privacy advocates, Bill Gates hadn't designed the personal computer for the benefit of those seeking to cover up a trail. But rather for those, like the Agency, seeking the benefit of a second bite at the apple.

Anand slid open the drawers of Rosewater's desk, looking for a change stash. He found a couple of coins rolling around with the pencils, and, using a old dime, he unscrewed the back panel of the computer.

Down on the ground floor, Ivo was changing to his last roll of film when he saw Anand take a half step into the lobby. "All right, now," Ivo said. "Just a couple more." He lifted the camera to his eye and began shooting.

Latisha Dixon, enthralled by the camera the way all people are, never heard or saw Anand Ashland walk past her and into the night.

When they met up twenty minutes later, at an all-night, all-black diner named Jehovah's, Ivo asked, "Did you find what you were looking for?"

"With luck," Anand said, removing a thin metallic box from underneath his jacket and placing it on the table with a sly grin. Uncharacteristically showing off and enjoying it.

"What's that?"

"Elliot Rosewater's hard drive...much easier to delete information than actually erase it from the drive, or so I'm told." He passed a thick envelope across the table to Ivo. "Thanks."

"You know," Ivo said, as he tucked the envelope into his jacket, "I'm thinking I may just actually do that book of photographs. I think some of those shots tonight are going turn out real good. Latisha put on a real good show for me. Yeah, I might just do that book."

24

Teresa Gomes ran the downtown gallery of the moment. She was beautiful and young, several years still shy of thirty, and she had named her gallery Sintra, after her beautiful birthplace in Portugal. But to her arteratti clientele, it would forever be known simply as Teresa's. As in, remember when Teresa's was the place.

When Kathryn Blaire arrived, dressed all in tight black but for the pendant still dangling from around her neck, Sintra was already filled with a typical opening night crowd of the hip, the rich, and the pretend hip or rich.

The artist of the moment was named C. Miller Wynant. And to Kathryn's surprise, Miller Wynant was a kind of sloppy fat guy. The kind of guy Kathryn expected to see at a football game with his shirt off and his face painted. But it was his show and it didn't matter how sloppy or fat he was. The hip and the rich just wanted a piece of him for the night, and he was surrounded by a cluster of smiling art babes.

Miller Wynant's metier was blue sculpture, a genre he seemed to be trying to make his own. Although Kathryn wondered if there were a lot of other contenders.

In the middle of the gallery, up on a stone pedestal, was a lifelike midnight blue Doberman Pincher. It made a nice contrast with the gallery's maple floors and white walls. In the far back corner stood a mock classical statue of a Roman god in azure. In another corner, a faux primitive stone icon dipped in a sky blue lacquer. Along the walls were a couple of large-sized photographs of people. Clothing optional. Also done by Wynant.

Kathryn stopped in front of a mostly black and white photograph of a nude woman with long dark hair and fabulous legs, a little Gucci handbag drawn in bright blue crayon over the woman's arm, and little blue crayon Gucci shoes on her bare feet. Cute, she thought. Before Kathryn had a chance to think of anything else, a woman slipped right up next to her.

Not just any woman, the woman in the picture, in real life. She was carrying a black Prada bag instead of blue Gucci, but she had the same fabulous legs under a short black dress. With the woman was a most handsome man with olive skin, jet black hair, and even darker eyes. He was in maybe his late thirties, and wearing a beautiful suit that possessed the graceful under-statement of fine tailoring.

"Do you like the photograph?" the woman asked.

"Very much," Kathryn replied.

The woman extended her hand. "Teresa Gomes. Welcome to my gallery." Her Portuguese accent beautiful. "And you are?"

"Kathryn Blaire."

"Lovely to meet you, Kathryn." Teresa gestured politely toward the gentleman with her. "May I introduce Paolo delle Bande Nere. A dear friend of mine."

Kathryn looked at him and smiled her pretty girl smile.

"Pleased to make your acquaintance, Ms. Blaire," he said in a soft voice with a southern European accent.

"All mine," Kathryn replied.

Teresa Gomes turned her own gaze back toward the picture of herself that was on display, and spoke to Kathryn. "Are you familiar with Miller Wynant's work?"

"No, not really. I knew Elliot Rosewater. We were going to meet here tonight."

"I'm sorry. So tragic his death." Teresa Gomes made an appropriately somber expression. "He was a wonderful man. My condolences."

"Thank you. He was dear to me."

"I read about it in the paper. Do the police know who did it?" Paolo delle Bande Nere asked.

"Not yet. But I understand they have some leads," Kathryn shrugged and smiled. "Anyway, life goes on, right Mister Bande Nere, or is it Mister delle Bande Nere?"

"Paolo, please. May I call you Kathryn?"

"Of course."

"How do you like the exhibit, Kathryn?"

"The photography is wonderful. This picture of Teresa in

particular. Is it for sale?"

Teresa Gomes shook her head. "I'm afraid, no. It was a gift to me. Do you collect photography, Kathryn?"

"I have some, but I wouldn't call myself a collector."

"Have you seen anything else you liked?" Teresa asked.

"I believe Elliot Rosewater was looking for something in amber. I haven't seen it though."

"Amber?" Teresa Gomes looked over at Miller Wynant, still surrounded by hipsters who hadn't come to buy, but to be seen. No way to sell art. "I don't believe Miller has done anything with amber, Kathryn. But I'll be glad to ask him for you."

"That would be great," Kathryn replied.

Teresa Gomes stepped back and politely separated herself from Kathryn Blaire and Paolo delle Bande Nere. Made a nice looking couple she thought.

Kathryn watched Teresa Gomes walk away and wondered what to do next. It was an opportunity, being left within arm's length of a handsome and wealthy man. And she looked good tonight, sexy clothes covering up inner doubts. But it wasn't as if she had managed this part of her life well lately. Lately being ever since she had turned seventeen and received that first tulip. There was a reason she was alone, and it wasn't because she wished to be. Maybe she could do better this time. She checked his hand, saw no ring, and was about to ask him something about himself, when he beat her to it.

Paolo delle Bande Nere smiled at her gently, and it surprised her. She hadn't been expecting gentle, there appeared something very substantial about him, perhaps the essence of wealth that touched upon him. But Kathryn didn't think so. He dropped his gaze and lifted a polite hand just a whisper toward the pendant that was dangling just below her breasts. "Do you mind?"

Kathryn hesitated. God only knew why she'd worn the pendant. Well…God and herself. She'd just wanted to look pretty and hip for the gallery of the moment. So she had to live with that decision. "No, not at all. Do you like it?"

Paolo delle Bande Nere cradled the pendant in his hand,

feeling its heft. Running his fingers over the image of the man hanging upside down by one leg. "It's fabulous. I love the tarot."

"Tarot?" Kathryn asked.

"The image. It's the Hanged Man. Didn't you know?"

"The Hanged Man? No. I just liked the way it looked," Kathryn said, with an innocently sweet shrug. "Do you know what it means?"

"Me?" Paolo pointed self-mockingly at his own chest. "No, I don't. But I know someone who might."

"So where do we find this someone?"

"She's nearby, if it's not too late."

Paolo delle Bande Nere checked his watch, a classic and elegant antique of the type that one saw listed in a Sotheby's catalog. Kathryn couldn't help noticing it, understated or not. It was only nine, not late at all for downtown New York in the summer.

"Shall we give it a try?" she suggested.

"What about your amber piece?"

Kathryn looked over to see Teresa Gomes in animated conversation with Miller Wynant.

"I think I'll come back in the morning. Shall we, Mister Paolo delle Bande Nere?"

Kathryn paused only to pat the blue doberman on his steel butt on the way out the door, Paolo delle Bande Nere on her arm.

25

They walked half a dozen blocks from Sintra, smiling and laughing softly about the blue dogs and little blue Gucci shoes, and talking about nothing that mattered, least of all themselves, because that is what Kathryn believed she wanted. Little blue Gucci shoes like a safe haven.

When they reached a curving cobblestoned sidestreet, Paolo delle Bande Nere drew to a stop in front of a new age shop that sold crystals and cards and amulets. The type of shop that Kathryn expected to find selling hash out of a back room, and not the type of place she would have expected a man of his wealth to frequent. But then, she really hadn't learned anything about Paolo delle Bande Nere, even whether his apparent wealth was real. He was still a beautiful blank cypher upon which she could project her own fairy tales.

In the classic fairy tales, the hero or heroine is restored from a place of severe indignity to his or her rightful place of honor by the end of the story: a frog is turned back into a prince, an orphan is revealed as the sole heir to a great fortune. That wasn't going to happen to Kathryn Blaire. She knew that. In all those tales, the hero was an innocent. Kathryn Blaire was a thief, a woman who had slept with too many men, a betrayer of trusts, and now a killer. One of Isaiah Hawkin's people. But it didn't mean, did it, that she couldn't dream for an evening?

Paolo took her kindly by the arm and led her into the shop. The owner of the shop was a young woman with extraordinarily fair skin that made her appear even younger. She was wearing a loose yellow sundress with big red flowers, and had blonde hair that draped past freckled shoulders. Her face was soft, with delicate, almost colorless lips and the bluest eyes Kathryn had ever seen. She looked nothing like a tarot card reader.

She greeted Paolo with a broad smile and an innocent air kiss on the cheek. Paolo made the introductions with an easy manner, then lifted the Hanged Man pendant from around Kathryn's neck and laid it on a counter in front of the blue-eyed woman. "What can you tell us about this, Cynthia?"

Cynthia pressed the pendant firmly against her palm, as if to leave an impression in her flesh of the young man hanging upside down from a tree by one leg. Then she thumbed through an almost new tarot deck until she came across the same image.

"They say the Hanged Man is based on Odin, the Norse God of war, wisdom, poetry, and magic. When he was old and dying, Odin struck himself with his spear and hung upside down from a tree to achieve a rebirth. He hung there for eight days, waiting for someone to rescue him. No one came. Just like real life, I suppose. No one ever rescues you. On the ninth night, as he was dying of hunger, Odin looked at his situation with new perspective and saw, just outside his reach, a set of small round stones with strange characters carved into them. Straining his ropes, forcing them ever tighter against his leg, he stretched down and seized one of the stones. At once, he was free and reborn with new youth."

Sure, that was it. Elliot Rosewater was fucking reborn. Kathryn smiled overly politely, and hoped Paolo didn't notice.

The blue-eyed woman smiled right back and replaced the pendant around Kathryn's neck. "May I ask why you chose that piece?"

"I didn't. It belonged to a…ah…a man I knew."

"I see." She fanned the tarot deck across the counter in front of Kathryn. "Pick a card for him, will you?"

Kathryn hesitated. This Cynthia looked so young. Elliot Rosewater was so dead. And she'd killed him. She looked at Paolo and shook her head. "I don't think so. It wouldn't be right. Besides, I don't even really know what tarot cards are for."

Cynthia explained as she put the deck away. "Some believe the tarot is a tool for unlocking your personal unconscious. That when you see an image, it brings to your consciousness things which you already knew to be true, but were not willing to admit to yourself. Others think the tarot are drawn from archetypal images, stored in the collective unconscious of men. Images which reappear in myths from all different cultures—serpents, the devil, death, and the like." She paused, and shrugged her shoulders. "There are, of course, others who believe something entirely more simple."

"And that would be?" Kathryn asked.

Paolo answered in his soft voice, "That the tarot are just fourteenth century Italian playing cards, around which a false mysticism has been built."

"What do you believe?" Kathryn asked, speaking to the woman.

"It doesn't matter what I believe."

"But what about the pendant?" Kathryn asked. "Why would someone put the image on a pendant?"

The blue-eyed woman shrugged. How could she know why? Because they liked the image. Or to make money perhaps.

•　　　•　　　•

After leaving the shop, Paolo delle Bande Nere asked Kathryn if she wished to go back to Sintra and check on Miller Wynant, and whether he had composed an amber piece. But Kathryn Blaire didn't wish the evening to end at the gallery of the little blue shoes, where they would run into temptation in the form of Teresa Gomes and the remaining art babes. She wished for magic.

So she lead Paolo away from Teresa Gomes' gallery of the moment, to a little Spanish restaurant that had been part of downtown New York since before prohibition.

"Tell me something about yourself, anything," she asked a little while after settling into a red leather booth. A glass of wine already half finished. "But, please, nothing I don't wish to hear."

"What don't you wish to hear?"

"What you believe in. What you don't believe in. The name of your last girlfriend. The name of your current girlfriend. That you are only in New York for one night, and that you live far away."

"Fair enough," he said. He was quiet for a long moment, as if determining the perfect piece of information to reveal. Then finally, "Here goes. I don't have a girlfriend or a wife."

"That's not something I wish to hear either," she said quickly.

"Why not?"

"It violates the rules. Nothing personal."

He shook his head slightly. "But you asked for something personal."

"Not exactly. I asked you to tell me something about yourself. They're not the same thing."

"I see," he said. "You'd like to know something of me that can have no possible bearing on this evening. Either way."

"Of course." Kathryn finished her wine and poured another glass and waited for him to answer. She wanted a cigarette, but that would have to wait until later, after the food came. Paella and chorizo sausage and shrimp in some unexplainably divine sauce verde. Then flan. They made a fabulous flan. "Well...?"

"I have a sister."

"Just one? No brothers?"

"Yes. Just one."

"Older or younger?"

"A year older."

"Do you love her?"

"Very much," Paolo replied.

"What's her name?"

"Bianca."

"It's a beautiful name."

"I'll tell her you said that. Now tell me something of yourself."

Kathryn hesitated. So much to choose from. About her beach in Brazil, the way the trees ran right down to the ocean. About the first time she'd heard a Billie Holiday album and was captured by the way Billie made each song her life, no matter what the song. About her favorite novel or poem or car, and why she loved them. But she chose something very different in the end.

"At my apartment, there's an old black and white picture post-card pinned to the frame of my bathroom mirror.

"The picture isn't famous. But it shows the same view that can be seen from my deck—a tree-lined park and flatiron building. My guests always assume the postcard came with the apartment.

Or that I saw the postcard one day after moving in and bought it. I let them think that. But it's not true. I bought that postcard when I was eight. I was growing up in a small town on a hundred and twenty-five acres of corn. I saw that postcard in a drugstore, bought it, and put it in my diary. Kept it there until the day I took it out and pinned it to my mirror."

Paolo leaned closer, to look at her closely. To see the light in her green eyes, and to ask a question that was most certainly personal. "Why did you tell me that?"

"Because I've never told anyone else. It was something I owned, that I could give you."

"Do you know you are beautiful, Kathryn?"

"No. But I like to hear it. I like it very much."

• • •

It was true that Kathryn Blaire belonged to Isaiah Hawkins. But not that evening.

She opened the door to her apartment with an old tarnished key and let Paolo delle Bande Nere in. She undressed him slowly in her mind, imagining his touch even as he stood still in the entryway. Then she led him to her bedroom, her eyes sparkling, hoping he would tell her that he loved her. The words, but not their truth, being all that mattered. The gold could turn to dust in the morning.

"Shhh," he said softly, as if he heard her thoughts, placing his hand on her forehead, and running it through her short hair.

"Tell me you love me," she whispered, barely aloud, lifting her hand to his chest, and placing her breast softly in his warm hand. He slipped the Hanged Man pendant from around her neck, undressed her with a delicate hand, and put his lips to hers. Touched her like she was the one woman he had dreamed of forever. Making her forget all the truths. Telling her he loved her.

And when she fell finally fell asleep, under the covers of her bed, her head on his chest, she knew nothing of him that she did not wish to know.

26

Ending up on a slab at the New York City forensics department was, to Ben Russo's mind, one rung shy of the very bottom of the pecking order for the dead. He always figured that up on the top rung was dying peacefully of old age in your sleep. After that came some of your other better deaths, like going in the line of duty. Then came your deaths in the hospital surrounded by your family, your deaths by tragic accident, and even, God forgive him, suicide. Somewhere after that came the type of endings that put you on a slab at forensics—getting stabbed, poisoned, garroted, shot, hacked, or otherwise savaged. In fact, the only worse death he could think of was dying homeless and being sent over to the medical school to be used as a teaching tool by twenty-year-olds.

He hated going to the lab. Most cops did. But he hated it even more than that. He just never did get used to seeing the bodies lying there, with pieces removed and hung on scales or stuck in jars. What's more, the lab never quite waited for you to come to it, and this day was no different.

He was not quite halfway down the corridor leading to the lab, still one hundred feet away, when he came to a middle-aged woman laid flat on a gurney, a quarter-sized hollow above her right eyebrow. Next up was a bearded man with a half moon cut into his throat. The man was maybe thirty, looked like he'd lived a hard life and had died in the same fashion. Ben crossed himself and turned away, just as a man in a medical smock emerged from the twin doors at the end of the hall.

"Detective Russo! You look great. It's been a long time."

"Not long enough, Richard."

"Detective, I'm insulted. What? I should give up my life's work?" Dr. Richard Klein said with a laugh, clapping Ben on the back with his arm. He spoke quickly, and with a thrill in his voice—like Quincy on uppers. "Let me show you what we got. I think you're going to get a kick out of this."

Dr. Klein walked him toward the back of the lab, making a

point of walking near an autopsy table where a couple of his colleagues were working on a new arrival. Another doctor raised an electric power tool to Dr. Klein to say hello. Then hit the power switch. A blade whirred, Ben blanched and turned away. If Dante came back and needed another level for his hell, he needed to look no further.

They stopped at a body that was mercifully covered by a sheet. Rare decency for the lab.

"Here we are, Ben."

Russo imagined Elliot Rosewater's body and quickly grabbed the doctor's arm before he could lift the sheet. "Why don't you just tell me what you found?"

"What would be the point, Ben. I could've done that over the phone."

"I wish you had."

"Come on, Ben. It's not like you haven't been here before. This one isn't even too bad. Remember the Carter Benford case, now that was a gruesome murder. Even I almost lost my lunch over that one. I didn't though, and I'm still proud of that. I've been here eighteen years and I've only tossed my cookies once. And that was because of something I ate, I'm sure of it. It was some bad tuna fish, I can still remember the smell."

Ben Russo's body, every ounce of it, slumped in resignation and he let go of the doctor's arm.

As Klein pulled back the sheet, Ben prepped for the worst: a naked body, chest cut wide open, no organs inside, the head sawed in two…

But when he opened his eyes Ben saw, to his relief, a fairly typical (if dead) naked man lying on his back. All things considered, Elliot Rosewater didn't make a bad corpse. His jaw was bruised, but the rest of his face looked more or less alright. And Dr. Klein, or his staff, had already stuffed the internal organs back inside and sewn up Rosewater's chest, leaving just a long scar shaped like a Y running from Rosewater's shoulders to his sternum, and going down in a straight line from there.

"What am I supposed to be looking at?" Russo asked. "I thought he died of internal bleeding."

"Yes, that's what we thought at first." Klein pointed to a bruise below Rosewater's ribs. "He was hit in the abdomen, right here. We figured that ruptured his spleen. But when we got in, we didn't find that type of damage. Some bruising, but not the kind of internal bleeding it would take to turn out the lights."

"You're sure?"

"Positive. We checked everything on this one super carefully. This guy, Rosewater, he packs some serious juice, even in his current state. Commissioner O'Malley himself called."

"Lovely," Ben muttered, with a smile because he figured he understood the game now. "That's why you want to show me everything. I had to come down here so you could cover your ass. Well, great. I've seen it. Can I go now?"

"Sorry, Ben. You know me. If that was so, I would tell you. I know you hate coming down here. Me, I love it. But it's not for everyone. I know that. But you really gotta see this."

Ben looked the body over again, not seeing anything else that could've killed the man. Involuntarily, he started counting the stitches that formed the Y. He got to twenty-nine before he got control of himself. "What am I supposed to be looking at, Richard, the bruise on his jaw? Saw that when I first saw the body. Didn't suppose it would've killed him."

"Naw," Dr. Klein, said waving his hand dismissively. "You had it right. That's just a broken mandible. He would've been eating all his meals with a straw for a couple of weeks, that's all. The good stuff is down here." He pointed to Rosewater's crotch, which had been completely shaved.

Ben looked, then stopped himself and rubbed a hand over his eyes. He figured this might just be a new all-time low, staring at a dead man's business.

"If you remember, our preliminary exam noted bruised testicles." Klein reached out with his right thumb and forefinger and pinched some skin at the bottom of Elliot Rosewater's scrotum, matter-of-factly pulling the skin up between Rosewater's balls and towards his belly, so that the underside of the scrotum was showing, revealing purple amoeba shaped blotches. "You can see that both testicles appear bruised. I didn't pay too much attention to it at first. I mean it might've hurt like hell. But a kick in the balls doesn't rate much...virtually never the cause of death." Klein lifted up Rosewater's small, limp penis. "Not much of a schlong is it?"

"Please, the man is dead."

"Dead, alive, it makes no difference. The man, he had no schlong. That's all I'm saying."

Russo rubbed his eyes, again. A new low. "Richard, do you think you can just tell me what killed him? Would that be too much to ask?"

"That's what I'm trying to do, Ben. Usual autopsy procedure is not to cut on the testicles. Don't really know why. We cut on everything else. Got the man's brain in a jar. Whatever. Since we couldn't find any internal bleeding and he had the bruises, I figured I better take a closer look. I was about to go to work when I finally noticed it."

Klein was now holding Rosewater's penis by its head and he pulled on it, stretching the penis far as it would go. The doctor pointed to a spot at the very base of the penis. "Here, do you see this? Come on, detective. Don't be a sissy. Lean closer."

Russo held his breath, leaned in, and saw a small round needle puncture, right over the big vein that runs the length of the topside of the penis. He blanched, again. He'd seen this kind of stuff before: on heroin addicts who'd shoot up wherever there was a good vein left—between their toes, in their tongue, wherever. Like leeches, going to any area with good blood flow. But this...this made no sense.

Russo shook his head, bewildered and them some. "What are you telling me, that Rosewater overdosed? What did he do, beat himself up, then shoot smack into his dick until he died? Come on."

"Slow down, Ben. After I found the puncture, we ran a complete toxicology. You understand, ordinarily we wouldn't run a full tox in a beating case. I got the report back right before I called your office and asked you to come down."

"What does it show?"

Klein picked a medical chart up from a nearby table. Even

though he already knew the answer he read the chart for confirmation, the way doctors do. "Curare. It's a muscle relaxant. In high enough doses it relaxes your muscles so much you can't breath. Then you die. That's what happened to Elliot Rosewater."

"So he didn't die from the beating?"

"The beating was just for show. It was the curare that killed him."

"You're sure?"

"Like I said, we checked everything on this one super carefully. The curare killed him. No doubt about it. It's actually kind of elegant, in its own way. Nice and neat. One press of the thumb and it was over. No noise, no blood. And it made his death look almost like an accident. Looked on the first pass like someone tried to rough him up, and killed him by mistake."

Ben nodded his head, like that made sense. But there was still plenty that didn't. He pointed at Rosewater's penis. "Why there?"

"Nice big vein, easy to hit. Plus, it's hard to see a puncture wound when the penis is flaccid and the flesh is all folded up. If there had been a needle puncture in his arm, I would've noticed it on my initial pass. As it is, we got lucky."

"Lucky?" Russo, responded. Oh yeah, he'd gotten real lucky. He and Rosewater both. Russo backed a step away from the body. It wasn't nearly far enough to make him happy.

"One more thing," Russo said. "That girl who fell thirty-nine floors the other night…"

"Sarah Ridell. I remember her. Wasn't much left."

"You do a toxicology on her?"

"No. She fell thirty-nine floors. We pretty much knew how she died without spending time on lab tests."

"Well, you might think about doing one."

"Why? Did those two know each other? Don't tell me they were doing the old one-two."

"Something like that," Ben said, and he walked out as fast as he could, breaking for daylight. The more he learned about Elliot Rosewater and Sarah Ridell, the less he liked.

PART THREE

They change the sky, but not their
souls those who cross the ocean.
—*Horace*

27

Isaiah Hawkins had briefed his first president, Lyndon Johnson, in the spring of 1965 during the Dominican crisis. After spending the prior six years of his life running Africa ops from the back room of a parish church in Nairobi with the active support of Father Juma, Isaiah figured he knew some things about third-world behavior.

"There are your items, Jimmy. That's right, the ones I promised you. Right there."

The crate of surplus Russian ammunition next to the hand-me-down Bibles from the States. Manufacture yourself a nice incident, General Jimmy. Blame it on the communist guerillas. Please leave Father Juma a donation on the way out. The Father thanks you. And have yourself a nice publicity day.

After all, General Jimmy had been one of the good guys in Kenya. The good guys in Africa discernable from the bad guys by luck, or intuition, or the simple act of closing one's eyes and choosing sides. The British and the French and the Dutch having cut and run after the war, leaving the continent to the likes of General Jimmy.

That was decolonialized Africa. A complete free-for-all, and a paradise on earth for a man with the talents and inclinations of Isaiah Hawkins.

After that, nothing Washington had ever thrown at him could compare. But Lyndon Johnson had tried to intimidate him just the same. The Dominican situation wasn't even really much of a crisis, more of an intramural-spat-with-guns between elites in the Dominican military and political establishments. Isaiah had told Johnson to handle it as such, which didn't stop Lyndon Johnson from sending in the marines.

That was Lyndon Johnson—a man who had volunteered for active duty in WWII while serving in Congress, and had won a Silver Star. This current president, Isaiah's immediate concern, was smart and tough. But he wasn't that kind of tough, nor that kind of smart.

Sitting now at his desk, Isaiah checked his watch, lifted the telephone and asked Anne to put the scheduled call through. A few minutes later, the president, Isaiah Hawkin's eighth, came on the line for his weekly briefing.

As usual, Isaiah mostly let the president speak, saying only as much as was strictly necessary, even though this was supposed to be the president's briefing and not the other way around.

Near the end, the president said, "Everything is coming down to the wire in Moscow, Isaiah, you know that. It's not looking too good. Vice President Lysenko is still behind in the polls, seven to nine points depending on which poll, according to my people."

"Yes, I'm aware of that, Mister President."

"Well, we want that guy to win. He's been VP over there for six years. Our diplomats know him. He's not supposed to be a half-bad guy. Believes in democracy. We don't want to see General Mikhailov and the communists win. The State Department tells me the general is supposed to be a tough guy."

"I believe he is, Mister President," Isaiah replied simply. There was no doubt that General Sergei Mikhailov was tough—he had survived a command in Afghanistan, protected his men, and fought to win in Chechnya. Some of that was even admirable, and it wasn't the general's toughness that presented the challenge. Plenty of men were tough, and there was nothing wrong with a leader who would vigorously promote Russia's self-interest. It was the general's embrace of a romantic Russian nationalism that was troubling to Isaiah Hawkins. Economic hard times coupled with the loss of national self-esteem had been a bad combination for as long as history, leading, almost inexorably, to authoritarian movements. And, authoritarian governments ruined the lives of their own people and anyone else who got in their path. Just the way it was. That's why it was so important to give Russia time to rebuild its economy and its pride. That's why it mattered that Vice President Lysenko win. Not because the general was a tough guy.

"Well, what are we going to do about the situation, Isaiah?" the president asked.

"There is something in the works, Mister President. It is a matter of timing. These things always are."

"I understand that, Isaiah," the president said quickly, running his words together in a rush. "You're always telling me that. Just hope your timing is right—we could use a little magic to pull out of the proverbial hat here."

"We do what we can, Mister President."

"Keep me informed."

"Of course, Mister President."

As Isaiah replaced the phone receiver, a small round red crystal illuminated on his telephone console. It was a rule of thumb in his business that only the paranoid survived, to reclaim a phrase that modern business had misappropriated for the trivialities of companies. As part of that philosophy, Isaiah's phone line was swept at thirty second intervals, twenty-four hours a day, the red crystal indicating that the line was clear.

He checked his watch again, 7:30 A.M., then lit a cigarette. Of his people, only Anand Ashland would be working this early, Kathryn Blaire not being the sort to get much accomplished at this hour. Not that it mattered, so long as everything came together in the end. With that in mind, he began to thumb through the set of reports that had filtered into his orbit during the night: an assessment of the ever-deteriorating situation in Mozambique; a white paper on crisis management by the new deputy director of the NSA; a field confirmation that a senior senator was, in fact, sleeping with a male member of Russian intelligence; and, the one that caught his eye, his own personal copy of the police autopsy report on Elliot Rosewater.

That cop, Russo, he'd be working already too.

28

A new, brilliant translation of Dante's *Inferno* rested on the end table next to Ben Russo's bed, along with a treatise on the symbolism of the Italian Renaissance. He tried to make a habit of studying each morning before starting his work day.

It was a fantasy—that the escapist life of a scholar was still open to a middle-aged cop, that he might find meaning in Dante that all the others had overlooked—but it was his fantasy and he believed it deserved a full, fair opportunity to thrive. After all, what was the *Inferno* but a meditation on crime? The *Inferno*—a world where Dante, as pilgrim and judge, had considered the worst man had to offer and decreed that sins of betrayal were the lowest of all, worse than murder, even. A view that was difficult for a policeman to share. And there, perhaps, Ben believed, lay the gap in which he could find meaning.

An hour later, after putting Dante away, Ben was standing on the Upper East Side, looking up and across the street at the window from which Sarah Ridell had been thrown. Boarded up with wood and tape, the window looked like a scar against the mirrored skin of the steel and glass building, a scar which Ben could only see in outline from the ground, but which would be clearly visible from the upper floors of the white brick building at his back.

He turned around and pushed through a tired glass door. He wanted the building manager's blessing to interview the tenants on the thirty-fifth through fortieth floors, in the chance that one of them had seen the fall and, perhaps, the push. Not that he needed permission to ask questions, but two decades on the force had taught him that good manners worked the best magic.

The building manager, a stout crewcut ancient from the Balkans, proved the point again. An apartment had been sublet on the day of Sarah Ridell's murder. Number 39G. Rented with cash, enough to convince the regular tenants to take up temporary residence somewhere else for a month. Yes, he remembered what the renter looked like: a small woman with short dark hair. She hadn't given a name.

That would be the woman, Ben figured. The one who'd killed Elliot Rosewater. The skinny one who liked reggae and curare.

It didn't require too much further prompting from Ben (just a gentle nudge) for the manager to add that, yes, detective, he suspected there might be a water leak in the apartment and, yes, he had been planning on checking it. Would the detective mind going up with him to take a look?

Not at all, Ben said, patting his pocket to make sure he had appropriate fingerprint paraphernalia with him.

It was fifty minutes later when Ben called the station house and asked for Detective Stacy Sparks. "Any luck with the prints in Rosewater's office?"

"Like you thought, sir. Too much. The print team pulled more than twenty different sets. We've already sorted out those belonging to the deceased. The rest we're running through the computer now."

"Um-hum," Ben murmured without much enthusiasm. None of those prints would amount to anything. Reggae girl would've been wearing gloves in Rosewater's office. "Stacy, how about...how about something our girl could have touched before she got to Rosewater's office. Or after she left?"

"I doubt there's much, sir. Maybe the elevator."

"That's not worth checking," Russo said quickly.

"There's the conference room where she dropped off the food for that associate. I'll get that checked, sir, but I think it's already too late for that. My understanding is that the cleaning people wipe down all the conference room tables first thing every morning." Sparks paused, reviewing everything they knew Rosewater's killer had done at Osborne, Crane. "I guess the only thing that leaves is the receipt."

"The what?" Russo asked.

"The receipt for the Chinese food, sir. I've been reading the notes of your interviews, like you suggested. That associate, Visser, he said he paid for the food and got a receipt. Maybe she didn't put her gloves on until after she was done with Visser. Would've looked pretty out-of-place, a delivery person wearing gloves in the middle of the summer."

Ben smiled and tapped his left forefinger five times against his temple, tapping out the letters like he was typing M-O-R-O-N. Should've thought of the receipt himself—what with the way Visser had gone on. Too busy with Dante, not busy enough with his job. At least Sparks was thinking.

"Excellent. Get to work on that right straight away, Stacy. The receipt is probably with the accounting department. And, there's another thing. I just pulled a couple of sets of prints that might be interesting. I'm going to drop them off with you, and I want them cross-checked against any prints on the receipt."

"What's up, sir?"

"Just a hunch. I'll explain at the station," Ben replied, although he had no intention of doing much explaining at all. He'd found two sets of good looking prints: one from an ashtray, which appeared to be a woman's, and another from the glass door of a microwave, definitely a man's. Ben didn't think he was looking for a man, but you never knew. Leaving him with two sets of prints and no warrant. Therefore, not much explaining. "Detective, that's good work you're doing."

"Thank you, sir."

"It's Ben."

"Right, sir."

29

Kathryn Blaire woke when the pale sunlight that had been streaming through a window for several hours finally breached her consciousness. Her head was turned toward the light, she felt sluggish, like she was hungover, and it took her a moment to remember where she was.

She was home, in New York, in her own bed, but there was something more. Something out of place. Someone out of place. Maybe her. She reached back with her arm and felt only wrinkled sheets and the bell tolling on her illusion.

She sat up and propped herself against a pillow, naked and suddenly self-conscious of it, the sun shining down now on her small breasts, exposing her. She pulled the sheets high and hugged them to her body, trying to hide and hold onto herself. She barely breathed and tried just to listen. But there was no sound of running water. No music playing on the stereo, or coffee being made on the stove, or newspaper rustling. No matter how hard she wished to hear, there were no sounds at all. At the foot of the bed, and draped across the floor, she saw one set of clothes, all black. Black cotton panties resting on black boots.

The black turning cloudy as she started to cry, the tears drifting into worries, the same ones that she had tried to escape: of chances that would never come again, of bad choices made, of being alone, and most of all, of the gap between who she wished to be and who she had chosen to become.

After a while, the tears slowed and she pulled on a robe and walked through the loft. She remembered Paolo delle Bande Nere waking up early and sitting by the side of the bed, the sun reflecting off something in his hand. She had opened her eyes and had seen him staring at her and she hadn't felt naked at all. Then he kissed her on the forehead and told her to go back to sleep. Kissing sleeping beauty good-bye. But not leaving so much as a note on the kitchen table. Telling her nothing of himself that she did not wish to hear. Following her own rules.

She made herself tea, peppermint, found an album she loved by the Brazilian diva Virgínia Rodrigues and put it on the stereo, and told herself that it had been worth it. Cognitive dissonance, the shrinks at the Agency would have called it— convincing yourself after the fact that you'd done the right thing. But it wasn't that at all. She had known it all before- hand. Paolo delle Bande Nere had been everything she wished for last night, and every night—gentle, sweet, strong, and all hers. That was all she could really ask for. Anything more than that was neither promised nor guaranteed. Tomorrow wasn't promised to her, nor to anyone really.

With a smile, she went back to the bedroom, straightened her bed, and picked up her clothes from the floor, folding them and placing them in a neat pile on top of her comforter. Then she hopped in the shower.

While brushing her teeth, she stole a glance in the mirror above the sink, her eyes fastening onto the black and white postcard of the park and flatiron building she had described to Paolo the night before. She had wanted to tell him something that he would see and remember, and also to let him know he would be coming home with her that night. She wondered if he understood, and supposed he did. But why had he told her about his sister, Bianca? Perhaps just because he hadn't played that game before, but she didn't think so.

With a towel wrapped around her waist, she returned to her bedroom and thought about starting her day. She hadn't really learned much of value about the pendant the night before, not unless the great god Odin was going to help her find the Amber Room, and she hadn't accomplished much at the gallery either.

She had to go back to Sintra to follow up that lead and see why Elliot Rosewater was interested in a show at a downtown art gallery. She would do that first thing, and was deciding what to wear to meet with Teresa Gomes—something sexy and smart—when she felt the first shiver that something seri- ous might be wrong. Her clothing from the night before was sitting neatly folded on the bed, where she'd placed it earlier. But she didn't see the Hanged Man pendant, or remember where she had put it. She remembered that Paolo had lifted it off her neck before undressing her. Before kissing her. Where had he put it?

She looked around the room, on her dresser, her chairs, and on the floor, and didn't find it. She ran her hands through the pile of clothing, slowly at first, then in an increasing rush, until finally she picked each item up and shook it out, hoping with increasing desperation that something would fall loose. But nothing did.

In her mind, she saw Paolo sitting by the side of the bed in the morning, looking at her. In his hand, reflecting the morning sun, was the pendant. He'd taken it. Stolen it.

She cursed under her breath and truly hoped Paolo delle Bande Nere had only wanted a sentimental memory of the night. She didn't even want to consider the alternative—that the evening, for Paolo delle Bande Nere, had always been about the pendant.

•　　　•　　　•

Kathryn arrived at Sintra an hour later. It was before noon, an unfashionably early time. The gallery doors were still shut to the public, but were open to her, now that she was known there as a friend of both Elliot Rosewater and Paolo delle Bande Nere.

Teresa Gomes greeted her with a warm smile and a question that preempted any immediate discussion of Miller Wynant and amber. "Kathryn! So nice to see you again. Did you and Paolo have a good time last night?"

"Splendid."

"I'm so glad. I just adore Paolo."

"Yes, he's wonderful," Kathryn replied, wonderful not exactly the word she would have chosen if she had been speaking to a girlfriend.

Kathryn looked at Teresa Gomes closely now, in a new manner. Teresa was dressed in blue jeans and a light pink T-shirt, no bra. Her nipples showing nicely in the cool air-conditioned gallery. She was beautiful, ever-so-hip, younger than Kathryn by a good five years, if not more, and her nude picture, with her fabulous legs, was still hanging on the wall of her gallery. Kathryn couldn't help wondering if Teresa Gomes had slept with Paolo. Couldn't help wondering what Teresa Gomes was like in bed, whether Teresa Gomes needed to be told she was loved, or whether she just lost herself completely in the moment. Those last questions not likely to get answered.

"So how long have you known Paolo?" Kathryn asked, innocently enough.

"Oh, I just met him this week."

"Really?" Kathryn was surprised and didn't mind letting it show. "I thought you said he was an old friend?"

"A dear friend, but a new one. I was introduced to him this week by another gallery dealer. He's been in New York buying art. I haven't been quite sure what he has been looking for. But maybe he found it last night." Teresa flashed a just-between-two-city-girls grin. "He told me you had a great time."

"We had what?" Kathryn paused, caught herself.

"Oh please, Kathryn," Teresa said with a light laugh, reading Kathryn with charming ease. "He didn't tell me anything really interesting. Not his style, I wouldn't think."

"What did he say?"

"That you were lovely and that he enjoyed your company."

"Well...good," Kathryn stammered, still a bit off her guard. At least he said she was lovely. But what was art girl here doing with a report on her evening? Especially seeing as Teresa Gomes had just met Paolo herself. Kathryn's life didn't work like that.

"When did you speak to Paolo, anyway?" Kathryn asked. "Did he call you this morning?"

"No, he didn't call. He came in. Several hours ago. Said he figured I would be here early the night after a big opening. He was right. I probably shouldn't be telling you this, but he wanted to discuss the amber piece that you were asking me about last night. I think he wished to get it for you as a present. I thought it was fabulous of him. You must have really had quite the time last night. I can only imagine. He's so handsome."

There was a long pause while Kathryn tried to remember to breathe. First the Hanged Man pendant. Then going back to Sintra for the amber piece. Lovely. Paolo delle Bande Nere was following the same paths as she, just taking it from a different angle. She didn't know enough about him to understand his interest in the Amber Room, at least not yet. But she knew it was no coincidence at all that they had both stumbled into Teresa Gomes. And from there, the game just played out as they took it.

Kathryn thought about asking Teresa Gomes whether Paolo had the pendant with him that morning at the gallery. But she couldn't. The words wouldn't come. It would be just too embarrassing, and she didn't need that right now. She needed to believe, did believe, that at least some part of the last night had been true.

"Are you OK?" Teresa asked.

"Sure. I'm fine." Kathryn hesitated. Her throat so dry all of sudden. "Is there someplace we could sit?"

Teresa led her to a private room at the back of the gallery. An assistant already had made morning cappuccino and poured some into a cobalt blue mug for Kathryn. Surrounded on all sides by works that Teresa Gomes kept for her best clients, they sat at an exquisite blonde wood coffee table. The table the signature piece of a famous '50s designer, although Kathryn didn't care to remember which one.

"So, can you tell me more about the amber piece?" Kathryn finally asked. "And I don't mean by Miller Wynant, or whatever his name was last night."

"No of course you don't. How much do you know about the piece, Kathryn?"

"Not much really. I just know it was something Elliot Rosewater was interested in."

Teresa sipped her cappuccino. "Well, it's rather interesting. A gorgeous mirror, about eight inches square, surrounded by an amber mosaic frame. It's the type of piece that would be interesting on its own. But I'm told it's part of the Amber Room. And that makes it much more interesting."

"How much more interesting?" Kathryn asked, knowing Teresa Gomes was talking about money here.

"I'm not sure."

"But aren't you offering it for sale?"

"Me?" Teresa pointed at herself, almost the same gesture Paolo had made the night before. "No, I don't have it. It was offered on consignment to this Gallery. There were issues over its provenance. The owner was not very forthcoming on how he obtained the piece. So I passed. Which is the same thing I told Paolo this morning."

"Interesting," Kathryn mused aloud. "Do you know where I can find the owner?"

"Certainly. But I hardly think that's necessary, Kathryn. As I said, I believe Paolo is interested in acquiring it for you."

Kathryn leaned forward in her chair, to draw Teresa further in. "Just between us, let's just say, perhaps I'm not looking for a gift right now."

"I suppose that's your call," Teresa Gomes said politely. "The owner's name is Shokovitch. A Russian émigré, must be at least eighty years old. I don't know where to find him, he had contacted me."

"Shokovitch?" Kathryn asked, vaguely remembering the name Shokovitch from somewhere, but unable to place it, a feeling that had been happening to her with some frequency lately.

"Yes, almost like the composer. But not quite." And, without pausing, Teresa Gomes stood and began pitching Kathryn on a lovely painting that had just arrived at the gallery by a brilliant new artist.

30

Anand Ashland spent his morning at the New York Public Library in the same Main Reading Room where, unknown to him, Sarah Ridell had researched the Amber Room.

He slowly turned through the glossy pages of a four volume set of oversized books. Each glossy page divided into four quadrants. Each quadrant occupied by a small color picture of a shield. Each shield similar, but slightly different, with various geometric markings and bright images of wild animals drawn upon them. An array of stripes, diamonds, circles, lions, tigers, and panthers crisscrossing the glossy pages.

Anand gave no attention to the stripes, nor to the diamonds, nor to the creatures, saving his particular scrutiny solely for those shields dominated by circles. Circles or spheres, depending on the limited perception of depth offered by the images. Either way, he was seeking circles, six circles set against an oval or triangular background; a crude drawing of which had been rendered in Elliot Rosewater's desk calendar and seen by Kathryn Blaire. The calendar and drawing Anand had subsequently recovered from the inadequately cleansed hard disk drive of Rosewater's computer.

Now, it was a matter of matching that image to a family name. Which would have appeared a daunting task. However, and quite fortunately, somewhere in Britain there was a man named H.L. Bruce, a member of the fading nobility with too much time on his hands who had made the study of coats-of-arms a life's work. These glossy books were the fortuitous result.

Anand started with the coats-of-arms for England. Lots of lions and crosses. Not much on circles, the English. Then the rest of the Empire: Scotland, Ireland, Wales. An hour and a half later, he'd given up on the British and turned to the French, his eyes soon blazing with pictures of dancing horses, golden lions, silver crowns, and multicolored diamonds. The illusory grandeur of the French on display on every page.

Tragic, really. Other than impressionism, what had the French given to the twentieth century? They were not much for circles on shields, either. And he moved on to Italy.

It was there, in the genealogical records of a nation whose finest days had arguably come and gone five hundred years before, that he finally found success. Of sorts. A golden shield with six round red balls. A perfect match. Another man's heart might have leapt, but Anand didn't generally go for that kind of drama, and he simply examined the picture more closely. Underneath the shield, printed in capital block letters, was the name MEDICI.

The legendary Medici. The family that had ruled the golden age of Florence. The family that had stoked the fire under the Renaissance, commissioning one masterpiece after another, from the likes of Michelangelo, Donatello, and Brunelleschi. All paid for by the fat profits of the Medici bank, a global institution with branches spread throughout Europe. That much Anand knew without needing to do any further research.

If any family might have sought to obtain the Amber Room after the war and add it to their collections, it would have been the Medici. But then it couldn't have been the Medici; not if the historical note entered in a fine type beneath the picture of the Medici crest was correct.

In 1434, Cosimo de' Medici, became the first Medici to lead the Italian city-state of Florence. The last Medici to rule Florence was Gian Gastone Medici, a senile drunkard, who died in 1737. His sister, Anna Maria, was the last surviving Medici. Upon her death in 1743, she donated all of the family's art treasures to the city of Florence.

All the Medici were dead. Elliot Rosewater wasn't taking any meetings with the Medici to discuss the Amber Room or anything else. Which meant that whatever Elliot Rosewater was doing, he was apparently just doodling while doing it.

31

After leaving Sintra, Kathryn walked uptown to Isaiah Hawkins's office, using the time and anonymity of the city streets to collect her thoughts. Once at his office, she started explaining.

It was less a conversation than an audience actually, and not much of a pleasant one at that. Things had not exactly been going to plan. First Sarah Ridell dying on her watch. Then Elliot Rosewater. Then losing the Hanged Man pendant to a man she'd just met (and slept with, couldn't very well leave that part out). By the way, the symbol on Elliot Rosewater's calendar hadn't panned out either. At least she had a lead on an amber piece—a mirror, said to be from the Amber Room—that Elliot Rosewater was also interested in. But then, the man she had slept with, who gave his name as Paolo delle Bande Nere, was onto that lead as well.

She paused there and waited for a response. While waiting, she looked past Isaiah to the plainly painted wall behind his desk, to the Edward Hopper print that hung there—of tired people drinking coffee in a late night diner, each one very much alone, even those seated together.

The Hopper had been there as long as she'd known Isaiah; and who knows how long before that. Besides his beloved map, it was the only decoration in his office: no photographs, no letters of commendation, no mementos from his years in Africa, no religious hints, not even a picture of his wife. There were no clues into who he was or what he believed, except for the Hopper. And she'd never understood what it was supposed to mean—perhaps something about being alone in the world, but that was too obvious. A longing for small town life? Hardly. She turned her attention away. She just didn't get it, and she figured she never would.

Isaiah picked up a nearby cigarette box, flicked its bottom with his thumb and offered her one of the exposed cigarettes. She didn't crave the nicotine just then, but she accepted, as always, because there were some rituals one just couldn't break.

"The good news. I don't care about Elliot Rosewater, Kathryn," he said. "Never have. Don't care if you did kill him. But you might be pleased to know you didn't."

"What?"

"You knocked Rosewater around good. You know that. But not good enough to kill him. Someone else did that favor for us. We have company on this one now."

"I know we have company. I've been telling you that. But I don't understand. How do you know I didn't kill Rosewater?" she asked, anxiously.

Isaiah handed her Dr. Klein's full autopsy report.

It made about the best reading of her life. Not that it was a particularly nice way to go—a shot of poison straight in the dick, after getting your balls racked and being knocked unconscious to start the night. It definitely made a most touching story for someone to explain to Mrs. Rosewater and the kids, and that didn't even include the part about him screwing Sarah Ridell. But to hell with it. Elliot Rosewater was dead, they had company now, and personally, she was pretty pleased—because at least she actually had not killed anyone. That was a win, and you always took your wins as they found you.

Isaiah broke the short silence. "Now tell me again about this Paolo fellow."

"Paolo delle Bande Nere. That was name I was told. Met him at the Sintra Gallery, introduced as a friend of the owner. He took me to a woman who explained the Hanged Man tarot. The explanation made no sense whatsoever. We went home," she paused but didn't flinch. "We slept together. I woke up, he was gone and so was the pendant. I went back to Sintra and the owner, Teresa Gomes, told me that Paolo had been there, asking about the amber piece. It's a mirror, some old Russian guy has it. His name is familiar. Shok...Shokov...like the composer, almost."

"Shokovitch," Isaiah said real slowly, as if he was relishing or perhaps reliving the name. "Mikhail Shokovitch. You might

remember it from Professor Greene's memo."

It came back to her now. Not perfectly, but she remembered the gist of Greene's very specific words:

> In the course of my joint investigations with Isaiah Hawkins, a final theory has emerged. In the early-1980s, a Russian defector by the name of Mikhail Shokovitch informed the Agency that the Amber Room had in fact been recovered by the Russians from Königsberg. Shokovitch asserts that the Room was secretly transported back to Moscow to be installed in Stalin's personal residence. However, rather than being so used, the Room remained in storage until being sold by Stalin to a private collector in the early 1950s along with some other items, also of apparently great value. We have been unable to confirm any of the details offered by Shokovitch.

"I personally interrogated Shokovitch in the eighties. I got tired of the son of a bitch," Isaiah said. "I want you to handle it this time. Take the professor with you. Find out what that old man knows."

He turned away from her and toward the crisp new map with the red and green and yellow pins. Her eyes followed. The green pins Isaiah's, the red pins belonging to the other side. It wasn't always so clear now, she supposed, who was the other side. But maybe it had never been that clear—except to Isaiah. He just knew how to work the board.

Her eyes settled on an expanse of open land to the west of Russia proper. She, and others, had worked on a project there when that land, Kazakhstan, had still been very much a part of the Soviet Union. But Isaiah had seen Kazakh independence coming for a decade—before the fall of the Soviet Union was fashionably inevitable—and he'd used that time to build the temple foundation. He'd laid the stones one by one, to put a man and a party in place for when the time was right. He'd worked so much in the background that no one had ever seen his hand. And he'd planned so precisely that he had been sure to succeed. Kazakhstan and its oil riches still had a red pin last time she'd been in Isaiah's office. Before her fall. It was a green pin, now, the prime minister of Kazakhstan a man with a personal debt to Isaiah Hawkins.

She was about to reach out and touch that green pin, feeling a somewhat proprietary interest in its presence, when Isaiah pointedly ground out his cigarette, stubbing it down until Kathryn looked back at him.

"There's one more thing," he said slowly.

"There always is, isn't there, Isaiah?"

"Just be careful. Like I said, we've got company on this one now."

"I know. Whoever killed Rosewater," Kathryn said, relieved again just to say the words that someone else had been the killer.

"That's right, whoever killed Rosewater. Plus maybe whoever has the Amber Room, if that's not the same person who killed Rosewater. Plus this cop Russo. Plus maybe this fellow Paolo delle Bande Nere. Plus whoever else knows what's going on and wants the Room. And now with Shokovitch involved you can't count the Russians out either. So be careful, Kathryn."

"Or stay aggressive, I suppose," she replied, saying the very words Isaiah Hawkins had brought her back to hear.

32

In a beautiful city across the ocean, a young servant girl walked onto a sunny patio in a carefully practiced manner: demurely enough not to disturb her mistress, sternly enough not to catch her unawares. Her footsteps barely rising above the soft sounds of a wide river flowing nearby. The girl was dressed in pure black, which matched her hair, and that of her mistress. She was perhaps sixteen, soon to come into her own, and already visibly possessed of perfect touch and grace.

Her mistress turned around to receive her, revealing eyes that, like her hair, were jet black. Like cosmic black holes. But she showed the girl a gentle smile. "What is it, Marina?"

"Paolo is on the phone, signora Bianca. From New York."

Bianca answered the phone at the large wooden desk in her library, a magnificently well-appointed room filled floor to ceiling with books and letters. Many of the books and letters hundreds of years old.

"Is it ended? Has the circle been closed, Paolo?" Bianca asked.

"Not yet, and not completely." Paolo's voice softer than Bianca's, yet a certain resemblance in their tones unmistakable. "Elliot Rosewater was really most indiscreet. His carelessness and his girlfriend's greed were remarkable. The rumors Sarah Ridell spread, they are like feathers from a pillow that has been slashed open and shaken into a wind. In the right rooms, you can still almost feel the whispers of the Amber Room she let loose. I don't know that we'll ever be able to fully control that."

"And the mirror?" Bianca asked, the mirror having started all of this.

"It's still the hunted. But I'm nearly close enough now to seize it."

"And it's still worth the risk?"

"I believe so."

"As do I," Bianca said with decisiveness and determination,

family traits of the delle Bande Nere that matched well the family desire for vast rewards and for taking the chances that brought them. "What of the pendant, Paolo?"

"I have it. The woman I met, Kathryn was her name. She had it." There was the smallest hesitation in Paolo's voice. It could have been the long distance transmission. But it wasn't and it was noticeable to his sister. "I took it from her—the pendant. While she was sleeping."

"Go on."

"That's all."

"Perhaps," Bianca said. "But I hear something else in your voice. What is it?"

"It was odd."

"What was?"

"The way she looked at me. She opened her eyes as I was leaving. She looked strangely innocent, lying there. Although one really couldn't call her that. Maybe she was not so much innocent as unafraid. And beautiful. She closed her eyes and went back to sleep, and I took the pendant and left."

"You only did what you had to, Paolo."

"Not what I had to. What I wished to. I wished the mirror. But I can still see her there looking at me." He paused. "Anyway, I shall be home soon, with the mirror. We'll celebrate then."

Bianca placed the phone down. She understood the look Paolo was describing. This beautiful woman, Kathryn, she was hoping that Paolo might be the one. Instead, he had taken her body, then betrayed her intimacy and her trust. She would be coming after the mirror and the Amber Room even harder now. Bianca delle Bande Nere was nearly certain of it. Either that, or Kathryn wasn't the woman Paolo perhaps wished she was.

33

At the precinct house Ben Russo turned to Stacy Sparks. "Please, tell me you got a print, Stacy."

"That's what I'm trying to do, sir. Picked it right off the Hunan Harvest receipt. Guess what?"

"What?"

"It matches one of the prints you found."

"Cool," Ben said, dragging out the "oo" sound, relishing a word he didn't use often. That was a real piece of luck, combined with smart thinking on Stacy Sparks's part. "Do we have an ID on it yet?"

Sparks's face showed a brief, out-of-place loss of confidence. "Sort of."

"Sort of?"

"From the FBI computer, sir. There's a match in the computer. But the bureau won't release any information to us. Not even a name."

"Come again?"

"The file's marked CONFIDENTIAL CODE 801, with a notation that authorization is needed from a deputy chief to get the underlying data. Otherwise, all I could access was the name. I called our liaison at the New York FBI office to request authorization."

"And?"

"It was denied."

"Why?"

"No reason, sir. I pressed, but they wouldn't tell me anything."

"Goddamn feds," Ben muttered. The feds just couldn't be bothered to explain themselves to the lowly locals, as if the locals were the ones responsible for screwing up federal investigations; as if, he supposed, it was the locals who had fucked up Waco by ordering in the tanks against a civilian target. Now that was a bright idea. Well, he had other ideas. "That's another nice piece of work, Stacy. I'll take care of it from here."

"May I ask how?" she asked.

"I rather you didn't," he replied rather hastily. Then added, almost as an afterthought, "How about the other prints I found? The man's?"

"Still working on it, sir. They were a bit smudged. Thought we were looking for a woman."

"Never know, Detective. Never know."

●　　　●　　　●

Ben drove across town toward the East River, stopping at a payphone on Elizabeth Street before continuing on to a weather-beaten pier. A heavily muscled man with ebony skin stood at the edge of the pier waiting. The man was wearing a workman's white T-shirt, jeans, boots, and a beeper, and was both half a generation younger and half a foot taller than Ben.

He clasped Ben around the shoulders. "It's been too long, brother," he said in a soft, fluid voice. "Come on, I'll show you the way."

They walked down the wooden pier toward the river and a cavernous hangar of corrugated metal and rust, about as long as a football field and twice as wide. As soon as they entered the structure, Ben was hit by the rush of a sweet odor, both vaguely familiar and entirely fresh, which was obviously emanating from canvas sacks stacked in rows throughout the warehouse. Thousands of the sacks, a good hundred pounds worth of something in each sack.

Ben breathed in suspiciously, trying to place the substance in its proper place in the criminal code.

Then the ebony man pointed him towards one of the sacks, which was lying open nearby. Ben leaned his head over the bag, seeing that the contents were a fine dark powder.

He breathed in deeply once again, dipped the tip of his index finger into the powder, then licked his finger. Not as sweet as he would've figured, but extraordinarily rich.

"That's some of the best stuff in the whole world," the man said, "just in the from the Ivory Coast."

"Fucking unbelievable," Ben muttered, with a smile. Thaddeus Jefferson Lake—a cocoa merchant. The king of cocoa, from the looks of things. Ben shook his head…should've been a doctor.

They kept walking past bags of cocoa until they nearly ran out of warehouse. A huge longshoreman's union banner, Local 434, hung down over the back wall. Thaddeus Lake drew it back to reveal a hardened steel door, which he opened with a long round key and a hard push. Letting them into a bright room with a white linoleum floor, a buzzing fax machine, blinking telephone lights, and a half dozen desks arrayed in a grid.

Thaddeus Lake strolled up to the center of the room to an unoccupied wooden desk with metal folding chairs on either side. The desk was bare but for a two-line phone, a computer, a stainless steel thermos, and two white ceramic mugs resting on the far corner. *DEA* emblazoned on the mugs. Lake settled down behind the desk.

"So what brings you down here, Ben?"

Ben shrugged his shoulders. "Slight problem with your brother bureau, the FBI."

"What else is new? Fuckin' fibbees, half the time you'd think they're working for the other guys—bunch of whitebread, bureaucratic pencil pushers if you ask me. We try to get cooperation, all we get is paperwork. Of course, you know that already. That's why you're down here: the enemy of my enemy is my friend, and all that medieval Italian shit you were always telling me to read when I was still on the force. Now what can I do for you?"

Ben handed Lake a set of the prints he pulled from the ashtray of the apartment on the thirty-ninth floor of the white brick building. Same prints that were on the Hunan Harvest receipt.

"Department's computers down?" Lake asked, with a knowing smile, not expecting an answer. He took the prints and walked over to a scanner-like device.

Ben sat back and waited. Drifting in a policeman's thoughts, he didn't notice the dismayed look that came suddenly over Lake's face. In fact, he didn't look up until he heard Lake's voice.

"Motherfuckers..." Lake pulling his hands back slowly from the scanner like it had an infectious disease. "Motherfuckers. CODE 801. That's a fucking Agency code, Ben. Should've told me. I've seen it before."

"DEA?"

Thaddeus Lake's dark brown eyes turned a shade darker. "Not exactly."

34

"Young lady, it wasn't even until I'd been here five years, living the grand life in America, that the fools in Moscow even realized I was still alive. Ha! Gotta love that! Incompetents! No one is as incompetent as an incompetent communist. They are the kings and queens of the incompetents! The Greek gods of the incompetents!"

Mikhail Shokovitch clapped his old hands together to finish the punctuation. "Isn't that right Professor Greene? And you thought academia was the great refuge of the inept, the befuddled, and the bewildered!"

Professor Greene tried to think of a response, none came immediately to mind.

Kathryn Blaire just looked back at Shokovitch in dismay. An eighty-year-old piece of work sitting in his apartment on Central Park West in New York. The old man just loving his life, which, by the way, was being funded by the American taxpayer at a rate in the neighborhood of fifty grand a year. And his English was better than most of the people she'd grown up with.

It was a long way from the piss-ass horse town in the Ukraine where Shokovitch had been born and joined the Communist party. And it was a hell of long way from WWII and Stalin's purges and the collapse of Soviet communism, all of which Mikhail Shokovitch had survived. In fact, he had done more than survived. Mikhail Shokovitch had beaten everyone— outlived some, out-tricked others—and he knew it. No wonder Isaiah Hawkins had punted this one right back to her.

Shokovitch clapped his hands again. "You understand young lady, and you too Professor Greene, those morons in Moscow were fed a story that I had died in a train accident. An Amtrak tragedy involving a switchman who was shooting heroin, a faulty switch, and a truck carrying pigs. Swine! Love that! Think of the headlines in Moscow—Mikhail Shokovitch, WWII hero, counselor to Stalin, and most recently attaché to the Russian embassy in Washington, dies in a horrible train collision with pigs while traveling to Florida for a conference on global agriculture. Genius! Your Mister Hawkins played a part in that."

"Really?" Professor Greene said.

"Oh yes. He actually arranged for an Amtrak train to derail as part of the cover story. While the train was lying on its side in a ditch, I was dining in a four star restaurant. I knew right then that defecting was going to be good for me. What a meal! The mental midgets at the KGB had no clue. Later I heard the KGB agent in charge said it sounded like Aeroflot, just swap out the heroin shooter for a drunken Cossack! Took them five years to figure out that I was alive and had defected."

Kathryn looked around the apartment. In contrast to Isaiah's office, it was littered with mementos of Shokovitch's life. Red army decorations. Eastern Orthodox church icons. A prominently displayed, signed first edition by Solzhenitsyn. A framed picture of the one-time communist elite—Stalin, Molotov, and Bukharin. That picture bookended by one of Mikhail Shokovitch with President Reagan. She wondered when and how the KGB finally figured it out—maybe when Shokovitch was at the White House for a photo op.

"And what about the Amber Room?" Kathryn asked.

Shokovitch simply grinned and pretended not to hear.

Kathryn grinned back, figuring anyone who was a friend of Bukharin and had survived the Stalinist purges must have been interrogated more times than she'd been laid. So she had best go at it with a hard twist and see what gave.

"The mirror, Mikhail Shokovitch," she said.

"Mirror?"

She exhaled. "The mirror from the Amber Room. If you tell us what you know about it, we'll leave you alone to enjoy your life. If you want to play it the other way, I'll be the first to admit I'm probably screwed. There's probably not a damned thing I can do about it. You've been getting the best of people like me for fifty years."

"Sixty years, Ms. Blaire," Shokovitch corrected.

She stood and walked over to one of the religious icons

displayed in the apartment, a silver cross inlaid with gems. No doubt seized by the Communist party from a Russian church and then seized by Shokovitch from the party. She picked up the cross and held it up to the light. Beautiful. "Where did you get this?" she asked.

Shokovitch smiled. "A long time ago, I told your Mister Hawkins what I know about the Amber Room. No doubt you've read the transcript by now."

Of course she had. The typeface twelve-point courier, the type of choice worldwide for interrogation transcripts. In the upper right hand corner of each page, in capital letters, the name SHOKOVITCH. Mikhail Shokovitch, the interrogee. The other name typed on the pages, HAWKINS, the interrogator:

```
A: As I said, Mister Hawkins, the room was
   brought back to Moscow in crates. While
   the war was still on.
Q: Where was it kept?
A: In the crates, just like the Czar Peter
   had kept it in crates—in the basement of
   the palace that Stalin had taken for his
   own.
Q: And now?
A: Now, I don't know.
Q: What do you know?
A: I don't know anything. I've heard rumors.
   Seen documents. A receipt.
Q: A receipt?
A: Yes. It was important to keep records, you
   know that Mister Hawkins. Even the execu-
   tions...there were always excellent
   records.
Q: Tell me about the receipt.
A: It was for ten million in British pounds.
   It didn't give the name of the purchaser.
   The year was 1952. The party was desperate
```

for hard currency then, you know that.

Q: What was sold, the Amber Room?

A: Yes, that and some papers of historical interest.

Q: Tell me about the papers, Comrade Shokovitch.

A: I'm not a comrade.

Q: The papers, Mikhail.

A: Letters, Mister Hawkins. From Lenin and others. That's all I know.

"The mirror isn't mentioned in the transcript, Mikhail Shokovitch." Kathryn almost absently dropped the silver cross into her own purse.

Shokovitch smiled again. "Please, Ms. Blaire. Don't embarrass yourself. Rogue behavior will not do anything for your career at the Agency. I can assure you of that. I have on good authority that the Agency ordinarily promotes the timid. Not much different than the KGB, really."

Kathryn moved over to another icon. A silver chalice. She hefted it in her hand.

Shokovitch still didn't lose his smile, but Professor Greene sat up more upright in his chair, a seriously concerned expression on his face.

"Maybe this really isn't the best way, Kathryn," the professor interjected.

She just ignored him, as did Shokovitch. Instead, Kathryn Blaire sat back down next to the old Russian, the chalice still in her hand. She spoke to him calmly and confidentially, putting it out there open-kimono style, like she was confiding a secret to her best girlfriend.

"What you don't know, Comrade Mikhail, is this. I stole three million dollars from the Agency a couple years back, and while I still have most of the money, I don't have a career. I'm owned by Isaiah Hawkins. And what I have here is a mess—no Amber Room, two dead people, a son of bitch who slept with me last night and ran out this morning, the cops wanting to know what's going on, and Isaiah Hawkins all over my ass. I'll walk right out of here with your stolen art or just throw it out the window and let you deal with trying to get it back. Because, truly, I don't give a damn."

Kathryn sat back and waited for Shokovitch's reaction. She thought it was a good speech, and she was glad she'd decided at the last instance to leave out the part about knocking Elliot Rosewater around and leaving him unconscious. That kind of threat would have sounded so heavy handed and empty to be laughable. Still, good speech or not, she didn't know exactly what reaction she expected from Shokovitch. And she certainly didn't expect the one she got.

Shokovitch stood and began clapping his hands with glee, almost like a child. Like he'd gone senile.

"Brilliant! That was truly brilliant, Ms. Blaire. He didn't tell me he fucked you last night. That must have been magnificent. Mister delle Bande Nere, I mean. He told me you might be coming. But he didn't tell me he fucked you first. Now please, put back the chalice and the cross. That's truly fabulous. First he fucked you, then he beat you here. And all this time, I thought this was simply about the Amber Room."

"It is," Professor Greene said.

"Not for Ms. Blaire, Professor," Shokovitch said beaming. "Oh no. Ms. Blaire says she doesn't give a damn. And she may not about me or her career or the Amber Room. But I do know people. And she gives a damn about what happened to her this morning. It's personal now, her and Mister delle Bande Nere. Isn't it, Kathryn?"

She didn't answer, didn't even try, just looked at the old man crossly.

"Please, Ms. Blaire. Don't fret. You see, I grew up a communist, Ms. Blaire. Communism is all about false symbols and systems. Isaiah Hawkins wants the Amber Room as a symbol. That's not interesting to me, so I figured, why should I help him? But you want it for the right reasons, as a woman who has been hurt. And that's interesting to me. Do you understand that?"

She still didn't answer.

"No matter," Shokovitch said. "I'm sure you do. The point is this. During the war, a number of pieces were removed from the Amber Room in Leningrad before the Nazis captured it. Those pieces were kept in a party repository. I had access to that repository. In the tumult of the war, nobody missed a mirror. Recently, I let some parties know it might be for sale, including Teresa Gomes at the Sintra Gallery. On her recommendation, Mr. delle Bande Nere came by here earlier today. I sold him the mirror for seventy-five thousand dollars. A good price, I believe. I do not know where he lives or even if delle Bande Nere is his correct name. He paid cash and I gave him the mirror. Good luck finding him, Ms. Blaire."

•   •   •

On their way down in the elevator, Professor Greene asked the only question he could think of. "I'm not sure I understood all that. About it being personal for you?"

"Not now, Professor," she said sharply.

It was personal and it was business. The old man was living on fifty grand a year, which probably sounded like a lot when he defected, but didn't buy many four star meals in New York anymore. So from time to time he sold pieces from his personal collection—pieces he had stolen, of course—to supplement that income. Now, the last thing Mikhail Shokovitch needed was a pissed off Agency and Isaiah Hawkins screwing up his gig dealing in stolen Russian art. So he rolled. That was the business part. But only after she let him save face by humiliating her first. Which was personal.

It stung like a bitch. But she would live with that, if it got her closer to finding Paolo delle Bande Nere and the Amber Room.

35

Later that afternoon, Professor Greene was staring out from the window of his Columbia University office, when his phone rang at a prearranged hour.

"It's Victor," said the voice at the other end of a distinctly distant connection. The voice of an older man, still vigorous. The words chosen slowly and carefully, as if English had been a hard-won skill that could slip away at any moment. The accent, Russian. "Are you now interested in my proposition, Professor?"

Greene hesitated for a very long time. "I'm not sure."

There was a cackle of a bad connection. "It would seem that Isaiah Hawkins and his team are stumbling badly. You've told me that yourself."

"Yes, I'm aware of that."

"Then what is your hesitation, Professor? You owe nothing to Isaiah Hawkins. You do not work for him."

"No. No, I don't," Greene said, trying to build up his own confidence. "Isaiah really doesn't appear to be what he was."

"Then what are you waiting for? Now is the time to be bold, Professor. I am ready to devote substantial resources to this venture, money included. To be used at your discretion. I don't believe Mister Hawkins has put the same at your disposal. Are you ready?"

There was another long pause while Professor Greene stared blankly out his window, as if looking to find the answer to that question somewhere outside his own sphere of control. "I don't know. I suppose I really don't know."

"One never does know for sure, Professor. Trust the facts—this is the best chance to recover the Amber Room in your lifetime, maybe the only chance, and Isaiah Hawkins is not getting it done. But then, does he even really care? To Isaiah Hawkins this is just one job of many in a long career. To you, the Amber Room, well, you have been studying art your entire life, Professor. The chance to recover a masterpiece.

What that would mean for your career?"

Professor Greene tried to respond, but the words wouldn't come. He was momentarily paralyzed, as if all the expertise he had acquired during a lifetime of study was of no value at all to him. Finally, he mumbled, "Tomorrow? Would that be OK, Victor? May I let you know, tomorrow?"

"Yes, of course, Professor. Let me know tomorrow. Tomorrow morning. I'll call you at seven, exactly. But do you really believe the situation will change between now and then, or will you only be one day closer to losing the Room?"

"I don't know."

"No, you don't. And that's the problem, isn't it?"

Professor Greene hung up the phone. Alone in his office, he went back to staring out the window and contemplating a course of action that he would have believed inconceivable only a few days before. Betraying Isaiah Hawkins wasn't a step to take lightly. But then, what did he owe Isaiah Hawkins?

•   •   •

At a desk in a deteriorating office on the outskirts of Moscow, an old school KGB officer named Victor Prokhanov looked at a fading map of the world hanging on a water stained wall in his office and lit a cigarette.

Victor Prokhanov had known Isaiah Hawkins for the better part of three decades, and he didn't believe that Isaiah Hawkins was no longer what he once was. Isaiah Hawkins was everything a man wished for in an adversary—formidable, resourceful, and focused on his objectives—and always had been.

But Victor Prokhanov was willing to let Professor Greene believe whatever nonsense he wanted, just so long as it would help push the professor to jump over the invisible wall dividing honor from ambition.

Prokhanov looked at his watch and did a little quick math, counting the time difference between Moscow and New York, wanting to be sure to place that next call at exactly ten minutes after seven New York time. Just late enough to give the professor concern that the call wouldn't be coming.

Always play to a man's ambition. Either that or his bank account. Victor Prokhanov had lived by those maxims for far too long. Rules that he knew his old rival, Isaiah Hawkins, would call his own.

36

Ben Russo walked up the steps of a magnificently restored Harlem brownstone and rapped the iron doorknocker. No one would ever have had any difficulty identifying Ben Russo as a cop, but he still showed his badge when the door swung open.

Ivo ignored the shield and looked at the man, evaluating this detective and checking to see if his jacket pocket held a warrant. It didn't.

Ben kept his voice low so that no one else in the house would hear him. "Mister Jenkins, I'd like to speak with you. If you don't mind."

"Why would I mind, detective?" Ivo smiled and bellowed, the same smile and bellow he'd once reserved for hot-shot-new-in-country officers. "But I'm finishing dinner with my family. My woman, she's a hell of a cook—fish and grilled peppers today. She's working with my diet. I'd like to invite you in, but I'm sure you'll understand if I don't. You don't mind waiting out here on the steps, do you? Just 'til I'm finished."

Ben Russo killed the time reading a *New York Post* that had been discarded on top of a nearby garbage can. He made no mistake, Ivo Jenkins had just won round one. But this type of thing, it wasn't ever a matter of who won the first round.

Eventually, the door opened and Ivo came out, looking well fed and ready to take a walk. Ben Russo came up alongside him.

"I always thought you were an urban legend, until today," Ben began. "Ivanhoe Jenkins…a colossus…a night phantom. Story went you did gallery quality work, black and white usually, preferably of politicians, although businessmen would do."

"I own some fried chicken franchises, detective. A black man with a successful business, does that make me a legend?"

Ben opened a small manila folder and handed two sheets of paper to Ivo. The first summarized the District Attorney's file:

Ivanhoe Jenkins...decorated Vietnam veteran...owner of six Papa's Fried Chicken franchise restaurants...believed to be the most significant blackmailer operating in New York...a four-year investigation that had turned up no hard evidence...no victims who would cooperate.

The second sheet of paper was a photocopy of Ivo's thumb print.

"Took it off the microwave from an apartment on Lexington Avenue, fortieth floor. Matched it against your service records," Ben explained. "You had a good war. Understand that's where you learned recon. Care to tell me what you were doing in that apartment?"

Ivo shrugged his massive shoulders. "Nothing much to tell you about. I was having a turn with an immoral woman. Pretty thing. Couldn't very well do it at home."

"No, guess not," Ben agreed. "I had a nice conversation with the building manager. Talkative fellow. Said the apartment was rented, with cash, by a small woman with dark hair. That your friend?"

"That's no business of yours, Detective. Not how I see it."

Ben walked on in silence for a couple of steps, as if mulling over whether it really was his business. "How about Elliot Rosewater? Is he my business?"

"Elliot Rosewater?" Ivo seemed to roll the name around in his mind. "You mean the lawyer who got killed. I read about that in the paper. Fancy lawyer. Got himself kicked in the nuts and died. Good story for the tabloids. Park Avenue Lawyercide. Yeah, I guess he's your business now. But not mine."

"No, I guess not, Mister Jenkins. Because you weren't black-mailing him. I mean, from that apartment on Lex you could— if you wanted to—see right across the street into a girl's apart-ment. Girl named Sarah Ridell. You could watch her fucking Elliot Rosewater. Take some pictures. But you wouldn't do that. You own chicken franchises, right? You were just up there getting laid by an immoral woman, right?"

"That's what I said, Detective."

"Right. Then you wouldn't have seen Sarah Ridell fall. Or

heard her scream. Because that might stick with a man for a while."

They walked on for another two or three blocks without saying anything, their strides matching step for step in tandem. And they might have kept that up a good bit longer, except they came to a corner grocery store with fresh fruit piled in wooden crates on the sidewalk. There were yellow-orange apricots, similar to the ones Ben got down on Mott Street, and he stopped to look them over, before buying a handful from the store's owner, a neat man dressed in a jacket and tie. Ben took a couple of paper napkins from the shop counter, and offered one of the apricots and a napkin to Ivo.

Ivo twisted the small fruit in two and ate the half which had separated from the pit. He wiped his mouth with the napkin.

"Seems to me," Ivo said, taking his time with the words, "maybe these two incidents you're raising are not coincidental. Maybe this lawyer might have been responsible for the girl's death. That is, if it's like you say, Detective, that she spent her last night fucking him. Maybe one of her friends killed him. Not much for the department to worry about, wouldn't seem to me."

"Maybe not, when you see it like that."

"No. At least, not if it had all taken place up here." Ivo gestured with his arms to take in his uptown neighborhood. "But this took place on Park Avenue, right Detective? So I guess that sticks with the department for a while longer."

Ben took a bite of his apricot, nodding his head, point taken—as if the sometime sins of the department were his burden. As if those sins were any reason to give curare girl a pass. He cleared his throat.

"Maybe I haven't made myself clear, Mister Jenkins. I got a thing about double murders. No matter where they take place. And you got an interest in rich men screwing pretty young girls. On the other hand, I don't give a good-goddamn about blackmail. It's not my beat no matter where it takes place. All I want is the woman's name. The one you were having a turn with, that is."

"Can't do that, Detective."

"How about if I told you she killed Elliot Rosewater."

"Wouldn't interest me much," Ivo said flatly. And he turned around to start walking back toward his home. "My family's waiting for me."

"Sure, I understand," Ben said.

"Glad you do, Detective."

Ben walked silently alongside Ivo for a long block, just eating an apricot. Then the detective began musing, aloud, "Your daughter, she's got a wedding coming up, right?"

"What about my daughter, Detective Russo?"

Ben took a last bite and spit the apricot pit into a nearby trashcan. "I've been thinking. I mean, it would be a terrible thing for a daughter if her father were to be arrested right before her wedding—let's say for attempted blackmail and suspicion of murder. Might make the front page of the papers, I would think. Would be a hard thing for a father to explain to his daughter. Wouldn't it?"

Ivo turned fast with an open palm, sticking it, without thinking, hard into Ben's chest. Pushing him back against the rough skin of a brownstone.

"You know that's a damned lie. I didn't touch Sarah Ridell. Or Elliot Rosewater," Ivo hissed, the words spitting from between clenched teeth.

They locked eyes. There weren't many people watching, and none of them would be watching too hard if it went that way. A small girl riding her bike pedaled faster. What was there to see? Nothing that anyone would want to discuss later with the cops.

It was Ben Russo's move to make, and it wasn't about pride. He brought one arm up slowly and pushed Ivo's hand an inch off his chest. Then he let go of Ivo's hand, giving him the next move.

Uncertain what to do next, but quite sure nonetheless that a street fight with this detective was not the answer, Ivo backed away.

"That never happened, Mister Jenkins. Now give me her name."

"That won't happen either, Detective."

"I work with what is given to me, Mister Jenkins. You have been given to me and, like I said, I don't have anything against blackmail."

Ben removed a business card from his pocket and handed it to Ivo. "Call me with your answer. Far as I'm concerned, you're just an urban legend, Mister Jenkins. I'd like to keep it that way."

37

Late that same evening, Billie Holiday's voice floated like trumpet notes across the breadth of Isaiah Hawkin's library, lightly touching the pages of the books and the grain of the wood.

Kathryn Blaire, Anand Ashland, Professor Greene, Isaiah Hawkins, a bottle of scotch, another of bourbon, four tumblers, cigarettes, half-filled ashtrays, spectacles, and a pile of books on the tarot, and related topics shared the space with Billie's voice.

The question of the evening was the Hanged Man pendant. Why did Elliot Rosewater have it? Why did Paolo delle Bande Nere steal it? And how could it help them find the Amber Room?

The room was quiet but for Billie's voice, until Professor Greene closed the book he was reading in disgust.

"Enough with all this Odin rubbish, what with Norse gods hanging themselves by their balls from sacred trees in search of self-renewal."

"By the ankle, Professor," Kathryn felt the compelling inner need to correct. She was still smarting from the embarrassment of the Shokovitch episode and blamed Professor Greene for being both a witness to it and being perfectly useless.

Isaiah put down the book he had been skimming, *The Dictionary of Symbols*. "In any event, I think it's clear that the Odin tree story isn't the answer. That's the type of half-mind analysis I can get from Washington."

There was, of course, an entire section of Agency staffers in Washington devoted to the analysis of symbols. Indeed, at one point in the Cold War there'd been an entire section of first rate intellects devoted to handicapping Politburo politics on the basis of such signs as who stood where at the Kremlin May Day parade. Hunched over satellite photographs in their air conditioned offices, they'd missed Yeltsin coming—because they weren't on the ground and they never understood that Boris was playing a different game. Isaiah hadn't bothered to ask their opinion of the Hanged Man.

"What else does anyone have?" Isaiah asked.

Anand Ashland cleared his throat. "I've think I've found something interesting from Dr. James Elias."

"From the television series on folklore?" Professor Greene asked.

"The very one." Anand held out toward the professor the book he was reading, *The Tarot Dialectics*, a particularly tacky-looking paperback. "It's filled with rather bizarre theories on the tarot. But it has a lucid introduction by Dr. Elias. This is what he says on the Hanged Man:

> A common belief is that this card is based on the legend of Odin. While this has a certain simplistic appeal due to the similarity of the Hanged Man's appearance and early Norse drawings of Odin, there is no scholarly evidence to support this supposition.
>
> On the other hand, it is known that the tarot were first developed in Southern Europe in the 1400s. At that time, in both Italy and Southern France, for a man to be hung upside down in public was a sign of extreme dishonor. This practice has been brought down to modern Italy. In perhaps the most famous recent example, Mussolini's body was hung upside down following his assassination."

Kathryn leaned forward in her chair, nearly spilling her glass of scotch. "But Elliot Rosewater wasn't hung upside down or any other way."

"No he wasn't." Anand paused, as if getting his thoughts in order. "But I do think there is something to this, thinking of the Hanged Man as a symbol used in a societal context. Maybe to express disgrace, like Dr. Elias says. Or maybe to express something else. Maybe someone was sending Rosewater a message. Or making a point. I'm not sure what."

"Well, figure it out," Isaiah said. "Or figure out some other way to find this delle Bande Nere."

Professor Greene hung his head. Figure it out? That was the best Isaiah Hawkins could do?

38

Bianca delle Bande Nere sat outside on the balcony that extended off her library, waiting for her brother to return from New York. He had called already to say that all was good. Now his plane was due in just a matter of hours.

The city of Florence spread out beneath her in a melange of gray stone towers, faded red tile roofs, thick walls, open squares, and soaring church domes. The Arno River flowing gracefully beneath its span of five heavy stone bridges. Most of Florence—at least that part known to the generations of tourists—lay across the Arno. Botticelli's *Venus* could be found there, properly displayed in its proper place during the proper opening hours. No point in coming to Florence without seeing Botticelli's *Venus*.

Everyone knew or at least believed that the *Venus* was more than a masterful painting, that it was an allegory of life. But almost no one knew anymore that the *Venus* had been conceived by Botticelli as something much greater than an allegory. That it was magic. Not magic like pulling a rabbit out of a hat, but Renaissance magic, the use of symbols and talismans and sacred words to pull the powers of the heavens down to earth. The *Venus* conceived to bring heavenly powers to its viewer through the images, symbols, and colors painted onto the canvas.

Botticelli had believed in the magic. So many had during the Renaissance, before the Church had decided magic was a threat and science had decreed it a fraud; before the priest Giordano Bruno had been burned at the stake for preaching that the earth revolved around the sun—a conclusion Bruno reached years before Galileo—based upon the study of magic as opposed to science.

Almost no one believed in the magic anymore, although its vestiges were evident in every new age shop that sold crystals. But even if you did not wish to believe in magic, if you wished to truly understand Botticelli, you had to understand his state

of mind. You had to understand the magic.

Bianca stood and looked over the city of her birth with great pleasure and anticipation. Paolo would be home soon. They would take a walk along the Arno, eat a wonderful meal, and celebrate the fabulous prize he was bringing with him. Later they would install that prize, the mirror, where it would be magnificent.

She did not believe she would ask Paolo about Elliot Rosewater or Teresa Gomes or Mikhail Shokovitch. They were all irrelevant now that they had the prize they had sought so dearly. But she would ask Paolo about the woman, Kathryn, who he had already described to her:

She opened her eyes as I was leaving. She looked strangely innocent, lying there. Although one really couldn't call her that. Maybe she was not so much innocent as unafraid. And beautiful. She closed her eyes and went back to sleep, and I took the pendant and left."

"You only did what you had to, Paolo."

"Not what I had to. What I wished to. I wished the mirror. But I can still see her there looking at me."

Yes, Bianca would most definitely ask Paolo about Kathryn Blaire. A strangely innocent woman who her brother might never see again, although he most certainly wished to believe he would. Bianca smiled. Interesting that Kathryn Blaire had opened her eyes as Paolo was leaving. That wasn't like Paolo, getting caught like that, his style so subtle and quiet. It was almost enough to make a sister believe that Paolo had taken the pendant in just the way to guarantee that Kathryn Blaire would follow him.

39

It was three in the afternoon in Moscow, seven in the morning New York time. Victor Prokhanov looked down at his reflection in the two-foot-square, quarter-inch deep pool of Moscow city water that had accumulated on the linoleum floor beside his desk.

The cause of the pool wasn't a leak from the roof, although there were presumably plenty of those as well. Rather, it seemed that the squat office building's antique ventilation system had developed a unique new flaw. It no longer filtered out humidity, as did the efficient western air conditioning Prokhanov had encountered during his years with the embassy in France. Instead, this system, installed years before by the idiot brother-in-law of the local Communist party head, managed to keep the humidity filtered in. Combined with Moscow's summer heat, a southern exposure, and windows that could not be opened, it created a tropical atmosphere inside his office—with water evaporating in the sun, condensing on his ceiling, then periodically coming down in short bursts of, well, rain.

He shook his head—a small movement belonging to a man past pointless recriminations—looked up from the puddle, and located the open pack of cigarettes on his desk. They were a Russian brand and they were both stale and rather tasteless, but they were also cheap and the nicotine still felt good. It seemed that all of Moscow now smoked Marlboros. They tasted far better and were, Prokhanov supposed, a sign that one was modern. Nor did it hurt that the franchise to distribute Marlboros had been awarded to several of Prokhanov's younger KGB colleagues, thereby ensuring both excellent distribution and limited issues with customs. They were wealthy men now—Prokhanov's colleagues—living in vast tasteless mansions that had seemingly descended from the air. Not that different, perhaps, than Lenin and Stalin and the other Bolsheviks inheriting the homes of the Russian boyars after the revolution, which was only the first sign of decay in the party.

Victor Prokhanov knew he had been born too late to be tempted by the trappings of wealth offered through the early years of the revolution. And he was still too much a man of the old to accept his friends' invitation to participate in the new game. He supposed he could have had an air castle of his own, if he could have just wrapped his heart around the new world. Instead, he sat in the rain and played the old game.

He rose from his chair and, making no effort to avoid the lakes and streams which coursed through his small office, walked over to his map. It was old and battered and still showed the empire. He drew his hand across Eastern Russia, toward the Baltic Republics where he had learned his trade as a young officer on his first assignments. Now, of course, the Baltic Republics were no more—replaced by the ridiculously inconsequential nation states of Estonia, Lithuania, and Latvia.

It was there in the Baltics that he had first heard of the Amber Room. Well, he had known of the Room vaguely before, as a great treasure lost by the nation in the war. That was taught in school. But in the Baltics, rumors danced that the Room had not been destroyed and was there for the finding by the right man. These rumors sparked the silly dreams of a young, idealistic, and ambitious officer. If he brought the Amber Room home to Russia, what a hero he would be!

Those first whispers had been followed by others, round-about leads and tales that had gone nowhere over a period of decades. His youth and his idealism were lost along the way, but he never gave up his young man's dream of recovering the Room. That alone made the chase worth the candle.

And that was before he'd learned of the Lenin letters. Before the KGB had finally figured out Mikhail Shokovitch was alive and had secured a microfiche transcript of that miserable traitor's interrogation. Before he'd learned what Shokovitch had told Isaiah Hawkins about the Amber Room and about the letters from Lenin and Molotov and the others. Before Isaiah Hawkins had joined the pursuit.

It wasn't a foolish dream he was thinking of anymore. It was besting Isaiah Hawkins in one last toss.

At his age, as he constantly told his younger colleagues, one couldn't afford to lose any more because there were no more chances. He wasn't sure whether his young colleagues understood that point, but he was sure that Isaiah Hawkins would understand.

He picked up the phone to dial New York. Professor Greene was ready to jump, he was certain of it. It was just a matter of hitting the right notes—ambition and, if necessary, greed.

40

Ivo Jenkins removed a sheet of Ilford paper from the enlarger with his left hand and slipped it, emulsion side up, into a shallow tray filled with developer solution. He set his darkroom timer to fifty-five seconds and gently rocked the shallow tray with both hands, the solution sliding up and over the paper.

He had started the morning with an image in his mind he didn't like: a picture of his face on the front page of his favorite tabloid under the caption: BLACKMAILER BUSTED IN ROSEWATER MURDER.

So he had paid a visit to Anand Ashland.

"Job was supposed to be 3K a night, no problems with the law, just take some pictures of a pretty young woman and her visitors. Now the woman is dead, her boyfriend is dead, and I got a cop squeezing me hard to give up the name of your associate, Miss Kathryn Blaire, who, by the way, I don't owe anything to. Now tell me—what are you, and Kathryn Blaire, and your Mister Hawkins, whoever he is, going to do about that?"

Anand Ashland had said all he could—that he needed some time to work it out.

Well, that much was pretty clear.

No doubt, Anand Ashland and Kathryn Blaire and Mister Isaiah Hawkins hadn't planned on having a couple of dead bodies and a New York cop poking around in their business. But the world was messy that way. Everybody was always looking for order and neatness and trying to figure out exactly how something did or did not fit into the master plan. But it was a truism that once people got set in motion, things got complicated in ways that no one could foresee.

All anyone could do was make sure they were prepared, because preparation allowed a man to deal with shit as it came up. Maybe Isaiah Hawkins was prepared, and maybe he wasn't. Maybe Isaiah Hawkins would figure that Ivo Jenkins had been paid for his services and should have known better than to not worry about the cops, no matter what he had been told. Maybe Isaiah Hawkins would decide Kathryn Blaire was expendable. Maybe not.

In the end, Ivo couldn't count on them. Hell, he didn't even know exactly who Isaiah Hawkins was. No, he couldn't count on anyone but himself. Which made it a good thing that he was prepared.

"Like I said, I don't have anything against blackmail."

That cop, Ben Russo, he'd just been doing his job. But Russo hadn't thought things through well enough. A man who blackmails for a living ought to have a few extra photos stored away for situations like this. Russo should have thought of that.

Ivo lifted the photographic paper out of its solution. The outlines of a woman slowly emerging from the white paper in shades of silver halide. His rainy day girl, the woman he'd been saving for trouble with the police, like cash under the mattress.

He remembered the day he'd taken her picture, focusing his lens into the hotel room where she was getting undressed. She'd turned and stared straight at the camera, walked right across a new white carpet towards the window and the telephoto lens. Naked and open as one could be. And she was more than fine. Long legs, thin waist, light hair, soft eyes, round shoulders. She was firm and she was natural, and she was abundant enough in the right places. A perfect rainy day girl.

Using tongs, Ivo transferred the photo to a water stop bath—he preferred water to the chemical solutions because that was the way he'd been taught—and shifted his gaze to the man in the background of the frame.

The man was older, giving a good thirty years to the girl. He was naked, his clothing on the corner of the bed, a gun and a badge barely visible. But that could be blown up later.

It would have been easy enough to step inside the man's thinking and empathize with him. But the man's thinking was more or less irrelevant right here. To Ivo's experience, the man's wife simply wasn't the type who would wish to empathize. First wives with grown children always had such

160

trouble with the empathy part.

Neither would the man's employer be pleased. No, it was not likely at all that the citizens of New York would be pleased about their police commissioner banging rainy day girls on city time and city expense accounts.

Ivo fixed the picture and washed it and set it aside with the others in the series. Ordinarily, line drying was his preference, but inartistic compromises sometimes had to be made. He had a deadline to meet, and he set the photo in the dryer and made the necessary arrangements. The least Anand Ashland could do was deliver the message.

41

Kathryn Blaire didn't need to be told by Ivo Jenkins that the wheels were coming off. It was clear enough now that Paolo delle Bande Nere had seduced her, all the while letting her think she was seducing him. Then he had stolen the pendant and disappeared, taking with him the mirror from the Amber Room. The cops were still dogging her for a murder she had not committed. Mikhail Shokovitch and Teresa Gomes had given her little. They had no clue what the Hanged Man meant. Isaiah was locked away studying books on symbols, as if that was proactive. And her future was hanging in the balance.

Against this fine backdrop, she met Anand in the catacombs of the museum.

"How did it go with the commissioner?" she asked.

"He took it well. He's a practical man. I don't believe the department will have any further interest in Ivo Jenkins or the Ridell or Rosewater matters."

"Good. And the cop, Russo?"

Anand shrugged. "The commissioner was arranging to speak with him when I left. Turns out they are old colleagues. Used to walk a beat together. Go to the movies together with their wives. That type of thing. The commissioner took one path, Russo another. According to the commissioner, Ben Russo is a most compelling man—refuses to take a cushy desk job downtown, even though it's his for the asking. Said it's a nice piece of work he's done so far in this case."

"What does that mean?" Kathryn asked.

"It doesn't mean anything," Anand said, which wasn't quite true.

Isaiah Hawkins had used the exact same words with Anand in referring to the cop. The cop, Russo, it's a nice piece of work he's done so far, Anand. I want to learn more about him. Make sure Kathryn handles this with discretion. No reason to make this hard for Russo or the commissioner.

Isaiah Hawkins didn't destroy people who were good, he collected them.

Kathryn let the ambiguity pass. She hadn't actually seen the pictures and there was something she wished to know. "The rainy day girl. Tell me, how was she?"

"Worth it, I would suppose. If one was into that sort of thing."

Pretty much the same thing, Kathryn thought, that Paolo delle Bande Nere would say about her. How was she? Worth it, I would suppose.

42

Professor Greene paid another visit to Mikhail Shokovitch that morning. On his own.

The old Russian Shokovitch greeted Greene with a grin and led him to his living room. A new bottle of vodka on ice and two shot glasses were waiting on a coffee table. Shokovitch twisted open the bottle and poured two glasses full to the top, the way he'd first learned to conduct business back in Russia.

"Drink up, Professor. It's from Scandinavia. Best vodka made in the world today. What a tragedy that my old country cannot even make a decent vodka anymore. Fucking communists, they couldn't make money running a whorehouse in a gold mining town. Anyway, drink up! I thought you would be back."

Greene downed a glass quickly. "Why is that?"

"A man survives Joseph Stalin's purges, Professor, he learns a few things. Or maybe he knew a few things already. Take your associate Kathryn Blaire for instance."

"What about her?"

"She was telling the truth yesterday—about not having a career. I know this for a fact, because I checked her out afterwards with some old contacts of mine. So the question is, why does she care so much? Why not just go through the motions, instead of pushing? I'll tell you why, Professor. Because all of life is psychological—Bukharin taught me that. Your Kathryn Blaire needs a win to prove to herself that she can still play at this level. And to show everyone else that she can too. Which also explains why I had to give her something. A person who will do anything for a win is much more dangerous to their opponent than someone who is thinking of their long-term future. With people thinking long-term there is always a certain undercurrent—if you don't hurt me, I won't hurt you. Your Kathryn Blaire could not have given a damn about hurting me or me hurting her. She was willing to stand in the center of the ring and trade punches."

"She's not my Kathryn Blaire."

"Of course not. It was only a figure of speech, my good professor." Shokovitch poured another glass for each of them and drank his right away, leaving Greene little choice but to do the same. "No, of course Professor, you would not be here today if she was your Kathryn Blaire. Tell me, Professor, what is the most important thing in the world to you right now?"

"Recovering the Amber Room," the professor said simply, clearly, and with the conviction of a believer. "It's why I'm here."

"I beg to differ, Professor. In my opinion, and I value my opinion, it's not the Amber Room you seek the most. Rather, it is the rewards and glory that recovering the Amber Room will bring to you. Am I not right?"

"No." The professor hastily finished a third glass. "No. That's not it at all—"

"Come Professor. There are points in a life when it pays to be honest with yourself, if no one else. You are a tenured professor of art at Columbia University. A fine post. It pays a nice salary, you get to travel to conferences and make speeches, occasionally you make love to a coed. Am I right? But for an ambitious man such as yourself, where is the upside? Outside your narrow field of colleagues, no one knows who you are. There are no riches. The coeds graduate. You see your friends who are bankers and lawyers and gallery owners making more money than you, even though you are smarter than they are. So what can you do to take a jump to the next league? That is what you have been asking yourself. And I think we know the answer to that question, Professor. Do we not?"

"You don't understand," Greene replied.

"Perhaps not. Perhaps I'm wrong." Shokovitch smiled and poured two more glasses. "But anyway, how can I help you, Professor?"

Greene pushed away the vodka now. "I want to know where you got that mirror. I want to know where the Amber Room is. And I think you know. I don't believe that story you told Kathryn Blaire yesterday about stealing the mirror from a storage room. As you said in your interrogation, the communists were always very good record keepers. For a mirror like that, records would have been kept."

"And as I said, you are a smart man, Professor. But you have told me nothing of interest so far."

Professor Greene leaned forward in his chair. "So tell me, is two hundred thousand dollars interesting?"

"Always. But where would a university professor find such resources?"

"There are other people interested in the Amber Room beside Isaiah Hawkins."

"Of course there are, Professor. But who?"

"Perhaps some of your old countrymen."

"I see, Professor."

Mikhail Shokovitch stood and walked over to a photograph of himself as a much younger man, standing on a stone bridge in front of a river. The setting was most obviously European, although Professor Greene could not identify the city.

"Let me tell you a story, Professor Greene. I joined the Communist party because I believed. And I went on believing until I was posted to the embassy in Paris in the 1960s. It was the first time I had been outside Russia. From the first day I set foot in Paris, I no longer believed. How could I? The city, the food, the wealth, the women—all compared to the hideous drabness that was Moscow. Only an idiot could still believe. That was when I began to make alternative plans for myself. There is an art dealer in Paris who you might do well to look up. A gentleman by the name of Rocard. His family has been one of the leading dealers in Paris for a hundred years. Like so many of the European elite—they were fellow travelers in the sixties. Maybe they still are today, poor fools. I acquired the mirror from them as part of a transaction where they wished the Russian government to ignore their illegal purchase of some Faberge eggs. I helped them, they helped me. And I believe they could help you find the Room."

As he stood to leave, Greene reached out to shake hands with Mikhail Shokovitch

"No need, Professor. I don't trust handshake deals. But I am rather certain that both Kathryn Blaire and Isaiah Hawkins would both find this visit of yours to be of interest. So I'm quite confident you will live up to your end of the bargain."

43

Ben Russo pushed through the heavy glass door, his eyes glancing at the silver letters stenciled onto the glass at chest height: ONE POLICE PLAZA.

Behind the reception desk sat a smartly dressed, attractive, young, blonde civilian. She looked up at his badge, then down at a calendar on the screen of her brand new computer.

"I'm sorry, Detective Russo. I don't see you listed. Do you have an appointment?"

She spoke with no trace of a New York accent, and nothing about her looked like original equipment—not her too bronze tan, her too full lips, her too round tits, nor her too bright smile. Must of been imported from L.A. Just another piece of the commissioner's ongoing PR campaign.

Ben could only wonder where they stacked the frizzy-haired women from Staten Island who used to watch this desk and do their nails—back when it was still acceptable for the receptionist's name to end in a vowel.

"Thank you, I know what time it is," Ben said with a smile. "I got a message straight from Irish Mike—"

"Excuse me, detective."

Her perfect face lost its perfect smile, as if she actually believed tribal nicknames could be legislated out of the so-called new police force.

"I said, I received a personal message from Irish Mike fifteen minutes ago, asking me to come down and see him. Now."

"I'll let the commissioner know you are here, detective," she said, with equal parts distrust and distaste.

Ben waited in a bright lobby on a new black leather couch. A half dozen copies of the *New York Times* lay nearby, prominently arrayed on a glass coffee table. In the old days, back on the beat, Mike O'Malley used to say he wouldn't waste his cigarette money reading that patron saint of armchair do-gooders. Now there was a no smoking sign next to the papers.

Irish Mike had certainly rolled with the times. The newspaper of record would probably say that Commissioner O'Malley had "evolved," a word Ben noticed the *Times* mostly reserved to describe public figures whose public posture had moved closer to their own. And, in a way, Ben Russo had to admire the way Mike O'Malley had come of age in one world and chameleoned right into the next. A trick that he, Ben Russo, had not quite been able to manage.

After twenty minutes on the couch, Ben was feeling like maybe he should have tried a softer approach with the blonde import, when a man's footsteps echoed toward him from down the hall.

He was a thick man of perhaps fifty-five, with carefully clipped short white hair. Even at a distance, the man was obviously beautifully packaged, wearing a crisp blue suit, white cotton spread collar shirt, maroon tie, captoe black leather shoes, stainless steel spectacles, and a thin black leather briefcase with gold locks. It was an expensive look. However, it was also an outfit that looked forced on account of trying too hard.

Ben stood up and offered out his hand, but Irish Mike O'Malley clasped him instead on the shoulder.

"Thanks for coming down, Ben. What do you say we get out of this stuffy place and get a beer? Down at Rosie's, like we used to. My treat."

•　　•　　•

The waitress, an Irish girl if there ever was one—freckled with red hair and a lilting accent—brought a pitcher of pale ale, tall glasses, and a basket of peanuts.

"At least some things never change," Irish Mike declared grandly, as he watched the waitress walk out of the booth with a swirl and a swish. "She looks just like that girl who used to work here when we first joined the force. Margaret...Margaret...what was her last name?"

"Wright," Ben said with a smile. Names stick to good beat cops like soot to New York City.

"That's right. Margaret Wright. Great lips on that girl. Remember?"

"Maybe not as well as you."

"Ah hell, Ben, I never did get more than a kiss and a feel. Which was pretty good for those days. Not like today." The commissioner laughed and took a long sip of beer.

An old black and white photo of Ireland hung on the inside wall of the booth and Ben stole a look at the picture while the commissioner refilled his mug from the pitcher. Ben hadn't been to Rosie's in years, but he remembered the photo. "This place still an IRA hangout, Mike?"

"I think it still depends who's asking."

The commissioner took another sip of his beer, settled deeper into the booth, and loosened his tie so that now he almost looked like he belonged at an Irish bar.

"I'm glad you came down, Ben. I really am. I don't get to share a drink with my old fellas much anymore. Tell me, how's Maria?"

"She's good."

"I'm hoping she's finally brought some sense to you."

"You know Mike, it's just not for me. Told you that a year ago."

"Tell me again," the commissioner said.

Ben shrugged his shoulders and turned his palms up in the air, doubling up on his what-was-there-to-say? gestures.

"Can't let you off that easy, Ben. Tell me again what's so bad about coming down to the Plaza. You'll work for me. It's a lot more money, you get more respect, some influence, an opportunity to use your experience. And when you retire, that extra money gives your pension a lift for the rest of your life. It's a good way to end your career. You should think about Maria. You could buy her some things with the extra money, take her on that trip to Milan—just to see the opera, like you always talked about."

"I know."

The commissioner took a long swallow of beer. "Of course, you know. But you won't take it. And, I'll tell you why."

"Don't."

"Hell, why not? Because we both know why already, Ben. You think I've become someone we used to laugh at."

"It's not like that—"

"Yeah, I know. Just do me a favor and think it over again. At least you know what it's like to walk a beat, which a lot of people who do want the job can't say."

Ben took a deep draught of beer, mostly to force himself to stop grinding his teeth. Irish Mike O'Malley was right enough. Right about Maria and right about why he didn't want the job. Wasn't much else really to say on that topic. And there hadn't been for a long while.

"Want to tell me what's really up, Mike?" Ben asked. The commissioner of police hardly needed to send him an urgent message just to go back over ground that was a year old. "Is it the Ridell-Rosewater investigation?"

The commissioner grinned. "You always did like getting to the point. Rosewater's old partner, Jack Osborne, noticed that too."

"Nice friends you've acquired, Mike."

"Supporter, not friend."

"Whatever. It's not right. A young girl dying like that. Had to use a high pressure hose to clean up the sidewalk."

"Osborne didn't kill her, Ben. Piece of garbage that he may be."

"I know that."

"Yeah, of course you do. I read all your reports. You have any doubts it was Rosewater?"

"No. I don't know if he pushed her himself. But he at least made it happen."

The police commissioner nodded.

Then he looked around the room thoroughly and lowered his voice. "That's good. I mean, seeing as Rosewater's dead anyway. Maybe not every murder deserves to get solved, you know what I mean."

"Fucking déjà vu," Ben muttered with a slight, sarcastic laugh.

"What?"

"Second time in two days that particular sentiment has been

suggested to me. He killed her. Somebody killed him. Move on. Next."

"I'm aware of that, Ben."

"What? You're aware of the prior suggestion?"

"That's right."

O'Malley's affirmation hung in the air for a while. How did the commissioner know what Ivo Jenkins had said? That wasn't in Ben's reports. Which meant Ivo Jenkins or reggae girl or someone else working with them had gotten to the commissioner. Ben cracked a peanut shell and spilled the nuts onto the table. He flicked a nut with his fingernail and, as it skittered across the wood and onto the floor, it dawned on him that this should have been expected.

Sarah Ridell was a nobody from nowhere, a girl from Johnson City, Oklahoma. Sure, Elliot Rosewater killed her, except nobody knew that other than Ben Russo, Mike O'Malley, and a couple of other cops on the force who could be expected to keep quiet. And there was no sense in dragging Rosewater's good name through the mud—irritating a good supporter like Jack Osborne—now that Rosewater was dead. So it was time enough to let everything go.

It would be better for everyone: the department, Rosewater's widow, Jack Osborne, Mike O'Malley and, not least, Ben Russo.

Ben cracked another peanut shell. "The big job downtown? That's my comp for letting this one go. Isn't it, Mike?"

Irish Mike let a sip of beer roll slowly down his throat, the way he did when he was embarrassed. "That's because you're my friend, Ben. I could use you and you could use the money. You can choose to believe that or not. The other situation is a separate matter."

"Sure. And your suggestion, Mike, that not every murder deserves to get solved, is that just advice? Or is that departmental policy now?"

"More than advice, Ben."

"I'll think about it."

"You got to do more than that."

The police commissioner lifted his briefcase onto the table

and removed a manila envelope. He handed the envelope to Ben. "Take a look through these. It's my understanding that Ivo Jenkins was doing a favor when he took them. Just do me a favor and don't look at the last one until I tell you. OK?"

Ben went through the glossies one at a time, deliberately. Sarah Ridell so beautiful and so full of life. Leaning back and laughing. Laughing. Her vitality in such vivid contrast to Elliot Rosewater's very being. He wondered how many minutes had elapsed between those final pictures of Sarah Ridell being taken and the end of her life. And he wondered whether finding justice for Elliot Rosewater carried much of a reward. Which was, of course, the point of showing him the pictures.

"Seen enough?" Irish Mike asked.

"What's the last picture?"

"Take a look."

Ben turned Sarah Ridell over, and saw another girl emerge. Ivo Jenkin's rainy day girl. She was looking straight at the camera, walking towards it. She was gorgeous and naked and young. Irish Mike O'Malley was sitting on a bed naked in the background, his shield and gun blurry, but visible.

Ben pushed the picture back across the table. "You should be more careful who you spend your time with, Mike."

"Fair enough, Ben. And I suppose that pulling the drapes shut would not have hurt me either. But what were you thinking going after Ivo Jenkins? If it wasn't me in that picture, it would be the mayor or the attorney general or a judge. A three-hundred-pound blackmailer with prominent victims hardly operates in a veil of complete secrecy. There's a reason the man has never been charged with a crime. And never will be."

Ben cracked another peanut shell. Point taken. There was no future in pressuring Ivo Jenkins. "So where does this leave us, Mike?"

"Elliot Rosewater killed Sarah Ridell. Someone killed Rosewater. Ivo Jenkins was a bystander—the man took a few pictures. And you should think about that job with me."

"Can I have a talk with her?"

"With who?" The commissioner's voice sounded exasperated that this wasn't over.

"Reggae girl. The one Ivo Jenkins is protecting. I'd like to know what she has to say for herself."

"What would be the point, Ben?"

"The point?" Ben shrugged his shoulders. "The point would be that I did my job. Took it to the end. After that, it's out of my control."

"I don't know why they would agree to that, Ben."

"I don't know why either, Mike. Just ask for me. Then it's over, either way."

44

Professor Greene crooked his neck to hold the phone receiver between his shoulder and ear. On a yellow pad, he scribbled a few notes longhand in a thin twisted script lacking in any grace.

On the other end of the line, a gentleman art dealer named Olivier Rocard spoke precisely, confirming his interest in meeting with the professor or his representatives in Paris.

The professor finished with Rocard, started to place a second call, and hesitated a long time, a silent calculator in his mind running in the background. He didn't owe Isaiah Hawkins anything. Hell, Isaiah had said he was going to give the Room to the Russians anyway. But what did he know of Victor Prokhanov? Only that Prokhanov was Russian, and that he wanted the Room too, and not as a gift. There was no obvious choice between them and, more than that, no obvious reason to choose yet. The object was simple: for Alexander Greene to recover the Room, and he would take anyone's help in doing so.

Greene placed a second call, routed to the desk of Victor Prokhanov in Moscow.

Prokhanov answered on the third ring and listened intently while Professor Alexander Greene, speaking in a professional voice with just the right twinge of excitement, relayed the information.

"The Amber Room then, Professor, it is in Paris?"

"Shokovitch has two hundred thousand dollars of your promised dollars relying on it."

There was a pause of perfect length on the other end of the line.

"That's a job well done, Professor." A quick note of joviality slipped into Victor Prokhanov's ordinarily careful voice. "I shall be packing my bags for Paris. We shall celebrate, Professor. Yes we shall."

In Moscow, Victor Prokhanov felt a drop of rain bounce off his shoulder as he hung up the phone. He ignored it. Paris—

that was a stroke of luck. His five years as attaché to the embassy in Paris had been exceptionally fruitful. The French were a most easily seducible people, and rather proud of it.

He looked at the old map on his wall, his eyes drifting across Europe from Paris to the remnants of the old Russian empire. He supposed all former empires dreamed of being restored. No different than old men dreaming of being young again. Now in Moscow, there were men from the past, lead by General Mikhailov, who sought to recapture past glory and piece the empire back together. To Victor Prokhanov, that idea was right enough in its goals—a strong Russia that was respected in the world. But the execution of the idea was pointless. Restoring the empire wouldn't solve Russia's problems, it wouldn't stop the corruption, and it wouldn't help the economy. It would neither make Russia strong nor respected.

Another drop of rain landed on his desk, and he blotted it with a piece of paper. Alexander Greene had told him of Isaiah Hawkin's reasons for wanting the Amber Room—his goal of influencing the general's election as president. But that was Isaiah's goal, not Victor Prokhanov's. His goals both simpler and more complex, to fulfill a dream, to best Isaiah Hawkins, and to protect a national myth.

•　　　•　　　•

In New York, Professor Greene was not yet done making calls. He dialed for a third time, reaching Isaiah Hawkins' private phone number.

"I'm a little concerned, Isaiah," the professor said quickly, as soon as Isaiah answered, rushing the sounds together.

"Why is that, Alexander?"

Alexander Greene could sense and nearly smell Isaiah smoking through the phone lines, and he wished now that he smoked. Just to put them on more equal footing. He took a long breath instead.

"I thought Kathryn Blaire was a bit rough with the way she handled Mikhail Shokovitch. In fact, it wouldn't have surprised me if she had tried knocking him around. I'd like to know where we are with this and—"

"Alexander, I usually think it's best not to discuss this type of thing over the phone," Isaiah cut in, almost lecturing.

"This isn't the Cold War, Isaiah. Your own people came by and swept my line yesterday. They said I'm clean."

"You're certain?"

"Absolutely. The line's as clean as a 1940s musical."

"I'd still rather discuss it in person, Professor."

"Right, fine," Professor Alexander Greene replied with a shrug. "Whatever you want."

"I'll arrange a meeting at the Museum with Kathryn and Anand. I'll be in touch to tell you when."

"Do you really think its best to invite Kathryn, Isaiah? It's not like she's really been of much value so far, if you don't mind my saying. I warned you about your people at the very beginning of all this."

"I'll be in touch, Professor," Isaiah said, pausing to light another smoke before hanging up the phone.

45

While a television droned in the background, Victor Prokhanov looked out the window of his spacious apartment. He saw the golden arches. Before Yuri Luzhkov was elected mayor of Moscow and opened the city to western money, there was a place called Restaurant No. 8 at that site.

Restaurant No. 8 had no heat in the winter, no light any time of year, a dirty gray linoleum floor, and grayer food. The specialty of the house was a particularly grim chicken dish, if you wanted to call the pale scrawny creature a chicken at all. Next door was a shop called Bread. Next to that, Clothes. Clothes didn't have fine cotton shirts or pretty dresses or even jeans. But if you wanted a dreary pair of gray trousers, Clothes was the place.

Was it any wonder that the people got tired?

McDonalds was clean, the lights worked, the food was hot, and the french fries really were divine. Not to mention the nearby Calvin Klein billboards, with their beautiful Russian women in pretty little things. What Russian woman didn't wish to look beautiful and to feel sexy and to own lovely things?

No, you could not blame the people. You could blame the party. And Victor Prokhanov did.

But tonight, about to be on his way to Paris, he didn't feel like stepping all the way through the blame, a topic that could occupy one's entire life in Moscow. He turned back from the window, just in time to catch the latest television news on the election.

A blonde newscaster with deep blue eyes—how could the old state-run television ever have hoped to compete with her?—read from a teleprompter with a bright red lipstick smile:

In the latest opinion polls, Nikolai Andreyovitch Lysenko, the darling of the Kremlin and the president's handpicked successor, continues to badly trail new-Communist Sergei Mikhailov. In this next clip, Mikhailov campaign spokeswoman Petra Labazanov says that the latest polls are further signs that the communist party will not be denied this election.

Prokhanov smiled. Nikolai Andreyovitch Lysenko, the darling of the Kremlin. That was a wonder of a phrase. Darling and Kremlin not often seen together in the same sentence during the course of Russian history. But then, things were different now and that blonde woman with the deep blue eyes and red lips could say just about anything she wanted so long as the people kept watching.

The news ended with a video montage—of well-dressed politicians and businessmen cavorting at a Black Sea economic conference. The inevitable long legged escorts in short black dresses at their sides. A good life, if it was for you.

Victor Prokhanov shut off the television and picked up the phone. His call was answered on the first ring.

"Phillipe," Prokhanov said. "The arrangements—I expect they've been taken care of?"

"Yes, Victor. Our mutual friend is awaiting instructions."

"Thank you, Phillipe."

Prokhanov hung up and smiled again. Our mutual friend. It was like dialogue from a Russian mob deal. The type of conversation where one moron named Yuri says to another, "Are the shoes in yet? You know, the shoes." Ten minutes of grunting dialogue about the shoes would follow—where they were going to be, when they could be picked up, how much the shoes would cost, whether the seller could be trusted or was a Chechnyan son of a bitch—and they were never ever talking about shoes.

He checked his watch. He had almost an hour before he had to leave for the airport, and he finished his packing rather methodically: two blue suits, the jackets turned inside out before folding. Three white dress shirts. Four ties. Black socks. White boxer shorts, several pairs. A set of brass collar stays. Cufflinks. Cologne. An extra pair of black leather shoes, captoe. A newspaper to read while waiting in the airport. A handgun in a diplomatic pouch.

179

To that he added his tickets on Air France, diplomatic passport, a map of Paris, and paper money in three different currencies. He placed these last items in his briefcase, which already held an English-language paperback copy of John Le Carré's great and under-appreciated spy novel, *Smiley's People*. Le Carré had gotten it right in that book. Not all the technical details, of course, but those were tedious anyway.

To all this, Victor Prokhanov needed only one more item, which was kept on a shelf with his work papers, mixed in casually amongst a lifetime's collected busywork. It was a thick transcript, photocopied onto 8½ x 11 sheets and held together with rubber bands like a manuscript.

The paper was faded and so were the rubber bands; the pages having come to him some years back in this very form, from his man in Washington.

The typeface was twelve point courier, the type of choice worldwide for interrogation transcripts. In the upper right hand corner of each page, in capital letters, the name SHOKOVITCH. Mikhail Shokovitch, the interrogee. The other name typed on the pages, HAWKINS.

It was well known in Moscow that Isaiah Hawkins liked to personally interrogate defectors—to weed out the Soviet plants from the true traitors. Isaiah Hawkins had an almost mystical gift for it, a gift some attributed to his years running Agency operations from a church in Africa, and reportedly listening in the dark while the priest took confession.

No matter. Mikhail Shokovitch was real. And Isaiah Hawkins knew it. In return for a new home, Shokovitch supplied the Agency with names of Soviet agents in the West, and of men in Moscow who might be susceptible to western currency. All because Shokovitch had lost faith in the party.

It was not until five years after Shokovitch's defection that Prokhanov's man delivered this transcript. For those five years, Soviet intelligence believed that Shokovitch was dead, killed in a phony Amtrak accident arranged by Isaiah Hawkins, a story which Shokovitch apparently took delight in recounting to this day. Or at least so said Professor Greene.

A win for Isaiah Hawkins.

Prokhanov now turned to the page where Shokovitch discussed the Amber Room. He mentioned a sale of the Room and he mentioned the letters, but he didn't mention a mirror or Olivier Rocard. And Isaiah Hawkins had not pressed. Even Isaiah Hawkins, it seemed, sometimes made mistakes.

46

Bianca delle Bande Nere leaned back in a rich leather chair and looked over at her brother, who was standing near their library's fireplace.

They had the same olive hands, the same lean body, the same dark cast of skin. Except, where Bianca was hard, her brother was gentle. His voice soft, hers less so, his eyes possessing a kindness, and his smile a warmth that hers would never have.

"You were right, Paolo, the circle will not be so easy to close. We've heard from our friend Shokovitch in New York. The Americans—your friend Kathryn Blaire and her friends—are still coming. And they have been joined in the chase."

"Shokovitch had been paid for the mirror and his information, but he is no friend."

"Only of himself," Bianca said. "And what of Miss Blaire?"

Paolo leaned over the mantle of the fireplace, where he had laid the Hanged Man pendant upon his return. He picked it up and held it in his hands, feeling not the cold iron of the pendant, but the warm flesh of Kathryn Blaire. "She may be coming. But she's not here yet, and Shokovitch was of no help to her."

"So we wait and see if she comes closer? Or if she loses the trail?"

"God favors the patient, Bianca. Or so I've heard it said."

Bianca leaned back in her chair and smiled. The God of the delle Bande Nere favored the aggressor. But she would wait for now.

47

The cop, Russo, had asked for a meeting with Kathryn Blaire. It was nervy of him, and Isaiah Hawkins didn't mind giving nervy people a shot. The business he was in, people like that were an asset. But a meeting alone with Kathryn Blaire probably wasn't a good idea for anyone.

So they met in Isaiah's library—Ben Russo and Kathryn Blaire and Isaiah Hawkins—the essence of cigarette smoke, bourbon, old books on Renaissance symbols, and Billie Holiday still lingering in the air.

Ivo Jenkins was also invited, and he was the last to arrive, the conversation already in progress.

"...they were watching Sarah Ridell for me. When they took the pictures, that is," Isaiah finished saying.

"So Irish Mike said," Ben replied. If he was nervous, he didn't show it.

Isaiah motioned for Ivo to sit in a high-backed ebony chair. "Of course, Mister Jenkins was working on his own time when he took the pictures of the commissioner. I hear the girl was quite beautiful."

"More festive than beautiful, I'd say. You should have seen her in person," Ivo offered with a grin.

"That's a nice business you're in, Mister Jenkins," Ben interrupted deadpan.

Ivo looked over at Kathryn. He might have said more about the rainy day girl and Mike O'Malley, but not with a woman present. Just because he was blackmailer didn't mean proper decorum had no place. So he let it go.

Isaiah exhaled a thin stream of gray smoke, the smoke cutting right between the two men. "The point, Detective Russo, is that Mister Jenkins is capable of handling himself. That said, I repeat he was working for me when Sarah Ridell was killed. And so was Kathryn."

Ben nodded his head and looked at Kathryn. He hadn't been given her last name. Not that it mattered. Whatever. Reggae girl worked just as well. She hadn't said a word yet anyway. But that had to be a cue from Isaiah that the time had come to ask her questions. So Ben decided to push it.

"I understand, Kathryn, that you're an aficionado of reggae music?"

"Yes, Detective," Kathryn rasped. Isaiah had told her to answer the cop's questions. Apparently Isaiah had something in mind for Ben Russo, depending on how he handled himself. And since Isaiah Hawkins owned her, she had no choice but to go along. "Peter Tosh in particular, Detective. But I believe you know that."

Isaiah Hawkins smiled. It was a nice detail from the cop. Carelessness got punished in the crime business, attention to detail rewarded. Kathryn had been careless. Leaving her finger prints where Ben Russo could find them. But that was Kathryn. So was dropping some reference to this Tosh guy. The Type T in her apparently outweighing the good this round.

"Did you know, Kathryn," Ben continued, "that Elliot Rosewater, prick that he was, had two children—five and eleven?"

"I didn't kill him."

"Really?"

"Accidents happen in our business, Detective. A man gets hurt in a fight, dies. It happens. But I had no motive to kill Rosewater. And that's not what happened here. I was there and I knocked him around, but I didn't kill him."

Ben moved to the edge of his chair. At least she was not denying the undeniable. Reggae girl was there in Rosewater's office. She smacked Rosewater around. Just didn't shoot him up with curare. Had no reason to.

"My personal experience," Ben said softly, "is sometimes you don't much need good reason to kill someone. Half the sons of bitches I've put away couldn't have told Jesus himself why they'd done it, not if it was the ticket to heaven."

"None of those guys worked for Isaiah Hawkins," Kathryn answered plainly.

"OK. Then walk me through this. For some reason you're watching the girl, Sarah Ridell. Right?" Ben asked, now spinning the working theory out loud. The theory they were all selling to him.

"Right," Kathryn said.

"Sarah Ridell hooks up with Elliot Rosewater. Ivo Jenkins here takes pictures. Sarah gets killed. You, Kathryn, go after Rosewater. Break into his office. Maybe you know what you're looking for. Maybe you don't. Rosewater walks in, unexpected. Maybe you have got the safe open by this point, maybe you don't. Either way, a fight starts and you win big, knocking him out. Then you take what's in the safe and leave. Someone comes in later, finds Rosewater, and finishes him off with the curare. Presumably, someone planning on killing him from the start. Or maybe someone just taking advantage of an opportunity—although they were prepared, having the curare and all."

"Yes, Detective," Kathryn said.

"That story works. I won't deny that," Ben said. "It has a neat logic. But so does murdering Elliot Rosewater in a way that makes it look like an accident. It isn't like one version of the story is inherently more believable than the other. It could go either way, you see that, don't you Kathryn?"

"No, I don't," Isaiah interrupted. "And neither should you."

Ivo smiled. "I think the commissioner would agree."

Ben nodded and slowly stood to leave. "You've got the cards, Mister Hawkins and Mister Jenkins. Even without playing Irish Mike, although that was a nice touch. In a fairy tale I would take you on, overcome my obstacles, and triumph. But this isn't a fairy tale. All I wanted was the truth. But I guess I don't have a right to that either."

"Hold off, Detective," Kathryn said. She didn't need Isaiah or Ivo or Irish Mike protecting her. She was innocent this time and she wanted this cop to know it, even if it didn't matter. It mattered to her. "Your theory has a flaw in it, Detective. We both admit that I was there and I fought with Rosewater. But if I killed him and wanted to make his death look like an accident, why would I have kicked him in the balls?"

"Excuse me?" Ben asked.

"I kneed him in the balls, Detective. Not very nice. But highly effective. I'm sure it left a nasty bruise. If I was then going to kill him by shooting him in the penis with curare, why would I call attention to the area, making it more likely that the curare would be discovered by your coroner, Dr. Klein?"

"I don't know," Russo said.

"Because I wouldn't," Kathryn answered. "Whoever used the curare on Rosewater didn't know about the other injury."

Ben looked at her puzzled. The I-kneed-him-in-the-balls-therefore-I-am-innocent defense. It had a certain logic as well as the sick ring of truth to it. She probably hadn't killed him. Only an innocent person would come up with that defense. But to hear that couldn't possibly be why Isaiah Hawkins had agreed to let him meet with Kathryn Blaire.

Ben turned to Isaiah. "Why did you set up this meeting anyway, Mister Hawkins?"

"Glad you asked, Detective. Two reasons. First, I believe the person who did kill Elliot Rosewater has something I'm looking for. My people are limited in the way they must operate. Sometimes it is hard for them to knock on the front door. I was hoping you might be of service to us going forward."

"And the second thing?"

"My people tell me you're an expert on Renaissance symbols, Detective Russo."

"How do you know that?"

"You probably don't wish to know."

Ben didn't say anything. No doubt Isaiah Hawkins had already reviewed all his public records and most of his private ones too. It was nothing to get bent about right now. Isaiah Hawkins had been through his entire life looking for anything of potential value. Symbols happened to be it. If it hadn't been symbols, it might have been something else. There was nothing personal or coincidental about it. It was simply the way Isaiah Hawkins maximized other people's usefulness.

"In any event, detective, I thought you might be able to help us understand a symbol that's giving us some trouble."

"And what is that?" Ben asked.

"The Hanged Man. Elliot Rosewater had a pendant with the Hanged Man on it. My original thought was that it wasn't much to die for."

"Really?" Ben replied, a strange knowing glint in his dark eyes. "My guess would be different. I'd say it's plenty to die for, actually."

Ben took a brief look at the open books out on the table. Books on the tarot and signs and symbols. Isaiah Hawkins was likely to get there anyway, to make the connections…Hell, Ben realized, Isaiah Hawkins might already have made the connections and know the answer. Or maybe he was just giving a cop from Brooklyn a chance to become part of the team. There was no harm in giving the man the answer.

"The Pazzi conspiracy," Ben said. "Took place in the late 1400s, I believe. Pope Sixtus IV conspired with the Pazzi family to kill Lorenzo de'Medici in church during Mass and install the Pazzi as the rulers of Florence. The plot failed. Lorenzo survived the attack, although his brother was stabbed and bled to death in a church pew. The conspirators were all caught, tortured in the best medieval fashion, and executed as traitors to Florence, except for one who escaped. His portrait was painted by Botticelli on the walls of the Bargello in Florence: painted hanging upside down by one leg. That's why Elliot Rosewater was killed, Mister Hawkins. Someone believed he was a traitor."

Isaiah picked up one of the books and began to skim greedily through the index like he was searching for Pazzi. "I suppose I should thank you."

"Personally, Mister Hawkins, I'd look in Italy for…for whatever or whomever you're looking for. Florence to be precise."

"Do you have a passport, detective?"

"Yes I do, Mister Hawkins," Ben said. "Yes I do."

48

After Kathryn Blaire, Ivo Jenkins, and Ben Russo had all left, Isaiah remained in his library, waiting for Alexander Greene to arrive for his scheduled meeting. The professor had wanted to meet alone, and Isaiah had decided to honor that request as well.

While waiting, he listened to a tape of his favorite Schubert symphony and thought about a gentleman named Frederick Lugard, who had been the British governor in Nigeria around the turn of the century.

He thought of Lugard often, not just because the high-backed ebony chairs in his library had once belonged to Lugard. But because, for Isaiah Hawkins, Frederick Lugard had long ago put a personal face on the fallacy of good intentions.

The accounts of Frederick Lugard's contemporaries left no doubt that Lugard first came to Africa from England because he was personally committed to halting the slave trade, which was still shockingly vigorous.

The same accounts also left no doubt of what had transpired. In 1906, Governor Lugard ordered two thousand weaponless Satiru peasants annihilated in retaliation for the killings of a white officer and seventy black infantry. It was said that the local Nigerian political leaders, and in particular the Sultan of Sokoto, supported the punitive expedition. Indeed, the evidence was convincing that the Sultan himself had demanded it as retribution against a low class upstart. Nevertheless, Frederick Lugard, as the British Governor, could have resisted the pressure. Instead, he issued his order, specifically using the word *annihilated*.

It really mattered not at all, whether it was Frederick Lugard or the Sultan of Sokoto who subsequently issued a directive to the troops that the heads of the two thousand dead Satiru be hacked off and stuck on spikes. Setting out with the best of intentions, Frederick Lugard had ended up with an unexplainable massacre of innocents as his legacy.

Just more than a half century later, Lugard's chairs and his twisted history had become a gift to Isaiah Hawkins from General Jimmy.

"It's about appreciating the tragedy; after all, the man had come to do good," the general had said, while his men backed up a truck to collect a load of firearms that were hidden at the bottom of a crate of Bibles.

General Jimmy, one of the good guys, and one of Isaiah Hawkins' prime tutors on human nature. No doubt the person who killed Elliot Rosewater had started out with good intentions. It was just so easy for intentions to get crossed along the way.

Isaiah checked his watch. The professor should be arriving presently. Isaiah shut off the symphony and placed a new tape into the cassette deck. He held off on pressing PLAY.

Moments later, Professor Greene arrived. He took note of Kathryn's absence.

"Thank you for meeting me in private, Isaiah." The professor sat in one of Lugard's chairs. "I really think Kathryn Blaire is not in control of herself. She was rather emotional when we met with Shokovitch, and I believe that cost us information. I appreciate your consideration on this point."

"So how can I help you, Professor?"

"I need to know everything that's going on, Isaiah. I want it to go through me. I'm not sure I trust your people right now."

"Interesting."

"Interesting?" Greene repeated with a look bordering on dismay.

"Trust, it is a fascinating topic, is it not, Professor?" Isaiah did not expect an answer. He lit a cigarette, taking it in slow time. "For example, Alexander, do you really think that a man like Shokovitch would confide in a man like yourself?"

Alexander Greene sat up stiffly. "I don't understand that question."

"You're not a professional, Professor. Mikhail Shokovitch is. Kathryn Blaire is."

"So what's your point, Isaiah?"

"Amateurs are dangerous, Professor. They make amateur mistakes. Shokovitch would be slipping if he confided in you."

"Exactly what are you saying, Isaiah? That we would be better off with Kathryn instead of me?"

"Perhaps."

Isaiah walked back over to the tape player and slowly depressed PLAY. Professor Alexander Greene heard Isaiah's voice, then his own, be played back through the speakers:

"Alexander, I usually think it's best not to discuss this type of thing over the phone."

"This isn't the cold war, Isaiah. Your own people came by and swept my line yesterday. They said I'm clean."

"You're certain?"

"Absolutely. The line's as clean as a 1940s musical."

Isaiah sat back down and spoke in a kindly tone.

"An amateur mistake, Professor. Letting my people sweep your phone line. Now, would you please tell me about your conversations with Mikhail Shokovitch and Victor Prokhanov. And, Professor, please don't leave anything out. I'd like to help you out here, if I still can."

PART FOUR

I have conquered them all, but I
am standing amongst graves.
—Isak Dinesen, quoting an unnamed
source in Out of Africa

49

Dressed in an old school tie of yellow and navy stripes knotted neatly against a starched white collar, Victor Prokhanov strolled west along the Parisian shopping avenue, the Boulevard St. Germain.

Phillipe, his man in Paris, strolled at his side. Phillipe was pudgy and looked like a baker. Pudginess being quite tolerable in a man who held a high-level position within the French Ministry of Cultural Affairs and who also had a twenty-year relationship with the KGB.

They turned left at the Rue du Bac. As they passed a chic Parisian boutique, Victor Prokhanov peered through the store's glass window. Inside was a tall, young woman in expensive black pants and a tight T-shirt who was considering a long and soft gray skirt. She was perfectly groomed and undeniably pretty, beautiful in fact—thin, but with enough substance for the eye to hold.

"She's lovely, don't you think," Phillipe said. "Reason enough to love Paris."

"Yes, she should be on a billboard," Prokhanov replied, thinking of Calvin Klein. "We have many billboards like that in Moscow now."

Prokhanov was certain that had you asked the boutique's owner to describe his ideal customer—it would have been this woman. He was equally certain the same answer would have held in Moscow. A young, rich, thin woman with money to spend. That is what the victory of the capitalists had come down to, was it not? The triumph of beauty and wealth. All throughout Moscow, businesses and restaurants and clubs had opened to cater to this ideal woman. To sell her the modern world.

Prokhanov tapped his index finger against his temple and smiled, as if gently rebuking himself for being a man past his time. There were others in Moscow who were smarter than he—they had seen this future and embraced it for themselves.

A piece of all those smart shops was owned by the government officials who had granted the licenses. Like his friends who distributed Marlboros. All those officials now floating high on a cushion of wealth and beauty, living in vast new homes that had sprung up as if from air. Air castles.

Of course, air castles were inherently unstable. The Russian nobility—whether the hereditary boyars of Peter the Great, or the Communist party cronies of Brezhnev, or these new princes of air—had always existed at the sufferance of the Russian tsar. Prokhanov smiled. They didn't use the word "tsar" anymore, it was an archaic usage. The tsar was now called the president to please the West, although it fooled no one at home.

With the current president old and no longer capable of maintaining even the appearance of command, a prerequisite of being tsar, all the air princes were desperately shoveling rubles into the fading presidential campaign of his hand-picked vice president and successor. Who could blame them? Air castles were a lovely thing, and who wouldn't want to keep them? But the old Communist party was winning, Isaiah Hawkins couldn't stop that, and the air princes would soon be proclaiming their devotion to the party once again. It would be a beautiful spectacle, Victor Prokhanov thought, watching the air princes grovel, almost regardless of what one thought of General Mikhailov and his dangerous illusions of glory.

Prokhanov and Phillipe continued down the Rue du Bac.

"Your meeting with Olivier Rocard is set for tomorrow, at the Musée Rodin, at the fountain." Phillipe said. "It is arranged for you to arrive first, with Rocard joining you at 10:00 A.M."

"Excellent," Victor Prokhanov said. He had no doubt that Olivier Rocard, art dealer, long-time fellow traveler of the effete European communist elite, and the man who had dealt the mirror from the Amber Room to Shokovitch, would be a man proud to turn a good deed for Moscow.

50

Isaiah Hawkins sat completely still, an unlit cigarette in his hand, a faint mechanical hum from the jet's engines in the background. Ivo Jenkins sat in a seat across the aisle, on the way to his future with the Agency. He would be one of Isaiah's people from now on. But Isaiah was on his way to the past.

Isaiah's role was behind the scenes now, his place conducting the symphony from behind his desk. Once it had been so different:

Be on the ground in a city, cross with a man or woman who believes in a cause, or is betraying a cause. Or perhaps who believes only in their own destiny, or wants only to destroy the destiny of someone they despise. Enable that dream, if you can, but only so long as it fits with the Agency's interest. Otherwise, sorry, got to play it the other way. Don't care if you understand.

Isaiah had not been on the ground in so long, using people like Kathryn Blaire and Anand Ashland as his proxies. But Victor Prokhanov had made a decision to be on the ground in Paris personally, and Isaiah needed to meet him there.

Isaiah Hawkins pulled out an old silver lighter from his pocket and carefully lit the cigarette. Like an aging juggler who only realizes during a performance that his timing may have finally slipped, Isaiah worried he had been caught with too many flaming torches in the air. The audience doesn't know, but the old juggler does. And if he succeeds in keeping all the torches aloft that night, he vows to retire in the morning.

The Amber Room, one torch, soaring away toward the sky; Professor Greene another, in his grasp; Kathryn Blaire and Ben Russo swinging off to chase down another lead in a different city; the green and red pins on his map twisting at apogee; and Paris a dot barely in focus.

He hadn't been to Paris in years. Had not been anywhere on the ground. The ground being the one place he loved most in this world.

51

Victor Prokhanov slid thirty francs in coins beneath a bullet-proof glass partition in return for a paper ticket and two francs change. He walked toward a heavy stone archway, handed the ticket to a casually disinterested man in a blue uniform, and entered the gardens of the Musée Rodin.

He would meet the French art dealer, Olivier Rocard, at the Musée the following morning at a fountain in the back of the gardens. They would discuss Rocard's dealings with Shokovitch, and Rocard's knowledge of the Amber Room, which figured to be most substantial. Perhaps a business transaction would be arranged where Rocard was compensated for his information, perhaps that would not be necessary. They would see in the morning.

For now, Victor Prokhanov told himself he had needed to come to the gardens in advance, to check out the meeting site, and that was true enough. But it wasn't the real reason he had come.

Some seventy-five yards straight ahead down a stone path stood the splendid, faded, yellow mansion where the sculptor had taken rooms in the last decade of his life. The home was now filled with Rodin's work, small pieces and drawings and studies.

Prokhanov had come here often when he was posted to the embassy in Paris (not many years after Mikhail Shokovitch had the same post), and the house was a wonder, but he didn't think it compared to the gardens. It was the sculpture gardens that gave the Musée Rodin a special peace.

A sandy gravel path led Prokhanov to the left, to a set of enormous bronze doors: *The Gates of Hell*, with sculpted grappling characters from *The Divine Comedy*—Dante's fourteenth-century literary illusions brought to physical life by a nineteenth-century French genius.

A small scale version of *The Thinker* was stationed in the center of the gate, just above the doors. *The Thinker*, representing Dante himself, was conceived by Rodin as an homage from the artist to the poet. It was an image that would survive as long as man. Not quite the same fate as that of the huge stone heads of Lenin and Stalin which had been so gleefully toppled by the mobs.

From *The Gates of Hell*, the garden opened into an expansive lawn, landscaped with powerful sculptures. Prokhanov strolled easily amongst them. There were *The Burghers of Calais*, six bronze men shuffling to their destiny. In return for a promise from the King of England that he would end a year-long siege of Calais and spare the city, these six men offered the king their lives and the key to the city. It was an action suitable for heroic treatment. But in Rodin's hands, the burghers were not triumphant. Rather, they were barefoot, downtrodden men, wearing sackcloths, struggling to be brave.

It was a sublime work, one that Victor Prokhanov knew could never have been created in the Russia of his party. The party had failed to unearth—if unearth was the right word— an atmosphere where a sculptor of genius could emerge. Rather, the hideous and lifeless busts of Lenin and Stalin that had poured out of factories by the tens of thousands were a physical manifestation of the loss of the soul that had permeated the party as it had sunk into decay and corruption.

The loss of that soul was a uniquely Russian tragedy, one that had begun with Vladimir Ilyich Lenin's death and had continued, with minor interruptions, until the party was only words and meaningless symbols. Perhaps Vladimir Ilyich would have understood the Burghers—and hated their weakness. But Joseph Stalin and Leonid Brezhnev would not have understood at all. And that made all the difference. Or so Victor Prokhanov wanted to believe.

He turned away, to walk toward the very rear of the gardens, toward the fountain some two hundred yards in the distance where he would meet Rocard the next morning.

Yes, he'd come to the gardens to prepare for his meeting with Rocard. To make sure the meeting went well, and that Rocard gave him the information that would lead to the Amber Room.

That was why he had ostensibly come to Paris, to have the glory of recovering the Amber Room and to earn a triumph over Isaiah Hawkins. He knew those were perfectly good reasons to be on the ground in Paris. But there was one more. The letters Mikhail Shokovitch had mentioned in his interrogation and the myth they protected:

```
Q: What was sold, the Amber Room?
A: Yes, that and some papers of historical
   interest.
Q: Tell me about the papers, Comrade
   Shokovitch.
A: I'm not a comrade.
Q: The papers, Mikhail.
A: Letters, Mister Hawkins. From Lenin and
   others. That's all I know.
```

But that wasn't all Mikhail Shokovitch knew. The Lenin letters that Shokovitch was talking about were as fabled in their own way as the Amber Room. They were letters that went to the very heart of the Communist party myth. Not that Victor Prokhanov gave a damn about the party myth. He'd seen too much to believe in that myth or any other.

But his job wasn't about belief any longer. You didn't allow yourself to have any doubts. The decisions all made so long ago. The Communist party was on the cusp of reclaiming its place as tsar. And a man of his age, of his chosen profession, backed the tsar, played the game out to the end, and hoped God judged you with understanding. It was all one could do. So he'd come to Paris to find those letters and to delete them from history.

But this afternoon, he'd simply come to the gardens to spend some time alone with Rodin and Dante and the Burghers. Perhaps, while looking at the Burghers through Lenin's eyes, he hadn't much liked what he'd seen—the disdain Lenin would have felt for their sacrifice. But it was too late for doubts, and so he kept walking.

52

Kathryn Blaire counted out fifty thousand lira in paper money and handed the bills, watercolor pink, blue, and green, to the bellboy of the Excelsior Hotel.

Her room at Florence's finest hotel was both delightfully charming and truly spacious. It was, according to the hotel's Milanese manager, the best room the Excelsior had to offer—an accommodation secured by a large tip and her best smile. She had no doubt that Anand Ashland's and Ben Russo's suites would also be lovely, but as she visually absorbed her surroundings, she could not believe their charms would be a match for hers.

A quartet of twelve-foot-tall French doors lined one side of her suite and she pulled them open to step out onto the balcony. There, underneath a gray morning sky, she looked over Florence and the Arno river, which flowed slowly alongside the hotel.

She felt momentarily at peace, standing there, and she hesitated to leave the safety of the balcony, nervous she was about to do something that would cause that feeling to end. It was, after all, only an illusion. She had come to find the Amber Room, not inner peace. And she planned on starting at the monastery of Sant' Antimo.

The cloister was an hour and a half's drive south from Florence, the main road taking Kathryn past the city of Siena until she neared the walled, mountaintop village of Montalcino. At an abandoned olive oil press, she turned left and veered onto a one-lane road, traveled only by those going to the local vineyards. A wooden sign with a hand-drawn blue arrow pointed off to the Fattoria Barbi, and another, with its letters stenciled in black, led toward the Agricola Greppo. Kathryn drove past the small turnouts, the smell of dark red wine filling her senses.

At the end of the paved road, she turned right onto a dirt path that wandered alongside a row of grapevines. Some two hundred yards away, out in a small clearing, stood the apparent remains of an ancient, half-ruined church. She parked the car some fifty feet from the church and walked the rest of the way, a small mist of red dust hovering around her shins.

The church was built of huge blocks of rough, yellowing stone, rising to a small tower in the north corner, and holding a graceful curved apse to the east. It held power and beauty, and Kathryn walked its full circumference before approaching the front gates.

She only vaguely knew the legend of this place: that the great warrior Charlemagne had founded a monastery upon the site in the ninth century and that, some hundreds of years later, this later incarnation had been built upon the foundation of Charlemagne's work. To Kathryn, it seemed like little had changed since then, and carefully she stepped up a worn pair of steps, through a half-open wooden door, and into the twilight of the twelfth century.

The church was deserted, but not abandoned. It was illuminated by rays of sun which swept in through a rounded window above the apse. The pews, of which there were six long wooden rows, were in perfect repair, the smooth stone floor recently swept. A deep blue satin cloth, marked with a golden insignia, draped down from the alter. Near the alter, a single sheet, of what appeared to be music, rested on an iron stand.

Kathryn spent a few long moments wandering through the church, admiring the men who had built it so long ago. Then she looked down at her watch. It was ten minutes to noon, just a little early. In the far left corner of the pew that was furthest from the alter, she sat down to wait. An elderly caretaker came in and swept the already shining stone floor for a few minutes. Then he too sat down in a pew.

At noon, a door near the alter swung open and eight men, each dressed in a gray robe with a hood pulled up around his head, filed silently into the church. If the hooded figures sensed Kathryn's presence, they made no sign of it. They took their places on two small benches to the right of the alter and bowed their heads. Another man, dressed like the others, entered last and took his place at the iron stand. There was a long silent pause. Then they began to chant.

The sound of their voices filled the entire church, soaring off the stone walls and the cold floor to the reaches of the vaulted ceiling and beyond. The chants rose from that stone temple all the way to heaven, as they had risen each day at noon for the past thousand years. The last nine monks of Sant' Antimo fulfilling their duty to their God.

Kathryn listened in rapture. She lost herself in their voices as a feeling of tremendous joy swept her body, only to be followed by an aching sadness. She knew then the spiritual loss in her own life. It was the experience of all moderns who had visited Sant' Antimo for hundreds of years. And Kathryn could not have been expected to be any different. No matter the reasons she had come to that monastery on that summer day, she felt the touch of God. And that was sensed by the monks and all their brothers who had come before them.

Then the chants had ended, and the monks had stood to leave. And Kathryn sat there still, lost in a different age. It was not until the door near the alter had swung open once again, and the first monk had begun to file out, that the spell was broken.

Kathryn forced her thoughts back to the reasons why she had made this journey, and the words rushed out of her throat and she called across the church, "Brother Michael...wait..."

There was now no sound at all in that church.

The gray robed figure in the lead of the monks' procession paused. He had already taken a step through the doorway and he shuffled his feet slowly to face her. He had a short beard and piercing blue eyes. And in those eyes was recognition.

The monk sat next to Kathryn on the pew in the far corner of the church. It was the first time in many months that he had been this close to a woman. He waited for her to speak.

"I'm sorry, Michael."

"Please, don't apologize," the monk replied, lowering his hood so that his features were visible. A long scar ran down the side of his neck, from where the surgeons had removed the cancer. "I suppose I always knew that Isaiah would find me. Has he always known?"

She rolled her shoulders forward gently, less a shrug of ignorance than an admission of her own unimportance. With Isaiah, one never was told more than they needed. Go speak to Michael, Isaiah had said. Didn't matter what Michael had chosen to become, or that he had been her friend. Or Isaiah's.

"I'm sorry that it had to be me, Michael. I've only come for information."

"Yes, of course. Information is all I have, Kathryn."

The monk looked around the church, which he'd come to love so much. Here, no one cared about the secrets stored in his mind, the privileged knowledge of men and their acts that was his curse. This sanctuary had been indifferent to the affairs of the world for a millennium. It was the only place where he could ever be free. And now…

He closed his eyes and carefully considered his own interest for the first time in more than half a decade. He could stand and leave, and thereby send a message of one sort to his old associate, Isaiah Hawkins. Or he could answer, and send another. But really, it no longer mattered. He had been found and Isaiah would, once again, forever own a part of him. He opened his eyes.

"What is it you wish to know, Kathryn?"

She handed him a slip of paper, the drawing of a shield with six red balls she had seen on Elliot Rosewater's calendar, and that Anand had traced to Florentine royalty now extinct.

The monk looked at the paper, seemingly disarmed by the simplicity of the apparent question. "The Medici crest? You can see this on buildings all over this part of Italy. Sometimes with six balls, sometimes seven, depending on which member of the family paid for the construction." He paused and almost smiled. "Really, you've come to me for a history lesson?"

She shook her head. She had read the history books on the plane, learning how Giovanni di Bicci de'Medici had created the wealthiest bank in Italy in the late 1300s, employing savvy and divine intervention—a monopoly on handling the pope's finances. She'd read about Giovanni's son, Cosimo, the greatest of the Medici, and the manner in which he came to rule Florence. And she'd read how Anna Maria, the last of the Medici, had donated the family's art to the city of Florence upon her death in 1743. That information was not why she'd come to Sant' Antimo, as the monk well knew.

"We discovered the crest in New York," she explained. "Among a dead man's possessions. Marked in his calendar for last week." She hesitated.

Again, the monk almost smiled. Isaiah had not reached out to him about the past, but for information he might have learned since joining the monastery. How typical of Isaiah: to let the agent he had once been continue his slumber, while taking advantage of the Italian monk he had become. The monk lowered his voice to a bare whisper. "There are rumors, stories I have heard. About a forgotten branch of the Medici, descended from a bastard daughter of Lorenzo the Magnificent. It is said they have a magnificent castle in the Oltrarno, a secret place."

53

Bianca delle Bande Nere waited at the foot of a flight of black marble steps, a cylindrical silver key hanging from a silver chain draped around her neck. She had recent news of developments, matters playing out much as she had anticipated.

Paolo walked down the steps toward her. When he had reached her, Bianca slipped her arm around her brother's waist. Together they walked toward the library.

Bianca quickly explained the situation to her brother. "I just received a call from one of our associates, the old caretaker at Sant' Antimo. An American woman was there. He described her the same way you described Kathryn Blaire. Quite pretty, he said, lovely green eyes."

Paolo ran his hand through his dark black hair, remembering the way Kathryn Blaire had looked when he first saw her at the Sintra Gallery, and then later, when he had undressed her. How she had felt to his touch, how she looked lying in her bed asleep. He heard her voice, just tell me you love me. Left unspoken what a gentleman was supposed to understand: let me pretend, just tell me you love me. It doesn't hurt to pretend, does it?

He saw her open her eyes as he prepared to leave. He knew she was wishing he might be different. So she closed her eyes, and...and he stole the pendant. And he had kept seeing her, lying there, ever since. It did hurt to pretend.

He imagined her at the monastery. What thoughts must have coursed through the minds of the monks? The same one's driving through his. He knew then consciously that he wanted to see her again, to touch her again.

"I suppose," he said, "she was asking questions of Brother Michael?"

Bianca motioned toward the east wall of the library, where there hung a large golden shield with six red balls. "Yes, about us."

Paolo sat on the edge of a dark wooden desk. Behind the

desk was a portrait of a beautiful woman, composed with a fine hand. On the desk, holding down a set of papers, was a gold coin. He stared at the coin, as if looking for meaning. Then he looked across at Bianca and tossed it in the air.

"Heads," Bianca said.

The coin crashed down back into his hand. Paolo flipped it over and handed it to his sister.

"Heads it is," he said gently. "Tell me, what do you propose?"

Bianca held out the coin in her palm, heads up. Revealing an image of a hard man dressed in a simple Florentine robe, a look of reserved strength in his face.

It was the face of a man unafraid of using power, yet who understood that ultimate success lay in directing affairs so that he did not need to be so crude. That philosophy at the very core of Cosimo de'Medici's methods.

There was not a single doubt in Bianca's mind what Cosimo de'Medici would have done now. Kathryn Blaire was a loose feather that had been set free by Elliot Rosewater and Sarah Ridell. It was not acceptable to let the loose feathers continue to drift around. So Cosimo de'Medici would have gathered up the loose feathers. And what better way than by orchestrating the wind to blow the feathers straight back to you.

54

Ivo Jenkins waited patiently at an outdoor table of a cafe for Olivier Rocard to quit work for the evening. A half-eaten pastry—all butter with a little flour and some sugar tossed in—along with a cup of coffee in front of him. Enough money on the table to cover the bill and tip and leave without questions at any time. His Nikon stuffed in an open tourist bag along with maps, guidebooks, a French phrasebook, and an Eiffel Tower sweatshirt, size XXL.

Paris was outside the usual geographic scope of Ivo's business endeavors. There was plenty of business locally, in New York and D.C.—cities where he knew the rhythms, had an edge, and could be home for breakfast, if not dinner. But his skills traveled well. Paris wouldn't turn out much different than New York or the District—cosmopolitan cities were filled with rich and high-powered people doing things they ought not be doing, or didn't want other people to know they were doing. And not being careful enough about where, when, and with whom they did it.

Isaiah Hawkins had put Ivo on the payroll for this trip. Flown with him to Paris in a private plane, put him up in nice hotel, was paying for his meals, and had written a check for twenty-five thousand dollars. Kicked the hell out of his last experience with government employment, back in the service. Plus, Isaiah Hawkins was prepared.

Ivo's assignment was Olivier Rocard. Isaiah had provided a complete dossier on Rocard. He was forty-two, came from a prominent family, had lived in Paris all his life, was married with one child, and, by all accounts, did an excellent job of running House Rocard, the art and antiques dealership that he had inherited from his father.

The Rocard dossier also contained substantial information on art dealings that tilted toward the wrong side of French and international laws. Those dealings were too subtle to be of present interest to Ivo Jenkins.

Unsubstantiated accusations that House Rocard had, on occasion, retained the services of a forger of excellent repute were more interesting, had Ivo the time to develop the plot line. In itself, an art dealer being accused of dealing in forged works was not a very spectacular accusation. You dealt art for a hundred years, you sometimes bought or sold forgeries. People expected that. Hiring a forger was much more interesting, but that would require a sting operation to nail down and would take a couple of weeks—time Ivo didn't have because Isaiah Hawkins needed results within twenty-four hours.

That left Olivier Rocard's personal life as the only option. It was never a certainty, but Ivo's experience was that men with personal habits better kept private tended to make mistakes every single day. It was so easy to slip in a careless phone call, a purchase of flowers or lingerie, or a quick rendezvous for coffee or more. A man had a lover, he kept that lover in mind every day. A man liked hookers, he liked them Monday through Sunday. A man shot dope, he shot dope every day. That's just the way it was.

Ivo checked his watch. It was eight P.M.

He took the final bite of his pastry and stiffened up in the café chair. Olivier Rocard would be wrapping up for the day soon enough. They would see what the night would bring.

55

On the fourth floor of a tired municipal office building located beyond the Florence train station, Kathryn Blaire and Anand Ashland grappled with a book nearly as tall as Kathryn. Each leaf of old faded ivory paper slightly more than five feet tall and almost four feet wide.

The pages unwieldy enough that Kathryn wished Ben Russo was around to help. But he had been left at the hotel on Isaiah's instructions, at least until they had a clearer picture where this lead might take them. Brother Michael had suggested they come here. He said they wouldn't find the Medici by looking in modern Florence. The Medici—if in fact they existed as more than a rumor—would have erased all evidence of themselves from the present. They had to look to the past, Michael said.

The book dated back to the 1700s. It had twenty-five pages, one for the first year of each of the past twenty-five decades, running from front to back in reverse chronological order. Although the answer, if they found it, would be toward the back of the book, Kathryn and Anand started with the first leaf, dated 1990, so that they would have a point of reference.

It detailed, in thin black lines with the occasional handwritten script notation, the buildings, roads, bridges, and plazas of Florence, each marked with a reference number that would lead a searcher to the exact file in which its municipal and legal details were recorded.

Kathryn and Anand lingered over that first page, focusing on a set of long, thin lines outlining the buildings of the immense Pitti Palace, located just south of the Arno River on the eastern edge of the Oltrarno district.

The Pitti Palace, or so said the guide books, had been built by the powerful Pitti family in the 1400s, during the very same years when Cosimo de'Medici ruled the Republic of Florence as a virtual king. The Pittis accumulated vast wealth, but failed to achieve Cosimo's political influence. And great families, like the great nations on Isaiah Hawkins' beloved map, are ephemeral things. Mistakes were made—of marriage, of business, of politics—and the Pitti fell into a fatal decline. A mere hundred years after the Pitti Palace had been built as a monument to the glory of the Pitti, Cosimo de'Medici's descendants bought the place and moved in for themselves.

Come 1990, the palace had long been a museum. But it was still the most imposing structure on the Oltrarno side of the Arno River.

Kathryn finally shook her head. "He was talking about a secret palace. Rumors of a secret palace. This place could not be more open and known."

"Often the best place for a secret," Anand countered.

"Could be. But I don't believe so. Not from the way Michael said it. I think we're looking for something more anonymous, large enough to be a palace, maybe once known to the public, but now somehow hidden. Or something like that."

They turned to the great page for 1980. Then 1970...1960...and so on. Tracing back through the decades, studying the contours of the thin lines, seeking the one deviation that might obscure an underlying meaning, that might hide a gap in space.

They lifted the page for 1760 and turned to the final sheet in the book. It was stiff and cracked and appeared fairly certainly to be the original plan drawn more than two and a half centuries before. A hint of a large tear ran north to south through the sheet, countered by the offsetting hint of an expert restoration job, with the damaged black lines, letters, and numbers tenderly realigned so that they matched up nearly precisely on either side of the scar.

The text was in handwritten Latin. And, despite the passage of some 250 years, the plan was nearly as detailed as the most modern plan they had examined. Florence was, after all, already a mature city by the year 1750.

"So, what have we got?" Kathryn asked.

"Not much."

In fact, nothing. Not one set of lines large enough to hide a palace had vanished since 1750. Indeed most of the lines drawn upon the plans could have been traced in a perfect unchanged vision from 1750 to 1990. There was no secret palace to be found in an erasure from these pages.

It seemed hopeless. But the nature of secrets, which they both knew, was in their favor. Truth is that even the most precious of secrets have a life span. Information born in secrecy rarely stays that way forever. And the reverse is true as well. That the Medici palace was a secret now did not mean it had been when it was built. If they searched back far enough, they would find that palace on a map.

The Florentine clerk who had first helped them was sitting at his small desk, watching. They were his only customers of the day.

Anand spoke to him in an Italian that sounded as fluent as his perfect English. "May we see the book of plans prior to 1750?"

"I'm afraid not."

"Is there no book?"

"Not any more."

"Excuse me, since when?" Anand asked.

"A fire—in 1748—destroyed the building in which these records were housed. The plans for the year 1740 and all prior years were lost. It was the only building burned. A loss by misadventure, the magistrates ruled at the time."

"So all the records were lost?" Kathryn now asked redundantly, in English, holding her hands out wide to indicate the entire lot.

"*Si, mi dispiace,*" the clerk replied with a shrug. This was Italy. Records got lost.

56

Victor Prokhanov repeated his steps in faster motion—thirty francs slid under the glass, the ticket handed to a disinterested bald man in uniform, a first stride in the gardens of the Musée Rodin.

He headed straight toward the rear of the grounds where he was to meet Olivier Rocard at an agreed upon bench overlooking an ornamental pool.

"The bench near *The Shade*," Phillipe had said. "You know, Dante's *Shade*, not a shade tree."

"Thank you, I was aware of that," Prokhanov had replied wearily.

The plan called for Prokhanov to arrive first, approximately fifteen minutes before Rocard. It was a debatable decision. In Prokhanov's years with Soviet intelligence there had always coexisted two competing schools of thought on arrival order.

One school believed it imperative to arrive last. That way one could check out the lay of the land from a safe vantage point with the players already in place. If you liked what you saw, you showed. If not, you passed.

The other school believed, with equal fervor, it was imperative to arrive first, to take control of the neutral space and make it your own.

Of course, there was no all-purpose right answer. It was rather like trying to decide whether to kiss a girl on a first date. Or whether to speak your mind freely to your boss. Sometimes you did. Sometimes you didn't. Sometimes the Gods favored you and you made the right choice. Sometimes you didn't. Sometimes you got the girl. Sometimes you got fired.

For this meeting with Rocard, Victor Prokhanov had decided to come first. Why? Because Phillipe came from the school of first arrival, and Phillipe had handled the logistics. It was, Prokhanov supposed, as good a reason as any other.

He walked briskly now along a sandy path. The ornamental

pool was just beyond his field of site, but he could envision it completely in his mind: a splendid circle of shallow water with an agonizing statue of Ugolino in the center. Ugolino being a treacherous thirteenth-century Pisan who switched sides more than once in the battles between the Ghibellines and Guelphs.

If Prokhanov remembered the story right, our hero Ugolino was eventually betrayed in turn by one of his own coconspirators. He was thereafter locked up in a tower with his children and grandchildren. Since no food was provided, they all starved to death. Best of all, the gentleman who had betrayed Ugolino and locked him in the tower was an archbishop.

Tough times, Italy in the late 1200s.

For his trouble, Ugolino was consigned by Dante to the ninth and lowest circle of hell—below the murderers, the blasphemers, and the lusters. Seems Dante just couldn't abide betrayers.

A certain lightness came over Prokhanov's eyes as he now wondered whether the Frenchman Olivier Rocard, about to do a service for Mother Russia, would appreciate the irony of Ugolino's bronze presence at the event.

The next discomfort, however, belonged to Victor Prokhanov and removed the lightness from his eyes. As he came around the final bend in the sandy path, the pool came into his line of vision. Ugolino in the center. *The Shade* overlooking its bench. And, on that agreed upon bench, Olivier Rocard.

The Frenchman was blowing on his hands, obviously waiting for someone, and looking for all the world to be the only nervous person in the entire garden.

The Russian glanced at his watch: he was on time, Rocard was early. Now what?

Paranoid instincts told Prokhanov to leave. But his experience denied it. Arriving early was the type of mistake made by amateurs who wanted to impress, who didn't understand that choreography was safety. And the art dealer was no doubt thrilled about being in the game. Besides, if it was a trap, he was already caught. A man of his age, what could he do? Start running? It would only be laughable and demeaning.

Victor Prokhanov kept walking toward the bench. When he had closed to a distance of twenty feet he made eye contact with the Frenchman. On cue, Rocard rose and began to stroll around the fountain in a leisurely concentric circle. Halfway through Rocard's first revolution, Prokhanov fell in step along the dealer's right shoulder.

"You are early, Monsieur Rocard."

Rocard did not respond right away.

Prokhanov continued. "It is of no matter. My former comrade, Mikhail Shokovitch, speaks very highly of your family."

"Yes. I...ah...we," The Frenchman fighting to find his words.

"Relax, Monsieur Rocard."

"No...*Oui.*"

Prokhanov slowed his gait and pointed out Ugolino. "It's a wonderful piece, don't you think?"

"*Oui...Oui.*"

"Yes, it is. Everything is fine, Olivier. I'm interested in a piece your family dealt to Shokovitch a long time ago. A mirror from the Amber Room. Professor Greene may have mentioned this to you."

"*Oui.*"

"I wish to know where your family obtained that piece. I wish to know who had it, and if they had the rest of the Amber Room. Our friend Shokovitch believes you know where the Amber Room is. I'm prepared to pay handsomely for the information. I'm also prepared to give you a commendation in the records of the Russian state upon the Room's recovery. The commendation can be either public or private, whichever you prefer." Prokhanov paused. Money and ambition. Always appeal to money and ambition. "What do you think, Olivier?"

Rocard did not answer. It was almost as if he could not answer.

"Olivier, I assure you the financial arrangements will be satisfactory. Do you have the information I am looking for?"

Again Rocard simply did not answer.

The Russian now stopped and looked directly at Olivier Rocard. There was a tear in the Frenchman's eye. At first Victor Prokhanov didn't understand, either the Frenchman had the information or he didn't. Either he was interested in making a deal, or he wasn't. And then it sunk in.

Victor Prokhanov exhaled deeply and started walking around the circle again, Olivier Rocard at his side.

"Who?" Prokhanov asked.

"I'm...I'm not sure. An American. A fat man. He had pictures of me, with my lover."

"A man or a woman?"

"Does it matter?" Rocard said.

"He said they would show the pictures to your wife?"

"Yes."

"Your wife, she does not already know?"

"I don't know," Olivier Rocard said almost silently.

"And now what?" Prokhanov asked.

"I don't know," Olivier Rocard repeated.

"Did you already tell them about the Amber Room?"

"No, they are waiting for me. And I believe for you," said Olivier Rocard, the president of the hundred-year-old House Rocard, mouthing the words although no sound left his lips.

57

Kathryn and Anand stood on the corner of a cobblestoned street near the north bank of the Arno. Kathryn's head tilted down to peer at a map.

"We're at the Piazza Goldoni," she finally said.

"I know," Anand informed her, directing her attention to an engraved tile with the words Piazza Goldoni set into the second story wall of a nearby building.

"Whatever," she said.

From where they stood, a low heavy stone bridge led south from the Piazza over the river to the Oltrarno. On their side of the span, seven crooked streets spun off from the Piazza like the legs of a spider.

"Which one do we want?" Kathryn asked.

"Via del Parione. No. 11."

She peered back down at the map, twisted it sideways, then pointed toward a street slanting away from the Piazza and the river at a thirty-degree angle, toward the tourist center of Florence.

Their destination was 11 Via del Parione. An idea of Anand's. From the outside, 11 Via del Parione was simply a heavy door with massive stone walls. Set next to the door a tasteful bronze plaque that read, in Italian and English: Galleria Corsini, 10–1 and 5–7 daily. Closed Sunday.

It wasn't Sunday.

Admission was twenty thousand lira each. The money handled by a delicate woman with finely manicured hands.

"There's a tour starting in five minutes," she said, "Would you like to join? It's an extra ten thousand lira, each."

Anand graciously slid the paper money across the counter.

"Tell me again why we're here?" Kathryn asked.

"You'll see."

Anand led the way into the tall lobby of the gallery, where a small cluster of men and women had already gathered for the tour. In the center of the group was a tall, thin man, once beautiful, now handsome with age, his gray hair just a whisper of the blonde it might once have been. The man looked at his watch, then raised a slender, immaculate hand into the air.

"Vincenzo Corsini," he said, introducing himself to the group. "Welcome to my home."

The paintings virtually surrounded them. It was as if the house had been immersed in a bath of canvases. And it was no ordinary collection. That was made clear as soon as they reached the first display room—a rectangular drawing room with tall windows looking south to the Arno, and paintings seemingly draped upon the walls. Just inside the door hung a sizable canvas of a glowingly fat nude lady reclining on a velvet couch.

"Rubens?" Kathryn whispered uncertainly to Anand, seeking confirmation while her eyes examined the folds of pale flesh and flushed skin.

"Quite," Anand answered with a smile: both because he thought Kathryn's slight failure of confidence was becoming, and because he suspected that the woman in the painting was a woman of character, the company of whom his friend Ivo Jenkins might have most enjoyed. Had Ivo been born several hundred years sooner.

Vincenzo Corsini led the group smartly through his family's collection, seeming to have a story for each picture: describing how the Botticelli, with its nymphs, amulets, and flora was a Renaissance allegory; how the Bronzino was acquired by an ancestor in a game of chance with an archbishop; how the Filippino Lippi portrait of a very naked young woman had to be smuggled by the artist out of a convent, the model a reckless sister. Not that Filippino Lippi should have been inside the convent in the first place.

Vincenzo Corsini told the stories with evident delight. But after the Lippi came a picture that offered a different type of insight into the Corsini collection, although one not volunteered by the old gentleman.

It was a small picture of a well dressed lady, clothed, sitting stiff-backed in a high chair. It was framed in gold and, outside the yellow band of the frame, a second frame of slightly faded paint was just barely visible on the wall. Indicating that a larger painting had once hung in that place. Kathryn pointed it out to Anand. The larger painting perhaps sold to enable the Corsini family to maintain their homes and lifestyle. Or perhaps to satisfy the demands, legitimate or otherwise, of the tax authorities.

They went, in this fashion, through the entire ground floor of the house. A tour that took nearly two hours. When they had finished with the last painting in the last room, a study by Andrea del Sarto of a young student, and the group had begun to disperse, Anand quietly caught the old gentleman's attention.

"I had heard, Signor Corsini, that the collection includes some wonderful citiscapes of Florence."

"Why…yes," Corsini replied, somewhat surprised by the question. The citiscapes not among the works for which the collection was known. Instinctively, he appraised the well-dressed man, neither dark- nor light-skinned, who had asked the question. He seemed refined. And the pretty woman alongside him: a different sort. A mistress perhaps, in any event not a wife. Which was perfectly acceptable in Italy.

"May we have the pleasure of seeing them?" Anand asked.

Vincenzo Corsini cleared his throat. "They're kept in a room we usually keep private. But I'd be delighted to show them to you, Mister—"

"Ashland." Anand held out his arm toward Kathryn, palm open. "And this is Kathryn."

"Delighted," Vincenzo Corsini said with a perfect, barely perceptible bow.

He led them up a flight of stairs to a charming sitting room, its four walls decorated with citiscapes of Italy.

"We are particularly interested in the portrayals of Florence," Anand said politely, only after taking considerable time to study a wall of works sketching Pisa and Lucca, and a number of other Tuscan cities.

The images of Florence hung on the south wall. Anand and Kathryn viewed the pictures closely, paying particular attention to a canvas that was dark, and in need of a cleaning, but in which the streets and structures of Florence remained nevertheless, quite identifiable.

"This was done in 1502," Vincenzo Corsini explained. "You can see that much of Florence is now, as it was."

"Yes," Anand said.

It was true, much was the same. But Kathryn and Anand's attention were focused on what had changed.

Kathryn's eyes swept across the Arno, along an old stone bridge, then down a winding street, and another…before coming to rest at a majestic palazzo that occupied the entire block of Via San Giovanni. A palazzo no longer seen on modern maps. Her hand involuntarily rose to the painting, nearly touching it.

The significance of this missing palazzo not lost on Vincenzo Corsini. He looked at Anand with a wry smile. "You didn't tell me that you'd come to find Bianca, Mister Ashland. Looking for Bianca delle Bande Nere…that's rather a bold undertaking. I wish you well."

58

Victor Prokhanov walked back up the path from Ugolino's pool the way he had come. He walked alone, leaving Olivier Rocard to stroll in circles around the fountain.

Prokhanov's pace was deliberate, and he stopped once again to spend some time with the *Burghers of Calais*.

Isaiah Hawkins joined him there.

"I'm sorry, Victor," Isaiah said.

"Don't be, Isaiah." The Russian paused and let the set of events replay through his mind once more. "Professor Greene played me?"

"No. He was just careless."

"And Shokovitch?"

Isaiah shrugged. "Who knows, Victor. Your Comrade Mikhail is playing his own game and has been for a long time."

"So Rocard has the Room? Or knows where it is?"

"I don't know, yet," Isaiah answered.

Prokhanov nodded. It was he who had been careless, contacting Greene and putting his faith in Shokovitch. He supposed he had believed because he wanted to believe.

There was one thing Victor Prokhanov didn't quite understand, why Isaiah did not continue the charade and have their mutual friend Monsieur Rocard give him false information? He was about to ask, then held off. He knew the answer. Continuing the charade would only have embarrassed Victor Prokhanov even more, and it was not necessary. Besides, it would have kept the Russians stumbling around in the game when Isaiah wished them removed.

"I suppose there is a chateau in the country where I am to spend some time now?" Victor Prokhanov asked. "Until you find the Room or don't. Or perhaps until after the election. You would prefer that Nikolai Andreyovitch win, no? Because he is weak."

"Perhaps," Isaiah said.

"No great matter," Prokhanov said, with a measured acceptance. "I don't personally believe Nikolai Andreyovitch can win, even with your help. The people want to try the party again. Tell me, if you find the Room, what will you do? You know about the letters, of course?"

"Yes. Shokovitch told me a long time ago."

Prokhanov thought of the transcript of Isaiah's interrogation of Shokovitch that he had gotten from his man in Washington. It provided no details on the letters. Isaiah must have kept if off the record, just in case the transcript was ever leaked. "So tell, me, what will you do if you find them?"

"What would you have done, Victor?"

"Destroyed them."

"For the good of the party?"

"The good of the party? No. The good of the country? Who knows anymore. It was my job, Isaiah. I signed up for it. You understand?"

"Yes." Of course Isaiah Hawkins understood.

The Russian reached out a hand and touched the bronze key around the neck of the led Burgher. "There will be a reckoning, I suppose."

"Perhaps."

"I mean for Russia, Isaiah. I mean for Russia."

There always was a reckoning after a time of excess—the seven fat years and the seven lean years of the Bible being the rule that had yet to be disproved. And the men who had torn down communism and replaced it with opportunism, well, they too were subject to the laws of history.

The two men walked together toward the stone archway leading out of the Musée Rodin, and toward the van that would take Prokhanov to his villa in the country. As they neared the entrance gates, they both saw Olivier Rocard standing there despondently, waiting for Isaiah Hawkins to be done with him.

PART FIVE

Better a city ruined than a city lost...
—Cosimo de'Medici

59

The delivery arrived well before dawn. A metal box the size of a humidor, brought to a simple green door on Via San Giovanni by a man of few words.

A middle-aged servant who had been with the delle Bande Nere family for nearly his entire life received the box in the narrow entrance hall. He paid in cash and watched until the delivery man had driven away. Then he locked the green door and walked up a flight of eight stairs. The stairs led to a second door, and only upon passing through that private door could one begin to understand the palazzo which the delle Bande Nere had so painstakingly erased from public view.

On the second floor the servant entered a private reception hall, thirty feet square, with a black marble floor, marble walls, and a ceiling that rose to four times his height. The room was all the more stunning for being completely unfurnished, except for an ancient circle of black iron which hung down as a chandelier, and, at the far end of the room, standing guard in front of a pair of tall wooden doors, a slightly smaller than life-sized bronze statue of a helmeted Mercury.

Of the few visitors allowed to enter No. 33 San Giovanni, even fewer were allowed to advance past this Mercury, which bore an unmistakable stylistic resemblance to the famous *David* by Donatello. That *David*—sexually flamboyant, nude, and quite youthful—is on display at the Bargello. There is, however, no listing in any of the many treatises on Florentine art of this Mercury.

The servant, carrying the box which had been delivered, walked past the statue and opened the double doors. He brought the box upstairs to the library.

Paolo and Bianca were in the library reading. Bianca at her desk, a circle of light from a tall copper lamp illuminating what appeared to be a set of old handwritten letters. The servant stood patiently in front of the desk, the metal box clasped in his arms. Because Bianca was captured by the letter she was reading, it was only reluctantly that she looked up. Her warmth for the servant was nevertheless easily apparent.

"Thank you, Salvatore. You can leave that with me."

The man placed the box down carefully, as he did everything carefully, being sure not to scratch the beautifully grained wood of the desk. He then brushed away a fleck of dust with his handkerchief. He looked as if he was about to say something, then hesitated, and started to turn around.

Her voice called him back, "What is it, Salvatore?"

"It's nothing signora."

"Please."

He looked down at the black box, still hesitating, looked over at Paolo, then back up at her.

"Please, tell me."

"Yes, tell us," Paolo said.

"You shouldn't mind me, signora, signor, but I can't...I can't personally agree with what you're doing."

"I don't blame you, Salvatore," Bianca said evenly. "But a woman is going to show up here soon. An American, Kathryn Blaire. Paolo already knows her. But I'm not certain how serious she is. At least this way she'll know how serious we are."

"Yes, she'll know," Salvatore said. It was the Bande Nere way—test others, and burn your own bridges to let the others know how serious you were. It was heroic, but then you had no bridge.

"Will you be needing me more this evening, signora, signor?"

"Yes. Another package should arrive within the hour."

Salvatore glanced down at a clock on the desk. It was almost three. "Shall I bring it to you here, signora?"

"No, upstairs, please."

As Salvatore walked away, Bianca let the box be for the moment, instead turning her attention back to the letter she'd been reading. The letter, four hundred years old and written from a father to his son, was a small fragment of the library's collection of original correspondence. Some of it displayed in cases, most of it kept on the shelves. She often turned to the collection—for guidance, for illumination of the past, for insight, for the beauty of the writing. This particular letter exhorted the writer's son to think freely and challenge conventional wisdom. Advice any father could have given to a favored son. Except this father was Vincenzo Galilei.

Only when she was finished, did she walk around the desk and open the metal box. Inside were two flat spools of very fine gold wire.

Her body tensed, she saw Paolo tense as well, and for a moment, perhaps, Bianca doubted herself. But there was no room in her makeup for a failure of nerve. Nor was there time. Kathryn Blaire, would show up soon enough. Bianca and Paolo had made sure of it, their agents invisibly watching as Kathryn Blaire and Anand Ashland followed the trail from Sant' Antimo to the municipal records office to the Corsini Gallery. Bianca herself alerting Vincenzo Corsini to show Ms. Blaire and Mr. Ashland the old citiscapes, including the one which showed the palazzo. Giving Kathryn Blaire and Anand Ashland the illusion of progress, while all the while they were being drawn to the palazzo.

Yes, Kathryn Blaire would arrive soon. And the wiring needed to be in place before then. The threat needed to be real and credible. That was the key. So long as the threat and the will were true, Bianca was free to use any trick at her disposal to win, and Kathryn Blaire was certain of being put to the fire.

60

Isaiah Hawkins interrogated Olivier Rocard in a dingy hotel room in the Marais district for the better part of the Parisian evening.

Q: Where did you get the mirror?
A: In the 1950s. We bought it from a former Bolshevik colonel.
Q: Name?
A: Colonel Puchin. Vladimir Puchin.
Q: How did he get the mirror?
A: He said that it had been saved from the Amber Room in the early 1940s, before the Nazis captured the Room.
Q: Is that the truth?
A: That's what he told us.
Q: I understand. But was Colonel Puchin telling you the truth?
A: I have no idea. He dealt with my father.
Q: Where is your father now?
A: Dead, Mister Hawkins.

•   •   •

Q: Tell me again about Colonel Puchin. How did he get the mirror?
A: He said he stole it from a storeroom. The same story Shokovitch apparently told your people.
Q: Are you saying Shokovitch made up that story? Took Colonel Puchin's story as his own.
A: Yes, of course. My family got the mirror from Puchin. Shokovitch got the mirror from my family.

Q: How did Shokovitch get the mirror?

A: The House Rocard needed help smoothing over a purchase of artifacts from Russia. Shokovitch was with the Russian embassy in Paris and he helped us. In return we sold him the mirror at an excellent price for him.

Q: Is that all you sold him?

A: No.

Q: Did you sell him anything else related to the Amber Room?

A: No. Just the mirror.

Q: Are you certain the mirror came from the Amber Room?

A: Colonel Puchin said so.

Q: And you believed him.

A: The mirror was worth more if we believed him, Mister Hawkins. That said, it looked true.

Q: What do you mean, it looked true?

A: It's our business, Mister Hawkins, evaluating these types of claims. But it is an art, not a science. It looked true to us.

•   •   •

Q: Did you buy anything else from Colonel Puchin?

A: No.

Q: Nothing else at all?

A: That's right. Many people we deal with, Mister Hawkins, only have one object to sell. Especially if they have stolen it.

Q: How did Colonel Puchin get the mirror to you?

A: He smuggled it out of Russia through a dancer who was giving a performance in

Paris. They were lovers, Colonel Puchin
and the dancer. Does that make the story
more interesting to you, Mister Hawkins? I
suppose it would. You prey on people like
that.

Q: It's not personal, Olivier.

A: The hell it's not, Mister Hawkins.

* * *

Q: Did Colonel Puchin offer you any letters
with the mirror?

A: What kind of letters?

Q: From Lenin, Buhkarin, Molotov.

A: No. Like I said, all he had was the
mirror.

* * *

Q: Do you have any other objects relating to
the Amber Room?

A: No.

Q: Have you ever?

A: No.

Q: Do you know where the Amber Room is?

A: No.

Q: Just the mirror?

A: That's right.

Q: No idea at all about the Room?

A: Just what Shokovitch told me. Same thing
he told you. That the Room was sold by
Stalin to a wealthy collector. I have no
way of knowing whether that is true.
Comrade Shokovitch is a most excellent
liar. But then you know that already,
Mister Hawkins. Are we done now, Mister
Hawkins?

Q: I don't think so.

A: I have told you everything I know.

Q: Then no harm in going over it again. Tell me what you know about Colonel Puchin, would you Olivier?

•   •   •

At dawn, Isaiah Hawkins sent Olivier Rocard home. Rocard was not a hard man, and Isaiah had no doubt that Olivier Rocard was telling the truth. Rocard knew nothing about the Amber Room. The mirror was a one-time event. A random piece of noise confused by Isaiah Hawkins and Victor Prokhanov with data that mattered. Paris and Olivier Rocard were a dead end, a little fun played on Isaiah Hawkins and Victor Prokhanov by the ineluctable logic of the game. You followed leads where they took you. This one went nowhere.

Isaiah lit the last of the Kents that he had taken with him from the states. Maybe he was losing his touch. But he didn't think so. Kathryn and Anand were making progress in Florence. Perhaps so would Detective Russo. That's where the action was. That was the proper ground to be on.

61

Kathryn Blaire and Anand Ashland tried their best to look like just another set of tourists as they strolled along Via San Giovanni at twilight.

"Please, Kathryn, give me your arm," Anand said softly.

"Be glad to."

She held Anand's arm like she loved him. It wasn't the worst thing in the world, walking around Florence pretending to be with someone you loved.

Via San Giovanni was a winding block of townhouses. Three stories tall, the townhouses adjoined each other without gap, and turned a uniform facade of flat dull stone to narrow cobblestone streets. The result was a faded stone corridor punctuated only by brightly painted wooden doors and shutters.

Kathryn and Anand walked around the entire block twice, trying to imagine where the palazzo of the delle Bande Nere might be hidden. Twice they walked past a townhouse at 33 Via San Giovanni, a narrow building of pale yellow stone, with a fresh coat of dark green paint upon its heavy door and shutters.

On their second circuit, the green door opened for a moment, revealing a glimpse into the home's foyer. It was unremarkable: a bland narrow room of dark stone walls and old wooden floors leading up to a thin, crooked stairway. The home at 33 Via San Giovanni looked to Anand as if it had been a part of the neighborhood for longer than memory, but then that was true of virtually the entire block.

Anand turned to Kathryn. "What exactly are we looking for? I know we're looking for the palazzo. But it's not as if they are going to hang out a sign."

"Don't know what we're looking for," Kathryn answered. "I was hoping we would know it when we saw it."

"Well, do you think we have seen it."

"Yeah. I do. The palazzo is here, I'm quite certain of it. It's just hiding behind a mask."

"What makes you so certain, Kathryn?"

"I don't know. It just feels to me like what Brother Michael had described back at Sant' Antimo. A secret palace. Those were his words. It's here."

"Is that because you want it to be here?" Anand asked.

"No. It's here. And we'll find it." She paused. "Maybe our friend, Detective Russo, will work some magic for us. I asked him to visit with the Florentine police to see if they have any record of a family named delle Bande Nere. Unlikely, but he has a certain touch, you know."

"Apparently," Anand said, seeing as Ben Russo wasn't supposed to be able to find Kathryn Blaire either.

62

Ben Russo had arranged an appointment to see Lieutenant Tommaso Manetti of the Florentine police. Manetti, he had been told, was the official liaison of the Florence police with visiting policemen. Now he pushed through a glass door with brass fixtures to the lieutenant's office.

"Detective Russo, please sit down." Lieutenant Manetti sat behind a functional metal desk, not very different than Ben's own. Manetti noticed the look on Ben's face. "You are surprised at my English, Detective? I spent two years in San Francisco after college, before I decided to return home and become a policeman. A lovely town, San Francisco. Do you know it well, Detective?"

Ben smiled. Russo and Manetti would talk about the States and about Ben's family and about Florence. It would all be lovely. And Manetti would have the American detective out of the office in forty-five minutes feeling good about everything and knowing nothing.

"No, I'm afraid I don't really know 'Frisco. I'm from New York, Brooklyn. I've never spent much time in California, Lieutenant Manetti. I'm not sure it agrees with my temperament."

"Well, are you enjoying Florence, Detective Russo?"

"I haven't seen much. I just got here."

Manetti looked at Ben's hand. "Is your wife with you?"

"My wife? No. She might join me later, in Milan. Once I'm done with my business."

Now Manetti smiled back. It was so simple with the cops who came to Florence. Either they were on a job or on what the Americans would call a boondoggle. Four out of five were boondoggling—Florence being such a lovely place to chase down leads, eat a few meals, and relax in a fine hotel. But this cop Russo was on a job, and wanted Manetti to know it. Of course, Manetti had known that already. The delle Bande Nere had informed him that someone might be showing up, and

Bianca and Paolo's resources were most thorough and usually accurate.

"Of course, I can see you are on business, Detective Russo. So how can I help you?"

"I'm looking for a gentleman named delle Bande Nere. Paolo delle Bande Nere."

"May I ask why?"

"I'd like to ask him a few questions about something that happened recently in New York."

Manetti leaned over his desk. "What type of something, Detective?"

"A murder."

"Really. Do you think he did it?"

Ben shrugged. "No."

"So he's not a suspect then?"

"No. He's not."

"Because there are procedures to be followed, if he is a suspect." Manetti reached over to a nearby bookshelf and grabbed a thick manual. He started to leaf through it, as if he did not know the procedures.

Ben smiled again. "That's alright, Lieutenant. As I said, he is not a suspect."

"I understand. So you said, Detective. But even to interrogate a local citizen, there are procedures to be followed. Forms to be filled out. Approvals to be obtained from the embassy and our national government. This is no simple matter, Detective. But then, maybe you are not familiar with the procedures."

"I'm quite familiar. I'd just like to talk to him, informally."

"Ah." Manetti closed the manual with a solid hand. He placed it back on the shelf. "An informal conversation. Well, anyone in Florence is free to speak with anyone else, Detective. Why do you need help from the Florentine police?"

"I thought you could make an introduction. Perhaps give me a little background information on the delle Bande Nere first."

"Background. But I thought you would have researched that already, Detective. After all, the delle Bande Nere are hardly a secret." Manetti went back to the bookshelf and pulled out a thick book. "An invaluable history of Florence, detective. I don't believe it is available in English. I keep it here to inform my visitors, such as yourself. You are interested in the delle Bande Nere. Where shall we start?"

Manetti flipped through the pages until he came to the one he wanted. Whether it was actually about the delle Bande Nere was irrelevant. It was the show of looking it up that mattered.

"Giovanni delle Bande Nere," Manetti read aloud. "Giovanni of the black bands. Born in 1498. The great grandson of the brother of Cosimo de'Medici. Part of the Cadet branch of the Medici; the main branch of the family being descended, of course, directly from Cosimo. But the branches intertwine with Giovanni. He married Cosimo's great-great granddaughter, a woman named Maria Salviati." Manetti paused. "Shall I go on, Detective?"

Ben slid his chair back half a foot, as if preparing to leave. If he had wanted a history lesson, he could have gone to the New York Public Library. In fact, if this had been New York, Ben would have said a polite good-bye and left. This type of meeting in New York only ended one way—a stream of under the breath profanity and all sides pledging to remember how helpful everyone else had been. But Manetti had to have another agenda. Manetti had agreed to meet him, and would have done some checking before doing so. So there was no harm in playing it out.

"Please, Lieutenant. Please, continue."

"Wonderful. It's really quite a fabulous history. Giovanni became famous as being the greatest military commander of his day. Which would be, given the day we are discussing, detective, quite an achievement. Of course, he started young. His maternal uncle, Pope Leo X, had him led an attack by papal forces on Urbino when he was eighteen and he had his own command, known as the Bande Nere, at twenty-two. The Bande Nere were considered to be the best infantry in Europe since the days of Julius Caesar. Machiavelli himself is quoted as saying that he believed Giovanni delle Bande Nere was the only man capable of uniting Italy. But even Machiavelli was wrong, Giovanni died too young to help Italy. He was twenty-eight when he died in battle. A lot to accomplish by twenty-eight, am I right, Detective?"

"You said he was married, did he have children?"

Manetti flipped to another page in the thick book, showing a genealogical chart. "One. Cosimo I, ruled as the Grand Duke of Tuscany."

"Mistresses?"

"Don't know," Manetti said, closing the book and laying it on his desk near Ben Russo. "Not that kind of history book, Detective. Although perhaps it is covered in another book."

Russo pushed the book away. The point of the history lesson clear. The delle Bande Nere were not to be trifled with. As if Ben Russo didn't already know that. "And Paolo delle Bande Nere?"

"Yes, Paolo." Manetti leaned back in his chair. "Well, that wouldn't be history, would it, Detective?"

"It would make everything go a little smoother, for everyone, if you made an introduction."

"Smoother for me, Detective, would be going to my girl-friend's apartment for the afternoon. She gives an excellent massage. So perhaps smoother for everyone isn't the goal. Is it?"

"Smoother for Paolo."

"Smoother for Paolo?" Manetti asked the rhetorical question with evident relish. "Why don't we leave that up to Paolo, Detective. Without the official paperwork and approvals, Paolo delle Bande Nere would be out of my hands, and yours, Detective. Unless he chooses to see you, which is his business."

"So that's it, Lieutenant?"

"That's it, Detective. Enjoy your stay in Florence. I believe you will find it wonderful."

Ben walked out of the Florence police headquarters with a wry smile. Seemed it felt the same way to leave police headquarters, whether in Florence or New York. It felt good.

63

Bianca delle Bande Nere's fingers traced the surface of a sculpted bronze panel which showed the sacrifice of Isaac: an aged Abraham stretched upwards over a primitive alter of stone and wood, over the body of his only son, a knife in his hand, ready to do the Lord's terrible bidding. On Abraham's face was the fear of a man who desperately wished to believe.

The panel had been cast by Lorenzo Ghiberti in 1401. By all accounts, it should have been destroyed in that same year. It had been prepared by Ghiberti for a competition sponsored by the Florentine Merchant Guild. The winner to be awarded a commission to cast twenty-eight panels for the North doors of the Baptistry in the Piazza di San Giovanni. A commission that would bring honor and money and would take twenty years to complete.

But ultimately, Lorenzo Ghiberti had chosen not to enter the panel which Bianca's fingers traced. Instead, Ghiberti had submitted a revised version to the judges, one which portrayed Abraham full with belief, rather than fear.

It was easy for Bianca to understand why Ghiberti had chosen to enter the second version. The year 1401 was still the beginning of the Renaissance, before the corruption of the church had jaded the men who composed the Merchant Guild. In order to win the competition—in which his rival, Filippo Brunelleschi, had already submitted a brilliant work—Ghiberti chose to enter a panel showing Abraham in a state of mind most likely to appeal to the judges.

Ghiberti had made the right choice. His panel was awarded first prize in the competition, and that panel was now on display in the Bargello museum, a short walk from Bianca's home via the Santa Trinita bridge.

But Bianca preferred the Abraham which Ghiberti had chosen not to submit—the one which captured the awful ambiguity of Abraham's circumstances and which had now been in her family for generations. Lorenzo Ghiberti had loved that Abraham as well. On the day he was to melt it down to reuse the expensive bronze, he pulled the panel back from the fire, like Abraham pulling back his knife, and gave it instead to his most favored patron. The Abraham of the delle Bande Nere stood as a testament to both the fragility and survival instincts of men and art. The lessons of the Abraham still so applicable.

Bianca lifted her hand from the bronze. She thought of the gold wiring that had now been laid, of her brother, Paolo, of their possession that was so desired, and of their pursuer, Kathryn Blaire, who was also perhaps desired.

Each of them, Bianca and Paolo and Kathryn Blaire, would soon be faced with a similar choice to that made by Ghiberti—whether to destroy something they loved in order to achieve a worldly gain. Or perhaps, like Abraham, whether to destroy someone in order to satisfy their personal God.

Either way, that was the way Bianca had chosen to structure the end game. It was necessary in order to achieve finality, on that both she and Paolo were agreed. And there was no doubt in Bianca's mind that Kathryn Blaire would force the issue. All that was left was to offer an invitation.

From her desk drawer, Bianca removed two sheets of paper, each embossed with six red balls on a golden shield, and began writing in a beautiful hand, *Dear Kathryn...*

64

Kathryn Blaire had barely stepped back into her hotel room that afternoon when the hotel concierge rang. The concierge said a letter had been delivered for her, did she mind if it was brought up? Not at all.

She took off her shoes and waited in a big wooden chair that had a beautiful inlaid design, had to be at least two hundred years old, and was hard on her all over. There definitely was something to be said for plush. She was tired from walking around the Oltrarno and Via San Giovanni looking for ghosts with Anand, and hadn't even had a chance to catch up with Ben Russo yet. They would do that over dinner—drink a little wine and plan the next push. They were close, and now was no time to screw up or let up.

There was a knock on the door, and she answered in her bare feet.

The bellhop was wearing a lovely white uniform with gold trim and a red hat and carrying an envelope. It might have just been coincidence, but the way he was holding the letter, the upper left hand corner stuck out toward Kathryn. Six dark red embossed balls clearly visible against a gold shield in the upper lefthand corner.

She stared at the envelope, counted the balls twice, and tried her best to look casual. Then she handed the bellhop a thin stack of paper lira, she had no idea how much, closed the door, and held the envelope to her chest.

She assumed it was from Paolo and considered what that might mean. She imagined him sitting at some splendid desk, writing her a letter longhand, telling her that he was sorry. Sorry about the way he had left. Sorry about the pendant. About the mirror. Perhaps inviting her out for a romantic dinner at some restaurant in the Florentine Hills.

Then there was another vision altogether. A few clipped words from Paolo telling her that he had really enjoyed New York, that she was a nice enough girl, but that she would be

better to leave him alone now.

There were other possibilities, and she wasn't even sure what she wished for. But there was only one reality, so she sat down on the edge of the bed and slid her finger under the envelope's flap.

> *Dear Kathryn,*
>
> *I feel as if we must meet. Vincenzo Corsini tells me that you are quite interested in art and in my home, and my brother tells me that you are most lovely and beautiful.*
>
> *It would be my great pleasure if you could join me for coffee tomorrow morning. No. 33 Via San Giovanni, the green door. Not too early, I know you are a late sleeper. Shall we say nine o'clock?*
>
> *It goes without saying that this is a personal invitation. I'm sure that your associates are delightful, but I do wish to spend some time alone with you. I do hope you will join me.*
>
> *Yours,*
> *Bianca delle Bande Nere*

Kathryn read the letter a dozen times before she put it down, reading it like it was a Bible, looking for additional insight that was just not there.

First the brother, then the sister. Should have known it was going to be one of those types of completely fucked up deals. Should have known it as soon as Paolo mentioned his sister at dinner in New York.

She lay on the bed, knew she had to see Anand and Ben that night, and decided not to tell anyone else of the letter, including Isaiah. She just didn't want to deal with the questions, didn't need to go there. It was clear enough that Bianca and Paolo delle Bande Nere had been aware of all her actions in Florence to find them. It made her feel like a fool. But she would get over that. She had been played before, it was part of the game. An occupational hazard.

But she did not understand why they had done nothing to try and stop her. Why had they let her run all over Florence, getting steadily closer. And why would Bianca delle Bande Nere invite her to the palazzo? To show her that they did not have the Amber Room? To show her that they did? To offer a bribe? To complete a trap? To tell her to stay away from her brother? To complete her humiliation? Why not—it was all about the humiliation, wasn't it?

●　　　●　　　●

Anand Ashland also received an envelope embossed with the six red balls. An invitation to meet Bianca delle Bande Nere at her home at six o'clock the next morning. A driver would come to pick him up. Bianca had a business proposition to discuss:

> *My brother and I have done some research into your background, Mister Ashland, much the same way you and your associates have been looking into ours. It is my understanding that you are a gentleman who can assure the sanctity of certain deals. That is interesting to us.*
>
> *Please come alone, Mister Ashland, and do not discuss this with anyone, especially Ms. Blaire. I would prefer you not even mention this invitation to her. It would be truly unfortunate to begin our relationship in a manner that precludes mutual trust.*
>
> *Yours,*
> *Bianca delle Bande Nere*

65

Kathryn Blaire knocked on the green door at 33 Via San Giovanni at five minutes past nine in the morning. Salvatore, who had already picked up Anand Ashland and brought him to the palazzo at dawn, answered the door promptly. He looked Kathryn up and down, weighing and judging.

She had decided to wear all black—wool trousers, a form-fitting tightly weaved sweater, and a unconstructed wool jacket—choices which would please the signora. Also, a pistol underneath her jacket—so hard for a small woman to conceal a weapon, even in stylishly loose clothing.

"Please, step inside, Ms. Blaire."

She was a little taken aback at the English. She hadn't even had time to get out the few words of phrasebook Italian she had practiced.

"Please," Salvatore repeated, politely ushering her across the threshold.

She stepped in and he closed the door behind her. It took a moment for her eyes to adjust to the darker light of the entrance hall, and Salvatore kindly waited.

"Now, may I have your gun please, Ms. Blaire?"

She hesitated.

"This is not America, Ms. Blaire. Guns are not considered proper attire in this home. You are a guest."

"Right." She nodded. She was a guest. Of course Paolo delle Bande Nere had been a guest in her home when he stole the pendant. But that was different, she supposed. She slipped the gun out from underneath her jacket and put it into the man's callused palm.

Salvatore looked her over again, checking the flow of her clothes. There were no other bulges.

"This way please, Ms. Blaire," he said, directing her up the stairs.

He led her through the second entrance hall, past the statue of Mercury, and through the tall wooden doors.

It was there, through those doors, that whatever remained of the carefully drawn public illusion came to an end.

Where there should have been a well-furnished beautiful home, there were instead great rooms upon great rooms, with stone fireplaces and high ceilings and marble floors and grand hallways. There were tapestries thirty feet long and twenty feet high, paintings that should have been hanging from the walls of a great public museum, suits of chain mail armor, collections of stones and coins and silver chalices, and far too much more to be absorbed in a single pass through.

Where 33 Via San Giovanni appeared from the street to be one beautiful home among many lining San Giovanni, that façade was instead a false creation—not unlike the lovely villages of stage fronts built by Russian Field Marshall Grigori Potemkin in advance of Catherine the Great's visits to the Crimea.

The difference being that the illusion of San Giovanni was the reverse of Marshall Potemkin. The quaint homes of Via San Giovanni were a false façade built to hide not rural poverty, but a single palace of the most wondrous splendor.

Kathryn Blaire could not help but be awed. Her eyes flashed from object to object, trying to take in the immense wealth and power of it all, and she just couldn't. She was fathoms from her depth, and she knew it.

66

In the library, Marina brought out a silver service of smoky black coffee. "The signora will be with you shortly. Please make yourself comfortable, Ms. Blaire. Sugar?"

"Yes, thank you."

Marina stirred a delicate spoonful of sugar into the cup.

"Anything else, Ms. Blaire."

"No. That's fine."

"I'll be waiting outside the door if you need anything. Please, enjoy the library."

Marina curtsied—at least Kathryn thought it was a curtsy—and walked ever softly out of the room. Leaving Kathryn alone.

But why? Why leave her alone, Kathryn wondered. To see how she responded? Not likely. So that she might see something? Something too obvious if it was just shown to her? Possibly. Or maybe simply to remind her who was running this particular show. Hell, she already knew that. Might as well look around, then.

The library, like all other aspects of the home, was stunning, and revealing: the Medici shield with its six red balls on the east wall; the portrait of a beautiful woman; the gold medallion on the desk; in one corner, an eye-catching model of some sort of strangely wonderful solar system with planets set on tracks around a vast silver globe; in another corner, the study of Abraham. Everywhere Kathryn looked there was beauty and wealth and information.

Exquisite, built-in wooden bookshelves—the type constructed by two expert craftsmen working every day for a year—lined two walls of the library, floor to ceiling. She selected one wall at random, taking in the shelf square at her eye level.

It was no public library. The one shelf—about three feet long and containing some twenty-eight volumes (she counted)—was by her quick guess, worth more than all the money she would ever see in her lifetime, including the money she had stolen. Every book a first edition. Most of them more than three centuries old. Isaiah Hawkins had bought the entire governments of several semi-industrialized countries with less.

She walked over to the desk where the letters from Vincenzo Galilei to his son were fanned out, the way someone might carelessly leave their bills about. Kathryn didn't know enough Latin to read the letters, but the signature was clear enough.

The letters had apparently been taken from a free-standing glass display case, the back of which had been left open, and Kathryn peered over there next. There were several other items still in the case, among them:

A memo in French, directing a chief of staff to promote to general a soldier who had proven himself lucky in battle. Kathryn lingered briefly over the memo, surprised at the neatness of Napoleon's script.

A document in Latin with the papal seal, although she couldn't make out which pope.

A note to Joseph Stalin dated March 1918, signed "yours, Lenin."

She was working on the Russian to English translation, when a door at the rear of the library opened.

67

Even standing in a light shadow, Bianca delle Bande Nere was an extraordinary looking woman, with perhaps the richest features Kathryn had ever seen. Especially the eyes. So black and deep.

Bianca came forward, walking into the soft sunlight that filtered through the library's French doors. Exuding elegance and strength. Late thirties, olive skin, and black hair sliding past strong shoulders. Dressed in brown wool trousers and a black wool mockneck, the Hanged Man pendant on its chain around her neck.

She both judged Kathryn with her eyes and observed all the details. Seeing the woman, her beauty, her deceptive slightness of build, the nice clothes she wore, the barely noticeable, seemingly unaccustomed nervousness.

"Welcome to my home, Kathryn. Please, make yourself comfortable," Bianca said in English that was fluid, inviting Kathryn to sit near a small table where Marina had left the coffee service. Then she joined her there, refilling Kathryn's cup and pouring another for herself. Two girlfriends having coffee.

Kathryn replied to all this with a smile. She wanted to say something witty and polite, but instead her attention was drawn as if by magnets to the portrait which hung behind Bianca's desk. The woman in the picture—dressed in the clothing of the Italian Renaissance—was the most remarkable image of the woman sitting next to her now.

"Francesca delle Bande Nere." Bianca stirred sugar into her cup. "My direct ancestor. The daughter of Giovanni delle Bande Nere."

Kathryn reached into a corner of her mind, to recall what Ben Russo had told her of Giovanni delle Bande Nere's short and spectacular life. Detective Russo hadn't mentioned a daughter. "I thought he only had a son?"

"Yes, Cosimo I, Grand Duke of Tuscany. That is the official history. But at the time of Giovanni's death, his wife, Maria Salviati, was pregnant with a baby girl. She kept the girl a secret."

"Why?"

"The times, Kathryn. Giovanni was killed leading his troops in a battle fought at the behest of his uncle, Pope Clement V. His widow Maria didn't trust Pope Clement. She believed he had intentionally sent Giovanni into a battle he couldn't win. Although Giovanni and Pope Clement were allies and family, if Giovanni was dead, that would strengthen Clement's position by eliminating a rival. Do you understand?"

"Enough." Kathryn sipped her coffee. "I don't have the history to appreciate it in context. But I understand the idea—eliminating a potential rival, that is. But why keep the daughter a secret?"

"Because a little girl named delle Bande Nere could grow up to be a queen of Florence, and queens are threats. Maria believed Pope Clement would have taken the baby and placed her in a monastery. Nuns are not threats to the pope, they are servants. Maria had the baby girl, Francesca, raised by loyal retainers of the family outside of Florence—by a man who had served with Giovanni. Only much later, after her brother Cosimo I solidified his power, did Francesca move to Florence. This house became her house. She lived here as the sister of Cosimo I, part of the Medici family. My brother and I are her direct descendants."

"You have lived openly as Medici?" Kathryn asked, wondering why the history books all said the Medici had died out in the 1700s.

"As delle Bande Nere, Kathryn. Many people, of course, once knew that we were Medici. But people have short memories and perhaps they wanted to forget us. There was no advantage in us reminding them. We prefer to live in privacy. We're just a rumor now, something whispered in the wind."

Kathryn craned her neck once around the room.

"I'd say you're something more than that."

"Not really. Perhaps you are yourself more than you appear on casual glance, Kathryn Blaire. My brother believes that is possible."

"Really. What else did Paolo tell you about me?" Kathryn looked at the Hanged Man pendant dangling from around Bianca's neck. "Did he tell you how he stole that pendant from me?"

Bianca's gaze narrowed some now, again judging and evaluating the slight woman sitting beside her—her manner, her attire, her desire.

"This?" Bianca's fingers played with the iron chain from which the Hanged Man dangled. It swung lightly between her breasts. "You shouldn't judge so harshly, Kathryn. Paolo took it from your apartment, but he did not steal it. The pendant is ours, Kathryn. Paolo had been intending on retrieving it from Elliot Rosewater. But you beat him to it."

"You sent it to Rosewater...as a message? That he had betrayed you?"

"Of course."

Bianca stood momentarily and adjusted a small silver knob on the wall. The way someone might turn on the heat or air-conditioning, except the climate was perfect. The slightest hum emanated from the corner of the room, from the sculpted silver solar system. Slowly the silver planets began to revolve on their tracks around the silver globe. A seemingly bizarre touch. Bianca sat back down and poured a little more coffee into her cup.

"Elliot Rosewater was supposed to secure the mirror for us in a discreet manner, Kathryn. Instead, he spoke of us and the mirror to Sarah Ridell. She in turn tried to sell that information to others, including your Professor Greene. For that, Elliot Rosewater had Sarah Ridell killed. Not really justification for killing a young woman. That was most unfortunate."

Kathryn had allowed one eye to drift to the rotating planets. Now, she brought her full attention straight back to Bianca and cocked her head. "Is that what you call falling thirty-nine floors? Unfortunate?"

"We never knew Sarah Ridell. Her death isn't personal for us. Terrible for her. For her parents. Her friends. Just unfortunate for us."

"Right...right." Kathryn murmured. She rocked forward, closing the spatial and psychic distance that separated her from Bianca. "I'm sorry, but how would you describe Elliot Rosewater's death?"

Bianca delle Bande Nere smiled and leaned forward. So close for a moment that Kathryn could have counted the radial lines in her irises, had her irises not been pure black.

"How would I describe Elliot Rosewater's death?" Bianca asked, repeating Kathryn's question. "Inevitable."

"How's that?"

Bianca looked at the silver solar system, her eyes following the motion of a small planet, then she looked back at Kathryn.

Paolo was right about Kathryn Blaire. She was beautiful and worthy. Kathryn Blaire being more than smart enough to know that the Italian authorities would never cooperate, would never investigate Elliot Rosewater's death in New York, or Kathryn Blaire's death, if it came to that, in Florence. And yet she was fearless enough to be past the point of giving a damn. Perhaps even a seeker of such opportunities. Giovanni delle Bande Nere would have liked that.

"Rosewater betrayed us and compounded his error by killing Sarah Ridell. Would you like to know if I killed him? Or if perhaps Paolo killed him?"

"No. I know one of you killed him. Or had him killed."

"Does that worry you, Kathryn?"

"Not really," Kathryn said, sipping some coffee. "Rosewater was a son of a bitch."

"True enough. In any event, it was my decision. I've always been a bit firmer than Paolo. Thank you for leaving Elliot Rosewater the way you did—on the floor, unconscious and defenseless. It made it easier for my associates, I'm told. Independent contractors in New York, you understand."

"My pleasure to help," Kathryn rasped.

Bianca stood, the Hanged Man pendant swaying as she did so, swinging off her chest and then dropping back.

She looked again at the spinning planets and Kathryn's eyes followed her.

"You're wondering what that is?" Bianca asked.

"Yes."

"An astronomical clock—made by Lorenzo delle Volpaia for Lorenzo de'Medici."

"I see. It tracks the planets around the sun?"

"Around the earth," Bianca corrected softly. "It was built in the late 1400s, before Galileo. It's a Ptolemaic universe, the sun and the planets revolving around the earth. The clock tracks the positions of the heavenly bodies. It is also supposed to bring down the positive energy of the heavens to the earth. To this room, to be precise. Or so the magicians believed: Ficino, Pico delle Mirandolla, Giordano Bruno. Perhaps Botticelli himself."

"Right." Kathryn nodded her head, took a step closer to the rotating planets, nearly touching them with her hand. "And you believe that, that the energy of the planets is being transferred down to this room through that clock?"

"Lorenzo de'Medici did. As for me, it's like the afterlife. Why not believe?"

Kathryn didn't even attempt an answer. Astronomical clocks, the Hanged Man pendant, Francesca delle Bande Nere, and murder...all fair topics. But not a word yet about the Amber Room, the reason she had come to Florence. The reason she had met the delle Bande Neres. Kathryn turned her back to the rotating planets, looked at Bianca's black eyes, and decided there was no time like the present.

"The Amber Room...?"

"Yes," Bianca said patiently.

"You know it's what I came for."

"Perhaps."

"I thought we could discuss it."

"What do think we have been discussing, Kathryn?" Bianca smiled cryptically.

Without further explanation, Bianca walked over to the French doors of the library and looked through the glass at the sun, then looked at her wristwatch. They would be joining Paolo soon. That would interesting in itself. Answering Kathryn Blaire's question would make it even more so.

68

Isaiah Hawkins took his time traversing the old stone walkway on the southern side of Florence's Santa Trinita bridge. The Arno river flowing underneath in a broad, flat, and unhurried blue-green sheet. The sun reflecting off the water and rising over the red tile roofs. The bridge deserted of all other pedestrians.

He looked back for a moment at the great dome of the Cathedral of Santa Maria del Fiori, which hovered over Florence. The dome was the masterpiece of Filippo Brunelleschi, who had turned to architecture only after being bested by Ghiberti in the famed Merchant's Guild competition to sculpt the brass panels for the doors of the Baptistry.

Brunelleschi's dome had had its place in time. It could not have been built without the architectural innovations of the Renaissance that preceded it. It would never have been built if Brunelleschi had not lost the competition and turned from sculpture to architecture. And it would not be built today, in an era that prefers irony over majesty in its monuments.

It was all about timing. It had been when Brunelleschi built his dome and still was now. It was about keeping yourself alive and in the game and, when the moment was right, making the final play. The type of play that Bianca and Paolo delle Bande Nere had made by inviting Kathryn Blaire and Anand Ashland to the palazzo.

The delle Bande Nere had preempted the timing. There had been no opportunity for Isaiah to send Ben Russo in through the front door of 33 Via San Giovanni with a warrant or some other paper that looked official. No opportunity to fly Ivo Jenkins in from Paris and put his magnificent skills to use. Two chess pieces deftly removed from the board by the delle Bande Nere.

It was a smart and aggressive move. The delle Bande Nere had seized control of the end game, positioning the last moves to play out on their turf, on their terms, and with their choice of players. But like every play, it had also revealed information.

Whether the delle Bande Nere had the Amber Room was no longer an open question for Isaiah Hawkins. The answer apparent in their speed of action and in their choice of players, especially Kathryn Blaire. Kathryn being ever so susceptible to temptation.

Isaiah lit a cigarette and resumed walking along the stone bridge, heading in the direction of the Oltrarno. Crossing an empty bridge like a defector in some cold war tale. Hoping to make a play himself.

69

Bianca delle Bande Nere and Kathryn Blaire walked up the palazzo's sweeping flight of black marble stairs. As they climbed, Bianca played with a dull silver key, cylindrical with one notch. At the top of the stairs, and at the far end of a narrow corridor, was a heavy oak door.

Bianca reached out with the key, paused, and turned to Kathryn.

"It's the key to paradise, don't you know? Well, you shall see."

Bianca twisted the key into the lock and swung the door open to a world of amber. Floor to ceiling, the amber panels of Peter the Great lined the walls, a one-hundred-thousand-piece mosaic opening up before Kathryn's eyes. A dozen mirrors of various shapes and sizes mixed in with the amber.

"What do you think, Kathryn?"

The words this time were not Bianca's. The voice from behind. Deeper. And yet gentler. Kathryn turned slowly to see the same dark features, the same olive skin, the same black eyes. The same, yet muted.

Paolo spoke graciously, sweetly. "Welcome to my home, Kathryn."

She wanted to hurt him, and she wanted to touch him. She did neither, instead letting the truth inside her come out.

"You hurt me," she said.

"I'm sorry."

"If you were sorry, you wouldn't have done it."

"You're right." Paolo took a step closer to her. "I wasn't sorry at the time. I'm sorry now."

"Why?"

"Because I keep seeing you."

"Where?" she asked.

"In my mind. I see you sleeping in your bed."

"You see your triumph."

"No, I see my loss." Paolo walked another step closer to her.

252

"I was hoping you would forgive me."

Kathryn looked around the Room searching for the mirror. The mirror that would belong here. That would fill a gap and make the Room more complete. She did not see it, but knew it was there, as she saw no gaps in the amber and glass. She turned back to Paolo. "You did what you had to do."

"So my sister said." Paolo looked at Bianca. "I told her that I did what I wished to do. For that I apologize."

Kathryn smiled. "You don't have to apologize. If I owned this Room, I would have done the same thing, I suppose."

"I don't believe that," Paolo replied.

"Then you don't know me."

There was a momentary silence, when Bianca's voice intervened. "Well, at least tell us what you think of the Amber Room, Kathryn," Bianca asked.

Kathryn looked around the room again, trying to take it all in, the amber arrayed in wonderful shapes and patterns and colors. She shrugged. "It's beautiful. It's a beautiful piece of art. But I don't know. After all this, I expected something magical."

"Are you disappointed?" Paolo asked.

Kathryn walked closer to the panels, to get a better look. They were stunning, but very much of this world, very much the work of men. "I shouldn't be. But I guess I am."

"The tragedy of great expectations," Bianca said carelessly, but with intent. "Tell me, did you let yourself care too much?"

"Me?" Kathryn tapped her heart with a closed fist and gave a small smile, because it was only now that she realized she'd never cared at all about the Amber Room. She had cared about getting her life back, about helping Sarah Ridell, about maybe killing a man, about winning, about another man who left her apartment without saying good-bye, and about proving herself. But she had never cared about the Room until right now.

"No, I didn't care," Kathryn said. "Not about this Room. This Room wasn't ever for me."

"So who was it for?" Bianca asked.

"The Russians." Kathryn answered simply.

"The Russians?" Bianca all but exploded with delight. "That's priceless, Kathryn. Didn't you know—you must have known—Stalin sold the Amber Room to my family. Stalin wanted hard currency and knew he could blame the loss of the room on the Germans. Besides, it was the tsar's property anyway. What did Stalin care about the tsar's treasures? Sold it to my father for ten million pounds. That and some papers now in my library. But how lovely of you to try and get the room back for them."

"Lovely," Kathryn repeated, because that wasn't the word she would have used at all. So Shokovitch had managed to tell them at least one thing that was true. Stalin had sold the Room to the delle Bande Nere, and here she was trying to get it back for the Russians like some trained dog with a win and a future if she succeeded.

"So tell me, Kathryn, where does this leave us?" Paolo asked softly.

"Couldn't tell you," Kathryn replied. "The Agency knows you have the Room. Whatever I do, or whatever happens to me, Isaiah Hawkins won't give up. That's the way the Agency works."

"We know," Bianca said. "But we don't intend to give up the Room. We bought it. It is ours. You can understand that."

"Fair enough." Kathryn raised her palms upwards. "So tell me, what's your proposal?"

"We'd like you to spread the word."

"What word?" Kathryn asked, perplexed.

Bianca walked Kathryn over to the amber panels, stopping less than six inches away, then leaning in even closer. Both women bringing themselves right to the panels, the way one stares through a window.

Beneath the translucent amber, Kathryn saw a spidery golden thread. The thread transversing the back of the panel, not a part of it. She followed the thread over to the next panel, where it joined with another thread, then another. A web of golden threads.

Kathryn drew back haltingly. The golden threads were not of the panel, not of this Room.

From a rectangular panel built almost invisibly into the oak door, Bianca withdrew a thin silvery case. A single sapphire blue crystal protruding ever so slightly.

"A rather simple device. Primitive almost." Bianca said, her voice almost without emotion. This a moment she had so cautiously, thoughtfully, and recklessly prepared for. A course of action, the consequences of which she and her brother had already fully accepted. "I'm sure you are familiar with the mechanics, Kathryn. If the sapphire crystal is pressed, a radio wave will be sent to a control which will emit an electric pulse, which will go out through the gold wires and trigger a rapid series of small explosions. Still it would a shame if this was lost."

Bianca placed the tips of her own fingers on the amber, running her fingers over the precious mosaic, the way they traced the face of her Abraham. "A shame to be lost to others. Less of a shame to be ruined," she mused aloud.

Kathryn nodded. A nod that meant nothing, because there was nothing else she could think of to do.

Bianca walked to the oak door and opened it again, allowing Anand Ashland to enter. Anand acknowledged Kathryn with the slightest gesture of his right hand.

Bianca turned back to Kathryn. "It is our understanding that, despite my brother's fondness for you, Mister Ashland's word is nevertheless more highly regarded in certain circles than yours might be. Therefore, Mister Ashland was invited earlier, so that we could show him our preparations in some detail. He can vouch that he has personally been shown the wiring and that we are serious. You may stay here as long as you like, Kathryn. Enjoy this Room. Then you may leave and tell the others they may not have the Amber Room. If anyone tries to obtain the Room, we will destroy it first. Of that, I can assure you."

Bianca then placed the detonator in Kathryn's hand. "In the alternative, you may simply press the button yourself, if you prefer."

70

Isaiah Hawkins was almost surreally serene, like a monk returning to his monastery after a prolonged and unavoidable visit to the city. He was where he belonged, completely at ease. He knocked on the green door at 33 Via San Giovanni.

Salvatore opened the door partway and took Isaiah in with his eyes. "How may I help you, sir?"

"My name is Isaiah Hawkins. I'd like to speak to Bianca and Paolo, and I would like to see the Amber Room."

"I believe that can be arranged Mister Hawkins. You were not unexpected. But please wait here first."

It was perhaps ten minutes later that Salvatore brought Isaiah into the house. They went through the library, Isaiah slowing as they did so, taking in the silver solar system, the portrait of Francesca, the books, and everything else. Then he was led up the black marble steps and past the oak door.

Kathryn had her hand on the detonator, holding it tightly, keeping her fingers away from the sapphire crystal.

Bianca spoke first. "I've thought for a while you might be joining us, Mister Hawkins. You understand, Brother Michael no longer chooses sides."

Isaiah looked slowly, in turn, from Bianca with her black eyes like rivets, to her brother who was softer, to Anand, to Kathryn. But Kathryn's eyes seemed to disappear into the color of the room, and it was impossible even for Isaiah to gauge her. Then Isaiah looked at the silver case with the sapphire crystal in Kathryn's hand. It was unexpected and took a moment to register, but it didn't need to be explained to him.

He walked calmly over to the panels, looking carefully at the amber, then peering through it and seeing for himself the web of golden wires. The sapphire crystal pressed, a signal sent, the amber panels destroyed. Perhaps the entire room. Perhaps everyone in it. That was the way bombs worked—whether through brilliance or madness. This one was brilliance. And resolve.

It was a powerful but brutal tactic, threatening to destroy

one's own possessions to prevent an adversary from obtaining them. A tactic that had its place in history, but was nevertheless rare in its use for obvious reasons. Isaiah knew that during WWII, Joseph Stalin had burnt to the ground Russia's own grain fields in advance of the invading German army. As a result, the German army starved to death. So did hundreds of thousands of Russian peasants.

"Quite unexpected," Isaiah said aloud.

"You did not expect us to simply give up the Room, did you Mister Hawkins," Bianca said, focusing all her strength of will upon Isaiah.

"No, I didn't," Isaiah replied. He harbored no doubts that Bianca delle Bande Nere possessed the resolve. Her strength so visible in her person. Strong enough to hand the detonator to Kathryn.

Isaiah walked back to the center of the room, forcing himself to visualize not the room but the library as he did so. Seeing the silver solar system in the corner of the library, and drawing the connection he wanted. "Do you know the derivation of word revolution?" he asked, speaking to no one in particular.

"Excuse me?" Paolo asked, the strangely mystified look on his face shared by Kathryn. But not by Bianca or Anand. Bianca not letting anything show, and Anand's professionalism not letting him judge where Isaiah Hawkins was taking this...not until Isaiah was well and done.

Isaiah spoke slowly. "It comes from the Latin—*revolvere*. To revolve. It was first applied to the regular motions of the planets by serious astronomers, later twisted by astrologers to refer to discontinuous, abrupt events influenced by the conjunction of the planets, by magic. The original meaning of the word—based on the regularity of planetary motion—spun upside down to refer to sudden, unpredictable events. This meaning was then applied to human events. Like political revolutions. Which I have spent my life observing." Isaiah paused. "I was reminded of this by the solar system I saw in your library. Interesting. Ptolemaic, I believe?"

"Yes," Bianca answered, then turned her gaze toward Kathryn, who still held the detonator tight. "What is your point, Mister Hawkins?"

"I saw something else interesting in your library," Isaiah said. "I'm not sure what I expected to find here, signora. But I came for the Amber Room and for some letters, and I do intend to leave with them."

"Letters, Mister Hawkins?" Paolo asked.

From his coat pocket, Isaiah removed a folded sheet of paper. He was in no rush. That was the mistake so many made when they read aloud—rushing as if the written word deserved less time and merit than a newly formed spoken thought. Isaiah had learned otherwise back at Father Juma's parish, watching the Father prepare his sermons. The Testaments demanded time. Time and rhythm and respect. Old words more important than the new ones.

Isaiah carefully placed his reading glasses over his eyes and slowly unfolded the sheet of slightly faded paper.

> A: As I said, Mister Hawkins, the room was brought back to Moscow in crates. While the war was still on.
>
> Q: Where was it kept?
>
> A: In the crates, just like the Tsar Peter had kept it in crates—in the basement of the palace that Stalin had taken for his own.
>
> Q: And now?
>
> A: Now, I don't know.
>
> Q: What do you know?
>
> A: I don't know anything. I've heard rumors. Seen documents. A receipt.
>
> Q: A receipt?
>
> A: Yes. It was important to keep records, you know that Mister Hawkins. Even the executions...there were always excellent records.

Q: Tell me about the receipt.

A: It was for ten million in British pounds. It didn't give the name of the purchaser. The year was 1952. The party was desperate for hard currency then, you know that.

Q: What was sold, the Amber Room?

A: Yes, that and some papers of historical interest.

Q: Tell me about the papers, Comrade Shokovitch.

A: I'm not a comrade.

Q: The papers, Mikhail.

A: Letters, Mister Hawkins. From Lenin and others. That's all I know.

Q: I doubt that, Mikhail. From Lenin to who?

A: To Stalin and Trotsky and Bukharin.

Q: When were they written?

A: Beginning the summer of 1918.

Q: About what?

A: What else, Mister Hawkins? About the Terror. Letters from Lenin ordering the Terror.

"I believe," Isaiah said, looking at Bianca and Paolo, "that you have the letters. And I intend to leave here with them and with the Room."

"The Room I understand, but why the letters?" Bianca asked.

"It doesn't matter, does it?" Isaiah replied. "Personal vanity, perhaps."

"I don't believe that," Bianca replied.

"You don't have to," Isaiah said.

"May I have the Room and letters? Or shall I ask Kathryn to press that button?"

"That decision is yours, Mister Hawkins." Bianca said flatly.

Isaiah looked over at Kathryn, her finger over the sapphire crystal. "Go ahead, Kathryn."

Kathryn hesitated. Go ahead, Kathryn. Like she was being asked to take out the trash. Like she was being asked to prove herself. That decision is yours, Mister Hawkins. Like Bianca delle Bande Nere had no responsibility for what was about to happen. A masterpiece destroyed rather than preserved. Exactly what Alexander Greene had feared.

Bianca and Isaiah were playing on the same level and perhaps they deserved each other. But she didn't deserve either of them. Everything she thought she had wanted wasn't worth it.

Kathryn lifted her finger clearly off the detonator and walked over to Paolo. She leaned over to give him a gentle kiss good-bye, and he whispered something in her ear, words which made no sense. *Press the button, Kathryn. Press the button. Do it. Press the button.*

The words compelling her actions.

Shards of amber flew about the room in a symphony of noise and color.

71

Isaiah Hawkins walked alone across the Santa Trinita bridge, across the Arno, in his pocket, fragments of amber and a seventy year old letter. The letter a victory of sorts, obtained from an opponent who had the resolve but not the energy to destroy again.

The words were written in a script forceful and compelling. The work of a man without doubt of his intentions. The best of intentions. No doubt.

19 MARCH 1922
TO COMRADE STALIN FOR THE POLITBURO MEMBERS,

Regarding the famine in the Ukraine, the church—the Black Hundred—believe the famine offers cover to defy the decree on the confiscation of church valuables.

Our enemies would do well to remember the peasant wisdom, "Bad crops are from God, but hunger comes from men." It is precisely now and only now, when in the starving regions people are eating human flesh and hundreds of corpses are littering the roads, that we can—and therefore must!—carry out the confiscation of church valuables with the most savage and merciless energy.

We must—so as to secure the hundreds of million of rubles of gold that the church wishes to deny us. Without this, there will be no money for government work in general. As well, we must not be cowardly of seizing property for the good of the party and for ourselves. The sacrifices have been many, the opportunities to favor ourselves few.

At the next meeting of the committee, pass a secret resolution that the confiscation of valuables, in particular of the richest abbeys, monasteries, and churches, should be conducted with merciless determination, unconditionally stopping at nothing.

The greater the number of representatives of the reactionary clergy we succeed in executing for this reason, the better. As always, we must execute not only the guilty. Execution of the innocent will impress the masses even more.

I am to be informed on a daily basis of the number of priests executed. Appoint the best workers for this measure in the richest abbeys. We will need some hard men.

Yours,

Lenin

Isaiah repeated the words in his mind. I am to be informed on a daily basis of the number of priests executed…We will need some hard men.

A sanitized, fictionalized version of this directive had been released long ago from the party archives—to show that Lenin hadn't ordered the terror. The venality dimmed. The personal corruption stricken. The terror dulled. A mask offered to the world.

Now in Lenin's own script, the intentions so clear. The followers mere lambs compared to the prophet.

Isaiah Hawkins kept walking. Triumphant, one might suppose. The magic of the Amber Room only a flickering illusion for him.

Five days later, the world's major newspapers would each run the same led story in the main headline and upper right hand corner of their front page.

In the election for the presidency of modern Russia, Nikolai Andreyovitch Lysenko had surged to an improbable, come-from-the-dead victory over his communist rival. The victory by the pro-western Lysenko attributed to the release, twenty-four hours prior to the election, of a letter by Lenin, the existence of which had long been rumored, but never proven. It was claimed the letter had been found hidden deep in the secret archives of the Communist party.

According to the led paragraph in the *New York Times*, Lenin's own words had "shattered the communist myth forever." And it seemed, the *Times* reported, that with the myth shattered, the communists had nothing left.

The president of the United States, in the midst of a trip to

some strategically important place in the sun, was quoted as saying that the triumph was a testament to the strength of democracy and of his own foreign policy.

The president also sent a private cable to Isaiah Hawkins, inviting him to come to the White House for congratulations. But Isaiah Hawkins never seemed to make the time.

While Isaiah Hawkins walked along the Santa Trinita Bridge with Lenin's letter in his pocket, at the palazzo on Via San Giovanni, Kathryn Blaire was in tears.

Isaiah, Anand, Bianca, and Paolo all left the Amber Room after the explosion. Kathryn stayed. She slumped on her back on the floor, amongst the carnage of burnt amber chips. In all the images of her life that she had ever created for herself, this vision was never one of them, the gap between what she wished to be and what she had become never wider. Kathryn Blaire, an angel of the least sort, one who had chosen to destroy on command.

She kept hearing Paolo's whisper, his command—*Press the button, Kathryn. Press the button. Do it. Press the button.* It was like she was compelled, like she had given up her will. As if after all these years of fighting everything, she had given in.

But there was something else in Paolo's whisper. A silent emotion that had not been voiced, but which was there. And which was why she had pressed the sapphire crystal.

Do it. Press the button. Everything will be all right. Trust me. Trust someone, if just this once.

Kathryn picked herself off the floor, brushing amber dust and slivers from her clothes. She looked at the destruction all around her and wondered what trust had to do with it. Then she walked out past the oak door and wandered down the narrow hall. She was searching for something, although she did not know what.

The hall continued past the marble stairway, and opened to another corridor, at the end of which was a polished metal door.

She pushed the door open, and stepped into a world of brilliant yellow and gold light.

She was bathed in it, drenched in it, enchanted by it. Above her rose a ceiling of crystal—tens of thousands of pieces of crystal cut like the facets of an astronomical mirror, forming a chandelier of light and refraction. Below, a floor of polished platinum. Absorbing and reflecting at the same time.

And on the walls, were one hundred thousand pieces of cut glistening amber. Peter the Great's amber. Luminous and detailed and alive.

In the center of it all stood a gold solar system, like the one in Bianca's library, the planets and the sun revolving around a gold earth.

"As above, so below," said Paolo's voice softly from behind her.

Kathryn grasped for her own voice. She could barely absorb where she was. She was in a place beyond art. Beyond brilliance. Past madness and into magic. As above, so below. The virtues and powers of the heavens drawn down to earth, through a gold solar system in the Amber Room. The Amber Room was not destroyed, but turned into a kaleidoscope of light and magic.

She turned around as slowly as she could ever remember. Her feet unsteady beneath her, her eyes trying to absorb it all. She thought she saw the mirror that had been the object of Paolo's quest. Then she saw Paolo looking back at her with a smile.

"A duplicate room?" she asked. "The other a fake?"

"Of course."

She looked at him with a feeling between amazement and wonder. Trapped between Isaiah Hawkins' relentless cold war quest and Renaissance witchcraft, a third way found.

"You do believe, don't you?" she asked. "As above, so below."

Paolo drew close to her and took her hand. He placed it on the earth at the center of the gold solar system.

"I know that this system was built five hundred years ago and given to my family by a genius named Lorenzo Ghiberti who believed it could be manipulated to bring the energy of the heavens to earth. I know that it was my sister's idea to marry Ghiberti's solar system to the Amber Room. The effect is wondrous, and Bianca believes. Whether I believe is immaterial."

"But what if Isaiah had discovered this Room as well?"

"Take a closer look, Kathryn."

There was an eerie strength in his gentle voice and, unsteadily, she let go of his hand and walked over to an amber panel. It was radiant. It drew her closer. She placed her face against it, and shuddered. Golden threads of destruction running behind these panels as well.

From the pocket of his jacket, Paolo removed a second detonator, identical to the first except that the crystal was of blue amber.

"So you understand," Paolo said, "we would never have given up the Room."

"How did you know I would push the button, and blow up the other Room?"

"I didn't."

She smiled, believed she understood how she had been used again, as part of a trick against Isaiah Hawkins, and walked past the solar system and toward the door. Almost there though, she stopped and looked back.

"How come you let me see this Room?" she asked, taking a step toward Paolo. "It ruins everything, doesn't it? I'll go back and tell them I blew up a fake."

Paolo walked over to her and put his arms around her waist. "Not if you stay," he said softly, firmly. He lifted her off the ground, into his arms, and embraced her with a kiss that left nothing of his heart behind.

She closed her eyes and held her lips to his for the longest time. She imagined herself in this house, with this man, with this secret that he had entrusted to her.

Exposing himself to her so that she would know how much he wanted her. Telling her that he loved her.

She opened her eyes and took in the beauty of the Amber Room. Her room. She put her hand gently to Paolo's cheek and kissed him again. Their room.

Epilogue

Isaiah Hawkins sat alone in his office at the start of a new day. His map on one wall, freshly updated. A small pyramid of colored amber shards in a styrofoam coffee cup near his phone. An unopened lab report from Washington in a manila envelope on his desk in front of him. On the wall behind the desk, the Edward Hopper print of a few lonely people drinking coffee in a late night diner.

The Hopper, with its overwhelming sense of isolation, was believed by most who visited Isaiah Hawkins' office to be a window into Isaiah's soul, and maybe it was. But Edward Hopper himself always said that he was not trying to paint others, but only to capture himself. And, on that view, the print offered a window only into Edward Hopper's psyche. As for Isaiah Hawkins, it was another mask to hide behind.

Isaiah picked up the styrofoam cup and poured the amber fragments into his hand. They were a dullish yellow, marred by dark burns and scars and they had lost all their bright luster and shine. Slowly, he let the shards slip through his fingers and back into the cup. The amber pieces looked sad, almost pathetic, piled in a cheap white styrofoam cup, but then they never did have quite the right luster, even before the explosion. One expected a masterpiece to have a certain intrinsic aura.

He opened the manila envelope, removing a one-page lab report. A single, burned amber piece, was enclosed in a plastic bag stapled to the report. The report itself was primarily a chemical analysis. Seems that the amber collected by the Prussian kings and used in the Amber Room could have been expected to have a high concentration level of succinic acid, consistent with amber mined in certain regions of Europe. This burned piece fell short. Far short.

Isaiah Hawkins lit a cigarette and smiled. It was a hard thing to fake the truth.

Photo by Wynn Miller

Jonathan Harris graduated from Stanford University, Phi Beta Kappa, and Stanford Law School with highest honors. He started his career clerking for a federal judge before joining a law firm where he successfully practiced international white-collar criminal law. He lives with his wife, Trace, and their dog, Mike, in Los Angeles.